This was what family was like, extended or otherwise.

Becca smiled. This was what was permanently missing in her own life. Not that she'd ever belong with people like these in a living room like this. As a caregiver, she'd always be an outsider. She'd been fine with that for years. She planned to be fine with that forever.

"Becca's done a wonderful job with the house," Flynn was saying. "We bachelors aren't very good at cooking or cleaning or stocking up on toilet paper."

Hearing Flynn's voice, Becca's desire to belong increased. He was the carrot she happily plodded toward. But even if they explored their feelings for each other after her lawsuit was dismissed–crossing fingers, knock on wood– it may not amount to anything....

Still, the more they laughed, the more Becca felt connected to Flynn, and the more she believed in a future together.

But would Flynn agree?

Dear Reader,

Welcome to Harmony Valley!

Things aren't as harmonious here as they once were. Jobs have dried up and almost everyone under the age of sixty has moved away, leaving the population...well, gray-haired and peaceful.

Enter three young men—Flynn, Slade and Will—friends, newly minted millionaires and hometown success stories. Flynn Harris is balancing the trio's new winery against the needs of his stroke-burdened grandfather while caring for his young nephew.

Now that Flynn's wealthy, all kinds of people show up to try to take advantage of him and his family. Flynn is especially suspicious when Becca MacKenzie, caregiver in need of a job, conveniently shows up on his doorstep. Becca is smart, pretty and opinionated—and once his grandfather meets her, no one else will do.

If only Becca didn't have a secret that could break Flynn's trust.

I hope you enjoy Flynn and Becca's journey, as well as the other romances in The Harmony Valley series. I love to hear from readers. Check my website and sign up for email updates. Or you can chat with me on Facebook (MelindaCurtisAuthor), or on Twitter (MelCurtisAuthor), and hear about my latest giveaways.

Melinda Curtis

HARLEQUIN HEARTWARMING

Melinda Curtis

Summer Kisses

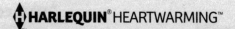

HARLEQUIN® HEARTWARMING™

Recycling programs
for this product may
not exist in your area.

ISBN-13: 978-0-373-36663-7

SUMMER KISSES

Copyright © 2014 by Melinda Wooten

This edition published by arrangement with Harlequin Books S.A.

For questions and comments about the quality of this book,
please contact us at CustomerService@Harlequin.com.

HARLEQUIN®

Printed in U.S.A.

™ www.Harlequin.com

MELINDA CURTIS

has lived in Georgia and Texas, but she's a California girl at heart. Her earliest memories are of life on an isolated fifty-acre sheep ranch in rural Sonoma County. Picture rolling hills covered in brown grass, a eucalyptus forest, a long gravel driveway lined with plump sheep, and no sidewalks. It was a big deal to drive into town on a one-lane road in a ramshackle, bubble-fendered pickup for an ice cream.

Fast-forward to today. Melinda lives in California's hot central valley with her husband–her basketball-playing college sweetheart. With three kids, the couple has done the soccer thing, the karate thing, the dance thing, the Little League thing and, of course, the basketball thing.

Melinda writes sweet to medium-heat contemporary romances as Melinda Curtis and red-hot reads as Mel Curtis.

With love to my family and close friends. It's not unusual for my spin buddies, household members or siblings to see me enter a room with a glazed look in my eyes and a new question—"What if...?"

With thanks to A.J. Stewart, Cari Lynn Webb and Anna Adams. Hardworking Bees, indeed.

And for Carrie.
I think of you every time I find a dime.

CHAPTER ONE

BECCA MACKENZIE WAS sweet and loveable and trustworthy.

At least, that's what people used to say.

But that was before. Before a Taliban bullet widowed her, before her smile felt scarred, before she got it into her head that everyone deserved the granting of their last wish.

Sure, go on, ignore trusts and wills and judgmental relatives. Never mind the necessity of paper trails to protect those left behind.

What had she been thinking?

Not about protecting herself. She'd been thinking, screw grief. She'd been thinking that if you loved someone and they loved you back, fulfilling that person's last request was an honor.

Sweet and loveable and trustworthy.

That's what Becca's clients would say about her.

If they weren't all dead.

Becca's lips were so tightly sealed grief had no chance to escape.

Death was an appendage of being a certified nursing assistant who cared for the elderly. Easing their passing was a sacred trust, whether they died of natural causes, of cancer or kidney disease, of heart failure or just plain fatigue. Life was exhausting, too short for the ones she loved, and, well, exhausting for those left behind.

Exhausted, Becca sat in her temporary home in Harmony Valley, a don't-blink-or-you'll-miss-it town in the northernmost corner of California's Sonoma County. Her home was mobile. Twenty-one feet long, with rusted bumpers, and an orange burlap dinette that doubled as her bed. She'd been in town less than three days, and was parked at the house of a prospective employer, waiting for him to get home.

When Flynn Harris showed up with his grandfather, she'd stand up straight, look him in the eye and ask him for the job. She would not think about the near-zero balance in her checking account, the accusations a previous employer's family made against her or the lawsuit she had almost no chance of winning without this job.

A cold, wet nose pressed against her side. Trust Abby to know when Becca needed reassurance. The black, tan and white Australian shepherd looked at her with dark, adoring eyes, as if to say everything was going to be as right as her nightly kibble. Becca stroked the small dog's silky fur, but even Abby couldn't chase away the tension knotting her stomach.

A classic black Cadillac the length of a small cruise liner turned into the lightly graveled driveway, moving slowly toward the army-green, ranch-style house where Becca was parked. The car stopped so that the passenger-side door was even with the front walk.

Becca hopped out of the motorhome and would have hurried to the passenger door, Abby trotting eagerly at her heels, if not for the penny she saw at her feet. Shoved between two small white rocks, the penny seemed bent and beaten. Becca shoved it into the pocket of her jeans and waved to the elderly passenger through the open Cadillac window.

Edwin Blonkowski's pale face was dominated by a bulbous nose, his expression stuck in a stroke-induced half frown, framed by a stringy gray comb-over. The T-shirt at the folds of his neck was a dingy gray, the collar curled as if clinging to life. He was so clearly in need of TLC that Becca's heart panged.

And panged again when she glanced at the driver, Edwin's grandson, Flynn Harris. Locals said Edwin was on the road to recovery. Flynn's eyes told a different story. They were the crisp blue of a morning sky, but sharp, so sharp. Sharpened by the fear of loss. Sharp enough to shred her hopes.

For a moment, Becca doubted the penny.

Flynn got out of the car and walked toward the trunk, adjusting his baseball cap over his shoulder length, reddish-brown hair. Faded blue jeans. A wrinkled white Comic Con T-shirt. He looked to be in his mid-twenties, same as Becca. His wasn't the domineering muscularity of a military man. His was the tall, wiry frame of an athlete built for speed.

For the first time in years, Becca looked at a man and her body buzzed in appreciation.

A totally unexpected response. She was looking for a job, not a date. And there'd been that penny.

She opened Edwin's door and assembled a smile as carefully as if it were an unfamiliar yoga pose. "I'm Becca MacKenzie, a certified nursing assistant. Agnes Villanova recommended I stop by and ask about the job."

"Wasn't expecting you." Edwin's words slurred as he shook her hand, his hospital identification bracelet too tight on his swollen wrist. "Told Flynn. I'm done with nurses."

"You're done with hospitals." Flynn's voice was deeper than she expected, rumbling along her nerves like drawn-out thunder after a lightning strike. "But we need a nurse at home. While you get better."

Hope strengthened Becca's smile. The sharpness in Flynn's gaze may have been due to worry, not lost optimism.

"I'm not muddle-headed," Edwin said. "Don't need a jailer."

Abby put her paws on the Cadillac's bottom door frame, stretching to sniff the old man.

Edwin patted the dog, his fingers exhibiting the bluish tinge caused by very poor circulation. "Who's this?"

"Abby." Becca snapped her fingers and Abby trotted a few feet away. "Can I help you out of the car?"

"Please." There was a determined twinkle in his eyes. "I can't dance like I used to."

"None of us can." Becca steadied Edwin as

he stood. She didn't dare look Flynn's way for fear he'd start a conversation with, "Thanks for coming by." And end it with, "But we've already hired someone."

"You did great," she told Edwin, rubbing a sweaty palm on her jeans, feeling the penny in her pocket.

Abby barked her approval once, high and sharp, pacing behind Becca as if she and Edwin were two sheep in her care.

Flynn closed the trunk. A walker appeared to Becca's left. "You're not from the agency. Those candidates are coming by this afternoon."

They hadn't made a decision. Becca wanted to sag with relief.

"I'm an independent C.N.A. I have letters of reference. And a résumé." Emotion tinged her voice, the way it did when she didn't speak the entire truth. There were gaps in her résumé, names and dates missing. She cleared her throat and produced the envelope with her qualifications from her back pocket. "Agnes told me you're looking for someone to help your grandfather regain his sea legs. And it just so happens I'm available."

Edwin gave her a half grin, and a thumbs-up. "Until I'm okay, I'm sold."

Becca grinned. Edwin was just what her lawyer suggested—a recovering client who'd give her a stellar character reference within the next few weeks. There would be no honoring a last request, no gift, no deathbed vigil. Edwin was recovering and after a few weeks, Becca would move on.

Flynn took the envelope reluctantly, as if it contained germs, and stuffed it into a plastic bag from the hospital. "Don't set your parking brake just yet, Grandpa. We should review all the candidates before we make a decision."

"Why?" Edwin asked.

"Because selecting a caregiver is almost as important as selecting a doctor." The edge to Flynn's voice was more pronounced. "You don't just pick one up off the street. Or off your driveway."

And then their gazes collided—hers and Flynn's. It wasn't a cursory glance like the one he'd given her from across the roof of the car. His scrutiny landed on her and delved deep in one surprisingly quick hit that left her breathless and panicky.

Because in his gaze she saw recognition.

Of her? Of her desperation? She didn't know which.

Becca pulled herself together, trying to salvage the opportunity, along with her smile. "I have eight years experience, mostly in transitioning patients from rehab to home life."

"Sounds super," Edwin slurred, at the same time that Flynn said, "We have to choose carefully."

Abby circled Flynn's ankles, doing a bit of character judging with her nose. Flynn leaned over to scratch behind her ears. She licked his hand approvingly and then ran up the front steps, giving them a satisfied smile as she sat.

"Even the dog thinks we should hire Becca," Edwin said.

At Flynn's frown, words tumbled from Becca's mouth. "I tailor my care to each client. I work toward my patient's goals as well as their doctor's orders. Abby's a licensed therapy dog. She's well behaved and loves everybody. I can work whatever hours you need if you'll let me park on-site." Becca pointed at her motorhome and rushed on. "I hear you're building a winery in town. You're probably incredibly busy and need someone right away…"

Flynn caught sight of the wedding band on her right hand and raised an eyebrow.

"My husband, Terry, was killed in Iraq three years ago." Saying it no longer brought tears to her eyes, just the memory of a nameless marine with bad news and a stoic expression.

Someday she'd put the thin band of white gold and its small, princess-cut diamond away. She'd tried a few times, but could only move it as far as her right hand.

"Becca, I appreciate you coming by. But you know as well as I do…" Flynn seemed determined. "I have to interview other candidates."

She knew, but she'd hoped—

"Nonsense." Edwin frowned with both sides of his mouth now. "She's a war widow. It's my duty to help her."

"Grandpa Ed, let me take care of this." Flynn edged the walker closer to his grandfather, dismissing her.

Because she wasn't sweet or loveable or trustworthy.

"I LIKE HER," Grandpa Ed said once Flynn had him settled in his recliner in the living room. "Hire her."

"Slow down." Flynn opened the ancient gold brocade living-room curtains, letting in the afternoon sunlight. It did nothing to cheer him. Instead, it aggravated the sledgehammer-like pounding in his head. He'd seen something familiar in Becca's expression. He just couldn't put his finger on it, not while he was preoccupied with his grandfather.

"I like her," his grandfather reiterated.

"It's time for your pills and to check your blood sugar." Flynn changed the subject, ignoring the light blinking on the answering machine. It was most likely the usual messages from Grandpa Ed's friends in town— help with a leaky faucet or something heavy that needed lifting. He'd become a go-to resource for the locals.

Flynn rummaged through the bag of medicine and paraphernalia they'd brought home from the hospital, searching for his grandfather's pill box and the flap that said Sunday lunch.

As he did all this, his mind flashed to the past, to a time without worry. To warm nights out on the back porch overlooking the Harmony River, while Grandpa Ed regaled him and his friends with stories of loyalty, honor and espionage.

How he longed for those days.

Flynn and his business partners had made millions in the dot-com world, but money couldn't buy health or happiness. Not for an eighty-year-old man with advanced heart disease.

"Why not hire her?"

"Because." Because people had tried taking advantage of Flynn's wealth already. He'd had to change his cell phone number twice and Grandpa Ed's home number. There'd been too many calls from out-of-the-woodwork entrepreneurs and college buddies wanting to manage, or rather, spend his money. Not to mention the temporary reconciliation with his mother. She disappeared after he'd written her a check. Only his ex-con father hadn't shown up for a handout. "If it'll make you happy, I'll call Agnes later. She's the one who recommended Becca."

"And then we'll hire her." Grandpa Ed sounded as if it was a done deal.

But there was something about Becca

MacKenzie that poked at Flynn's subconscious. He could see how his grandfather might be charmed by her warm smile and heart-shaped face. He could see how a man could be distracted by her sleek curves and ribbons of long black hair. But he'd been caught by something in her walnut-brown gaze. Something he had yet to identify. Something that was simultaneously familiar and unfamiliar.

"Knock, knock." Slade Jennings, Flynn's friend and one of his business partners, opened the screen door. "There's the big man." Slade crossed the living room and shook Edwin's hand, looking as if it was casual Friday in his black slacks, button-down shirt and yellow paisley tie. That was just the way the financial guru presented himself, even on weekends. "How're you feeling?"

Grandpa Ed's smile looked sad. "I've been better."

Flynn handed his grandfather two pills and a bottle of water. "He'll get better." He had to.

Grandpa Ed had raised Flynn since he was eight. That was the year his father had gone to prison for armed robbery. The year his mother decided she'd needed a new start in life, one that didn't include a son who looked exactly like his criminal father. The year Flynn learned that no matter what he did, his grandfather wouldn't leave him on someone else's doorstep.

If only Flynn had proven how much that meant to him before this, taken Grandpa Ed on the trip of his dreams to the cities and countries where the old man had made a name for himself in the intelligence community, instead of postponing the trip year after year while Flynn made his fortune.

"I picked up the bed." Slade smoothed his tie. "Are you ready to move it?"

Grandpa Ed turned questioning eyes toward Flynn.

"I ordered a new bed for you." One with rails and adjustable positions to keep the swelling in his extremities down.

Years of his grandfather's military service appeared in the form of stiff shoulders and a commanding tone. "My bed is fine. Just because you've made a lot of money doesn't mean you need to spend it on me."

The pounding in Flynn's head intensified. He exchanged a frustrated look with Slade. "I didn't buy you a hospital bed as a homecoming present. It's what the doctor ordered. If you don't manage your edema, you'll go into congestive heart failure." And die.

Grandpa Ed's weakened state from a fall a year ago plus the trifecta of diabetes, high blood pressure and high cholesterol had already tried to shut down his heart twice. The doctors didn't think he'd survive any heart procedures or live to see Labor Day, less than two months away.

"Oh," Grandpa Ed settled back down. "In that case, you can put the new bed next to mine. I don't want my bed moved out."

Impossible. "There's no room in there for two beds."

Grandpa Ed reached for the remote. "Slade, take it back."

"And while you're at it, Slade, take my grandfather and drop him off at the nearest hospital. He's going to need it." Flynn glared at his grandfather.

His grandfather glared back.

Flynn belatedly remembered stress could end things permanently for Grandpa Ed, as Slade backed slowly toward the door.

"Oh, all right." Grandpa Ed shook the remote at Flynn. "But don't you get rid of my bed. I'm going to need it when I get better."

Slade walked down the hall. "That's the spirit, Edwin."

His grandfather had spirit all right and he showed it to them. He showed it when they brought in a new recliner, one that helped him stand and sit. Unnecessary, he maintained. He showed it as they rearranged the furniture so he could navigate the house in his walker. Not how his wife wanted it, he declared.

At one point, Flynn pulled Slade into the kitchen, needing to vent. "Months spent trying to convince Harmony Valley that change is good and I can't even get my grandfather to accept little changes in his own house!" Ones that would help keep him healthy and safe and alive.

"He's been in charge most of his life." Slade peered through the kitchen archway at Edwin, who was snoring almost as loudly as the television news droned on. "This has to be hard."

It felt harder on Flynn.

"It's only short-term," Slade reminded him. "A little change to his diet, a little physical therapy, and he's back on his feet, right?"

Flynn couldn't look Slade in the eye as he

mumbled, "Right." He'd made his grandfather a promise—no one else would know the end was near.

As the job candidates started showing up, his grandfather found something objectionable in each one.

"I want Becca," he'd say as soon as one left.

And Flynn would always reply, "Keep an open mind. The agency stands behind their staff." He had no idea who stood behind Becca, other than Agnes, who was on the town council.

"I should be allowed to choose," Grandpa Ed wheezed after the last interview, clearly spent. "She's not going to be wiping your bottom."

"And on that note—" Slade gathered the paperwork they'd been reviewing "—I'm outta here."

After Slade left, Flynn counted ten sledgehammer strikes in his head before speaking. "I'll ask Becca to come by for an interview tomorrow, after the last interview we have from the agency." But when Flynn dialed the number on her résumé, it rolled directly to voice mail—not surprising given Harmony Valley didn't have cell service yet. Just as he was about to leave a message, the house phone rang.

The phone didn't stop ringing until nine o'clock, as nearly every Harmony Valley resident, of which there weren't many, wanted to talk to Grandpa Ed and welcome him back.

By then it was too late to call Agnes and ask her about Becca.

CHAPTER TWO

EARLY MONDAY MORNING, Becca stared through the window into what used to be the ice cream parlor on the northern corner of Harmony Valley's town square. The metal dipping freezers stood empty and forsaken. Cobweb streamers dangled from the ceiling. Most other stores on Main Street were just as deserted and decaying inside.

She rested her head against the cool glass and rubbed her chest.

Abby stood on her hind legs to peer into the store. She dropped to all fours and looked at Becca expectantly, as if asking what they were still doing in Harmony Valley.

"I was hoping, girl." Hoping that some of her childhood faith in the world and the world's faith in her would be renewed. Hoping that Flynn's grandfather would prevail and change Flynn's mind about the job. That she'd receive a call from them last night or first thing this morning. That maybe this time things would work out.

One thing she definitely was not looking for was love. She'd given up on happily-ever-afters once she'd cast her husband's ashes into the ocean. She was destined to be alone. But that didn't mean she couldn't fill her heart temporarily by caring for someone in need. She'd gotten good at smiling through the loneliness, at saying goodbye and letting go.

Since she'd parked in Agnes's driveway again last night, she'd checked with Agnes as soon as she was sure she was up. No call came. No second chance presented itself. It was time to stop hoping. Time to figure out how to pick up the pieces of her life elsewhere.

At the south end of town a parade of trucks made the same turn onto a side street. Utility trucks, beat-up work trucks, construction workers with orange coolers strapped to their truck beds. They lined up as if they'd been at the same coffee shop and had left at the same time for the eight o'clock whistle.

Curiosity set Becca's feet in motion.

The trucks parked up and down a long, freshly graveled drive leading to what looked like an abandoned farm. Men clustered about, finishing their coffee and adjusting tool belts. Their laughter lingered in the air, mingling with the scent of green growth.

Both sides of the driveway were bordered with palm trees some misguided soul had planted half a century earlier out of misplaced grandeur. Palm trees had no business in Sonoma County. As if to prove the point, hundreds of lush rows of grapevines flanked the palms, nearly crowding them out.

This must be where Flynn and his partners were building their winery.

The driveway branched at the end. To the right a white, two-story, craftsman-style home that had seen better days squatted. The porch sagged and windows were broken. To the left stood a large, red, prairie-style barn with winglike additions on either side, covered in a tin corrugated roof dappled with rust.

The instantly recognizable Cadillac was parked in front of the weary-looking house. Edwin sat in the passenger seat, head tilted back, snoring, an unopened bottle of water clutched in his puffy hand.

A rocket of exasperated anger launched from her toes to her fingertips, roaring through her ears.

Life was precious. Didn't Flynn know that?

She spun around quickly, almost tripping over Abby.

Flynn and his red hair were easy to spot. He was talking to a group of men in front of the barn. He held his lean frame confidently in the crowd, unconcerned that his wrinkled gray T-shirt looked like it had sat in a dryer for days. His grandfather wasn't the only one who needed looking after.

Flynn did a double-take when he saw her bearing down on him.

If she had any chance of landing the job, she had to be diplomatic and squelch the niggling man-to-woman awareness Flynn created.

Squelching awareness was easy. Unfortunately, diplomacy wasn't in her arsenal this morning.

Becca planted herself so close to Flynn, he could have heard her whisper. Instead, she chose her outdoor voice. "This is how you plan to take care of your grandfather? By leaving him sitting in a car at a construction site?"

Sensing the turbulence above her, Abby lowered her head between her shoulders.

Scowling, Flynn drew her aside. "There's a problem here I need to deal with."

"We solved that. You should have left thirty minutes ago." A tall man with crisp black hair and a crisper dress shirt and tie had followed them toward the barn. He extended his hand. "I'm Slade Jennings. One of Flynn's business partners. And you are…"

"Becca MacKenzie," Flynn said wearily.

Covering her surprise that Flynn had remembered her name, Becca shook Slade's hand and added, "I'm not a stalker. I'm staying in town." She blew out a breath, trying to release her anger. "I noticed Edwin's edema yesterday. He needs his extremities frequently elevated above his heart to help control the swelling. This isn't good for him."

"You're the one Edwin was asking about." Slade smoothed his navy striped tie and smiled just as smoothly at her, creating not a niggle in her awareness meter. "Weren't you going to call her to set up an interview, Flynn?"

"The day got away from me," Flynn said, looking uncomfortably like it was true and happened often. "Are you free around two, Becca? I'll be done by then."

Becca shook her head. Flynn didn't understand that old bodies weren't as hardy as

young ones. She could kiss this job goodbye.
Her lawyer was going to be disappointed. But
someone had to defend Edwin. "Give me your
keys."

"What?" Flynn's eyebrows nearly touched
the brim of his baseball cap.

Slade watched the two of them with un-
abashed interest and a hint of a grin.

Becca thrust her hand out. "I'll take Edwin
home. Give me the keys."

"I'm not hiring you, Becca. I haven't
checked your references."

"This isn't about giving me a job. It's about
what's best for your grandfather. I can't let
him sit out here without food or a decent bathroom. I won't charge you a cent, I promise.
Now, give me the keys."

"Are you always this bossy?" Flynn dug
into his jeans pocket for the keys and handed
them to her. He was kind of cute when he ca-
pitulated, not that she was looking for that in
a boss.

"I prefer the term *take charge*." She accented the label with air quotes.

"Okay, but just…don't get comfortable."

"I know, I know. You have to interview everyone and check into my past." Becca had no

illusions about getting the job if Flynn did a deep background check. It was enough that she could help Edwin through the day.

She hurried toward the black Cadillac, Abby trotting at her side. When she opened the door, Abby hopped up to sit on the bench seat next to the old man, touching him with her nose.

Edwin startled, bumping into the other door. "Oh, it's you." He scanned the area, wariness framing his gaze.

"Yes. Who were you expecting?"

"I saw someone I hadn't seen…" He blinked at her. "Where are we?"

"Flynn's winery. I'm taking you home."

"Oh. Flynn hired you." In a blink, he tucked wariness away, patted Abby and injected cheer into his voice. "I knew that boy would come to his senses."

She didn't tell him that boy had no sense, at least not when it came to taking care of his grandfather. When it came to hiring a caregiver, he had entirely too much.

"You should hire her."

Flynn stared at Slade as if his friend had just suggested he wear high heels and a thong to the construction site. "Hello? She was waiting for us on our doorstep yesterday. I can think of a dozen slasher movies that started that way. How can I trust her with my grandfather?"

Slade cocked an eyebrow. "You just did."

"I hate it when you're right." Flynn hated that Becca was right, too.

She'd moved with swift, purposeful strides over to the Caddy. All's well, said the sway of her hips. Mission accomplished, said the swing of her long, black braid. All woman, said the curves covered in black and pink spandex.

The wind picked up, rustling the silver-green eucalyptus leaves on the sixty-foot tall trees separating the river from the vineyards.

A wiry construction worker with a gray goatee and ponytail glanced Flynn's way, triggering the elusive feeling of familiarity.

Slade shifted, blocking Flynn's view and disrupting the path to recognition. "Hire Becca. She clearly has Edwin's best interest at heart. And if she moves here she brings skills to the town we don't have now. We promised to increase the population and the tax base."

The population in Harmony Valley was a

whopping seventy-seven. All but two of those residents—their business partner, Will, and his fiancé, Emma—were over the age of sixty-five. The construction crews commuted from other, larger towns, the nearest being thirty to forty minutes away. Flynn and Slade were temporary residents, staying only long enough to fulfill their promise to the town council—to create at least one business to revitalize their hometown.

What fools they'd been to think it would be easy.

They'd experienced a series of false starts, but now, construction on the winery was finally moving forward. Also in the works was a communications tower to bring internet and cell phone service to the remote valley. Today was the first big day of work—demo of unusable parts of the barn, utility work needed to upgrade water, sewer and electricity.

Grandpa Ed waved as Becca drove the Caddy slowly around the drive.

Flynn returned the gesture halfheartedly. "I brought him here because I didn't want to leave him alone."

There had been indignation in Becca's dark gaze today, with none of the subtle emotion he had yet to name layered in her eyes. Regardless, Becca was right. Flynn shouldn't have dragged his grandfather out here, much less left him sitting. As if he needed more guilt.

Guilt greeted Flynn when he awoke every morning, sat on his chest all day and wove through his dreams at night. Guilt that he wasn't doing enough, guilt that he wasn't home enough, guilt that he'd put off doing things with his grandfather until it was too late. If he could just speed up construction on the winery, he'd take his grandfather on the trip of his life. The doctors said Edwin needed a few weeks to regain his balance and what little strength he had left before attempting anything so taxing.

After the Caddy disappeared, a faded green Buick appeared between the palms, carrying three occupants—all councilwomen. They might just as well have been doctors, coming to chart his progress and, if required, give him a dose of medicine.

He walked across the driveway to meet them, determined to avoid their daily meds.

When the car stopped, he leaned down next to the open passenger-side window. With a nod to each woman, "Agnes. Rose. Mildred."

Flynn reached for his easiest smile. "Ladies, we're no longer open to visitors. This is a construction zone now."

"We won't be in the way parked here." Agnes, a gray-haired pixie who also served as the aging group's ringleader, turned off the ignition.

"We're old." From the passenger seat, Mildred squinted at him through lenses as thick as a hard drive. "We won't get out. You can tell us what's going on from here."

"Actually, I came to see the workers with their shirts off," Rose piped up from the backseat, her snowy ballerina bun windblown. "For efficiency's sake, you can call them out while you give us a construction update and then we'll be gone."

"Rose," Agnes scolded, her papery thin cheeks pinkening. "We are *not* here to ogle men."

Flynn's jaw ticked, tugging one end of his smile down. "Ladies, I have nothing new to report since yesterday. You'll need to move along. We're expecting delivery of a Dumpster." And they were parked right in its path.

"Young man, our town has a lot riding on this venture." Rose drew herself up regally, as if she'd already forgotten her shirtless desires. "As councilwomen, we need to be kept abreast of the activities here."

"I assure you—" as he and his partners had been for months "—that we have kept you up-to-date. But not only is it not safe here, my contractor won't allow nonessential personnel on-site."

The three elderly ladies looked crestfallen.

Flynn bent, just a little. "You can park out on Jefferson Street."

"I can't see anything that far away," Rose grumbled.

"We can go home and get our binoculars," Agnes suggested.

"Brilliant." Mildred patted his hand. "We'll talk later."

That's what he was afraid of.

Agnes reached for the key in the ignition, but didn't start the car. "Flynn, before we go, I'd like to put a vote of confidence forward about Becca MacKenzie. She's a wonderful woman."

"She knows all the songs from *Guys and Dolls*. And she can shake her bootie," Rose, the Broadway musical enthusiast, added.

"Any girl who can drive stick shift is okay

in my book." Mildred patted his hand again. "You won't make a mistake by hiring her."

Flynn doubted that. Becca had her secrets and worse: he liked her looks, her smile, her chutzpah. "How long have you known her?"

Agnes's smile stiffened. Rebooted. "I only met her Friday, but she stayed with me all weekend."

Flynn mentally chastised himself. The town council loved Becca. And she'd only been in town a couple of days? "Ladies, can you say con artist?"

Their laughter prickled and annoyed and re-assured. If they were laughing, chances were his grandfather was in good hands. Flynn had known these ladies most of his life. They were a handful, but they didn't misplace their trust. There was just that one look of Becca's to interpret before Flynn felt comfortable.

After they left, Slade walked over, chuckling. "Don't tell me you thought they'd stop coming once construction started."

"I had hoped," Flynn said.

Dane Utley, the project's general contractor, called them over to the blueprints he had spread out over the hood of his silver-gray truck. "I know we want to fast-track this project, but I'm warning you, old construction has a mind of its own." Broad shouldered, big-boned, Dane looked like a professional linebacker, but talked with the polish betraying his Ivy League education. "I don't know how that building has stayed up so long. The beams we examined this morning were either rotted away or split. We'll shore up everything before we do anything else, starting with the low beams on the north wall."

"We promised the Preservation Society this would be a restoration," Flynn said. "If we can't use the guts of the barn we may lose community support." And time. Every day they saved meant he had a better chance of fulfilling his promise to Grandpa Ed to take him on that trip.

"She's a beautiful piece of history and we'll save what we can," Dane reassured Flynn. "I stopped by the county office this morning and they were still missing a couple of key permits and agreements. We can demo today, but the lack of a public improvement agreement is going to stop us by next week."

"Will's working on it," Slade said. "He's in Santa Rosa this morning with our legal team."

They needed to widen a portion of Main

Street and do earthquake retrofits on the Harmony River bridge. Both projects impacted Mayor Larry Finkelstein's property. His lawyers, their lawyers and Will were handling the negotiations. Flynn was managing the building contractors and the councilwomen's daily updates. Slade dealt with finances. If they could obtain these last few permits, maybe things would finally run smoothly.

"We could use some good luck to get things back on track." Flynn voiced the understatement of the year.

Slade nodded.

A white car pulled onto the gravel driveway.

"It's one of the county building inspectors." Dane leaned around Flynn and shouted, "County!"

Power tools ground to a halt as word of an inspection spread. Workmen drifted through the red barn doors. The crew turned to watch the inspector approach.

The ominous sound of timbers snapping had them all spinning back to the barn. The southern wing undulated, wheezing and groaning as if straining for breath. And then it broke away from the middle of the barn, lurching to the ground in a drunken stadium wave, kicking up rolling plumes of dust.

Flynn felt the force of the collapse from fifty feet away. It eddied about his ankles, tugged at his determination, laughed at time-lines and plans and mocked promises made in good faith.

In the seconds after the barn's partial collapse, no one moved. Even the building inspector had stopped his car at the fork in the driveway, a safe distance away.

"Everyone back!" Dane leaped forward, gesturing for his crew to retreat. "She's not done."

The barn shuddered up to its hay loft and tilted precariously toward the collapsed south wing.

Flynn and Slade ran with the rest of the crew to the inspector's vehicle.

The wiry construction worker with the goatee and ponytail jumped into a dented white pickup parked in front of the barn. He sped past those running to safety.

"Head count. Now!" Dane focused on the man who'd saved his truck. "Idiot! Is a truck worth your life?"

"Can't make a living without my tools."

Unfazed by the reprimand, the wiry, gray-haired idiot strode purposefully past Dane to the cluster of workers wearing similar mud-brown Utley Construction T-shirts.

Flynn couldn't shake the feeling that he'd seen the man before.

"If you weren't such a good worker, I'd wring your neck, then fire you," Dane called after him, receiving a shrug in answer.

"I can't see a thing. And I don't hear anyone inside." Slade squinted toward the still-dissipating dust clouds. "Do you?"

"No," Flynn rasped, listening for any calls for help from the barn.

What if someone had been killed? What if their decision to salvage what they could from the barn instead of razing it meant someone wasn't coming home tonight? A dust cloud enveloped him. He pulled his T-shirt over his mouth, hoping that would help him breathe easier.

The world hadn't totally screwed him. The barn held. The sun continued to shine. Beyond that, Flynn was having a hard time finding a silver lining.

"Everyone's accounted for," Dane announced moments later.

"Thank God," Flynn murmured into his shirt. As favors went, that was huge. Unfortunately, his timeline had undoubtedly ballooned.

The balding inspector faced Dane looking like Christmas had come early and Santa hadn't fulfilled any of his requests. "What happened?"

"We were shoring up the beams on the north side," Dane said. "It must have caused instability on the south."

Slade tugged Flynn away from the others. "Let's tear the barn down and rebuild. It's safer and cheaper."

"I know you're worried about the budget, but this is a piece of Harmony Valley history. We promised to preserve it."

"Some promises aren't meant to be kept." Slade gestured toward the barn. "If someone had been hurt or killed trying to preserve the barn, we'd be ruined."

The inspector was shaking his head at Dane. "This got away from you. I'm shutting everything down on both structures until you can reassure me that any work—be it demolition or rework—is safe."

"Which is when?" Flynn quit pretending he wasn't listening.

"Until it's safe," the inspector repeated coldly.

Word quickly spread through the men that work was over for the day, sending them streaming like large ants toward the rows of parked trucks, until only a few of Dane's crew remained.

"It's going to be hell proving to County this is a safe construction site unless we take her completely down." Dane turned to Flynn. "I suggest we demolish the whole thing, salvage what boards, posts and beams we can, and resell the rest. There's a good market for old, weathered barn wood."

The promise they'd made to the community warred with the pressing need to speed things up. "How long?"

Dane looked toward the trees lining the river. "We'll lose three to five days from the collapse and a day or two in salvage. We're out in the boonies. County inspectors can't just stop by on their way to another job. We're at the mercy of their schedule."

Flynn hated when things were out of his control. A programmer by trade, he liked plugging in commands and seeing them work in predictable, stable order.

"I'd like to see the estimate for a complete demo before we decide how to proceed," Slade said.

Flynn nodded in defeat. "And we'll need to confer with Will."

The construction worker who'd rescued his truck appeared at Dane's shoulder. His gaze pierced Flynn's, distracting him for a moment from the outline of familiar cheekbones and sharp chin Flynn suspected was hidden beneath the man's gray goatee.

"Before you go, I'd like you to meet my job foreman, Joey Harris." Dane's voice sounded like it was coming from far away.

Flynn's vision dropped from those unapologetic eyes to the hourglass prison tattoo on his forearm.

It couldn't be…

He would never…

But it was. And he had.

Dane's foreman was Flynn's father.

CHAPTER THREE

Rose aimed her antique ladies birding binoculars out the window at Agnes hurrying back to the car. "Where did you get that ring?"

Drat. Agnes was hoping that her two friends wouldn't notice the ruby ring. And Rose hadn't until she'd retrieved her binoculars, a pair Agnes assumed would only magnify the appearance of a bird if she was standing beneath the tree it was in. And only if it was a small tree.

Agnes slid behind the wheel of her beloved Buick, a pair of binoculars draped around her neck. "I got a call from Mayor Larry. Part of the Henderson barn just collapsed."

From the backseat, Rose gasped.

"Was anyone hurt?" Mildred lowered her own binoculars.

"No." Agnes started the car and headed toward Jefferson Street and the Harmony River bridge. The morning sun had yet to chase away the briskness in the air. It reached through the windows and chilled Agnes to the bone.

"Agnes, about the ring?" Rose was doggedly annoying sometimes.

"Which ring?" Agnes tried to play dumb.

"The red ring as big as a stapler on your finger," Rose said sarcastically. "Do you think I'm as blind as Mildred?"

"I take offense to that," Mildred half turned, her eyes barely visible behind her thick lenses.

Rose huffed. "As if you noticed Agnes was wearing a new ring."

Harold's ruby ring glinted on Agnes's right hand. She'd returned the engagement ring to him decades ago on the Harmony River bridge. The same day the army informed her there'd been a mistake—her husband hadn't died in the Battle of Inchon. He'd been captured, freed and was coming home, leaving Agnes to choose between her childhood sweetheart and the man who'd picked up the pieces of her heart when she thought her first love was dead. "I can't believe we're talking about a ring when there's been an accident at the winery."

"Thank heavens no one was hurt or killed."

Suitably distracted, for now, Rose clutched the back of Agnes's seat as she took a corner faster than usual. "Do you think they'll realize this is an omen and quit?" Rose wasn't a proponent of change.

"More likely they'll realize the barn is past saving." Mildred raised her binoculars to her thick glasses, twisting the dials for a clearer view, which was nearly impossible given Mildred was legally blind. "Sometimes you need to cut your losses and move on. No regrets, right, ladies?"

Agnes pressed her lips closed and tried not to look at the ruby ring. She had regrets aplenty. If she'd chosen Harold that day instead of honoring her wedding vows, maybe her life would have been different. She was nearly eighty and she'd never gone skydiving or driven a race car, something both of her friends had done. Her days were spent cleaning and gardening, meeting up with Mildred and Rose to go to a museum or the botanical gardens. She'd been a boring, devoted housewife, and that was no doubt why her kids and grandchildren rarely came to visit.

The ruby winked at her, reminding Agnes

of all that life had to offer. She could hear Harold's baritone whispering in her ear: *come away with me.*

She'd been unable to run away. She'd needed to stand by the promises she'd made. She had more promises keeping her here today, as she tried to breathe some much-needed life into Harmony Valley before it became a ghost town.

"It's a shame when old things give out." Rose sniffed. "I just wish this winery business would go away."

"Rose, please." The winery was Agnes's only means to attract some of her family back to Harmony Valley. She wanted the chance to mention to one of the men starting the winery that her granddaughter, Christine, was an award-winning winemaker. She wanted the chance to mention that her daughter, Joanna, loved dealing with the public and might enjoy working in the tasting room. But she didn't want to appear as if she was asking for any favors.

She didn't want to be one of those old women who schemed and manipulated.

But if it was all she had left…

EDWIN WAS QUIET on the ride home. Abby rested her head on his shoulder. He squinted frequently into the side-view mirror, as if checking to see if someone was following them.

"Here we are at your house, safe and sound." Becca tried to sound reassuring. At her last job, Harold's edema had caused bouts of disorientation, especially when the old man was tired. A little grounding and reassurance were called for. "Are you expecting someone? Perhaps the person you saw back at the winery?"

"No. I thought I saw... But it couldn't be."

"Well, we're the only ones here now."

Abby was their chaperone as they made their way into the house, waiting patiently as they paused on each porch step so Edwin could catch his breath.

"You don't have to fuss over me. I was military intelligence." Settling into his recliner, Edwin smiled with the half of his face unaffected by the stroke. "Although you couldn't tell by looking at this old body, I directed campaigns and prevented wars."

Becca could have guessed the old man's profession by looking around the house. Edwin's good deeds had been acknowledged and rewarded with framed ornate military accommodations and medals. He'd be remembered as an honorable war hero, while she...

Becca's composure wavered like a flag in a hostile breeze. How would she be remembered? As a compassionate woman who helped the elderly she cared for? Or—as Virginia O'Dell's family accused—a woman who took advantage?

She never should have given Agnes that ruby ring. But how could she refuse Harold's dying request to prove he'd never stopped loving Agnes? Becca's protests to him about amending his will went nowhere.

It was the look on Agnes's face that made the risk worth it. The delight she'd tried to hide that a former lover had remembered her, tears she couldn't conceal when emotions overwhelmed her—grief, joy, regret, happiness. She'd hugged Becca as if she'd delivered Harold himself into her arms.

Just for a moment, Becca felt she belonged somewhere again. She'd welcomed the invitation to spend the weekend, hanging out with Agnes and her energetic friends. Baking banana nut muffins and singing show tunes.

A cool breeze coming off the river fluttered through the screen. Becca draped a deep green afghan over Edwin, who was staring at Flynn's graduation picture. His eyes were hooded, haunted. She rearranged the pillows beneath his feet and stepped back to survey her work, pausing to pat Abby's head. "Who did you think you saw back there?"

"Someone from the past." Edwin lisped slightly more than he had yesterday, a sign the morning's events had taxed his strength.

Abby padded over to the door, circled a spot on the foyer's black and white linoleum twice and lay down with a contented grunt.

Becca sat on the blue plaid couch. Dust puffed out of the cushions. She knew she shouldn't pry, but something was bothering Edwin, and she hated when her clients weren't mentally and physically at ease. "Was it someone from Flynn's past? Or yours?"

Edwin's gaze ricocheted to Becca's. Difficult as it was in the chair, he thrust his chest forward, and his shoulders back. "I didn't say."

"Of course, you didn't," Becca soothed. "It's none of my business." But she wondered nonetheless as she stared at the divots in the orange carpet marking where the coffee table had recently been moved. "Have you had breakfast? Do you like scrambled eggs?"

Edwin sighed. "I can make my own breakfast."

Not hardly, in his weakened state.

"It's okay to ask for help or accept a little help while you're on the mend." Why was independence the hardest thing for seniors to give up? When Becca was eighty, she wouldn't put up a fuss if someone wanted to cook for her.

"I've never asked for help and I'm not starting now." Edwin glanced toward the remote resting on the end table nearest him, just out of reach. "Could you turn on the television?"

Becca laughed. Edwin quickly realized he'd asked for help and did, too.

As their laughter died away, Edwin stared at Flynn's picture again. Worry etched a stockpile of wrinkles around his eyes. She'd seen that look before—in the eyes of her mother, her grandmother, and most recently, Harold Epstein.

"Sometimes..." Becca tried to stop herself. She didn't need any more trouble. But stress hindered recovery, and knowing Edwin had been in military intelligence, he probably had plenty of secrets, perhaps ones he still kept from Flynn, perhaps ones he didn't really want to take to his grave. She suspected he needed an outlet, a sympathetic ear, a keeper of secrets. Not her, of course. She'd made that mistake before and look where it'd gotten her. "Sometimes you might need help of a different kind. For example, you might want to get something off your chest or need help sorting through a box you stored in the attic."

There was a wounded quality to Edwin's gaze that indicated Becca's words struck a target the old man may not have realized he'd been harboring.

"Mostly, you should ask for a hand when you're unsteady. The rest of it—" the bucket list, the last wishes, the people he needed to make peace with. There was no hurry except to unburden himself. According to town gossip, he had years left in him "—just know that Flynn can help you if you talk to him." That was good. She didn't need to get involved.

Perhaps things would have turned out differently with Harold if he'd had a family member he was willing to confide in, instead of a daughter who considered him an inconvenience.

"Flynn's too busy to talk now," Edwin said gruffly. "We're going on a trip in three months. I'll talk to him then."

That seemed a long wait for an old man.

"We used to sit out on the porch every night and talk, weather permitting." Edwin shook a puffy finger at her. "Traditions are important in this family and in this town. I want traditions to live on. Like celebrating the successes of your neighbors every spring or walking the girl you're courting home and kissing her good-night on the Harmony River bridge."

"Did you follow that tradition?" she teased.

The old man had the sweetest blush. She was glad the world and Flynn weren't losing him just yet. "A good man doesn't kiss and tell. But I'll tell you this—I would never replace a good-night kiss on a bridge with a good-night text message or whatever it is young people do nowadays."

"I used to use Skype with my husband every morning when he was overseas." Becca's gaze caught on the picture over the fireplace of a young Edwin and his bride. Edwin wore his army uniform, his chest covered with medals, his stature approachably proud. His wife wore linen and lace, an unusual heart-shaped necklace and a smile Becca recognized—that of a joyous bride on her wedding day.

In his dress blues, Terry had looked just as proud the day they'd married, and Becca just as joyful. They'd taken pictures alone at the base chapel and then more pictures surrounded by Terry's family and friends.

Edwin noticed her staring at the photo. "Irma died nineteen years ago this July. She was volunteering at the veterans' hospital in Santa Rosa and had a brain aneurism. They told me she never suffered."

Suddenly chilly, Becca zipped up her pink hoodie. She knew all too well how quickly love and family could be stolen away.

"Flynn arrived soon after Irma died. If it wasn't for him, I might not have had the will to go on. I was almost grateful that my daughter, Maggie, thought I could give him a better life."

Needing a distraction, Becca pointed to a picture of Flynn and a redhead. "Who's that?"

"Flynn's half sister, Kathy. They're my daughter's children. I took Kathy in a few years after Flynn. She and my great-grandson live in Santa Rose. That's Truman on the mantle."

Truman had the ginger coloring of his mother and uncle, but the reserved smile was unexpected for a little boy.

"Becca, you're going to work for me and move to Harmony Valley permanently," Edwin proclaimed. "Someday soon we'll reopen the medical clinic here in town and you can work there. In the meantime, there's plenty for you to do. All we have around here are old people."

Becca would be happy with a few weeks of work and an impeccable employment reference.

The phone rang.

Edwin wrested a hand free of the afghan and answered. His face quickly drained of all color. "Thank, God. Keep me updated." He hung up.

Couch springs creaked as she stood. "What's wrong?"

"Part of the winery collapsed about half an hour ago."

"Is…is…" *Flynn all right?* She couldn't get

the words out, not past the stab of pain in her chest.

She would have thought she'd be unfazed by death after everything she'd been through. But she wasn't. It slipped in like a knife into a not-quite-healed scar somewhere in the vicinity of her heart.

"Everyone is fine, including Flynn."

Neither one of them spoke for a good minute. Maybe two.

"You should stay," he said gruffly, staring at the ceiling. "Harmony Valley has everything you're looking for."

"Except a job," she deadpanned, rubbing her hands on her thighs. She still felt shaken.

"Nonsense. I'm hiring you. I can't wait for Flynn and his background checks. He'll be busier than ever now with the winery."

That suited Becca just fine.

THE HARD MILES prison put on a man were inscribed on Joey Harris more indelibly than the numerous tattoos on his arms. It was apparent in the wrinkles in his sunken cheeks and the way his skin clung to him like a second-hand suit, worn and slightly saggy.

The man who fathered Flynn stood with his hand outstretched.

Flynn felt as if he was falling, jerked back, plunged into memories he'd buried deep enough he should never have been able to find them.

Father's Day. Eighteen years ago. His dad, looking young, strong and healthy, playing catch with Flynn on the front lawn of their apartment complex. Tall, handsome, those bladed cheekbones he'd given Flynn framing his infectious smile.

Flynn's dad wasn't like other dads. Sure, he was gone sometimes. He'd missed Christmas two times in a row. Sure, he had a temper. Flynn had gotten good at hiding behind the couch during his blowups, where everything from hammers to beer bottles might go flying across the room.

But lately his dad had been home every night, lately nothing more than a baseball had flown out of his dad's hand. He walked Flynn to school and picked him up afterward. His dad knew how to fix things. He was like a magician—starting cars and opening doors without keys. Flynn's dad was turning out to be the best dad ever.

The sirens were just background noise. The rhythm of the ball snapping into their gloves countered the volume-increasing announcement that the police were in a hurry. There must have been a car accident somewhere. Or a fire. The closer the sirens came, the more distracted Flynn's father became.

"Dad, come on." Flynn struck his eight-year-old fist into new, empty leather. Over the past few days, it'd been like Christmas in June. A new bike, a new video game system, new shoes and clothes for Flynn and his sister.

Instead of throwing the ball, his father turned toward the intersection down the block, watching as three patrol cars cut the corner on the wide turn. "Go up to the apartment," he commanded without turning around.

The first cold tingle of dread prickled in Flynn's belly. "Dad?"

His father spun, his scowling features a deadly, chalky white. "Go! Now!"

The jagged edge to his voice. The threat of more than a baseball being thrown.

Flynn fled, fighting back tears.

He got as far as the second-story balcony before the black-and-whites squealed to a halt, spilling booted uniforms and guns onto the sidewalk, aiming at his dad as if he were a criminal.

They couldn't kill him. He was the best dad in the world.

Flynn hadn't realized he was screaming until his father turned around, his hands high in the air, saying the words Flynn had assumed would be the last he'd ever exchange with him, "Get your butt inside!"

"Do you two know each other?" Dane asked, frowning when Flynn didn't reciprocate Joey's handshake.

The sun warmed Flynn's face, but his insides were making ice cubes. Now he could name the emotion he'd seen on Becca's face when they first met and he hadn't immediately hired her. It was the same look he'd seen years ago on Joey's face. Captured. Cornered. Trapped.

The question was: *Why?*

Slade stepped between Flynn and Joey, saving the moment that Flynn had no intention of saving.

Awkward? Who cared? The man had left him—no calls, no letters, no postprison visits. He didn't deserve the title Father.

Joey—Flynn refused to think of the man as

his dad—did a civilized meet-and-greet with Slade, all the while keeping his gaze trained on Flynn.

Presumably, he was still looking at Flynn when Flynn walked away.

CHAPTER FOUR

HOURS LATER, WHEN a long walk along the banks of the Harmony River had drained the resentment over the appearance of Joey Harris out of his system, Flynn's feet led him home.

He'd stayed away too long. Worry for his grandfather's condition had resumed its piggy-back position on his shoulders. Until the cell phone tower was completed, no one could get in touch with him if there was an emergency.

He didn't recognize the car parked in front of the house.

Becca's dog barked once. Her small nose pressed against the screen.

Flynn removed his muddy work boots, listening with relief to the sound of his grandfather's I'm-in-command voice. "I see you live in Santa Rosa. We'd want you here by seven every morning."

It came back in a rush—another candidate for caregiver—shoving his shock and hurt over Joey aside. Grandpa Ed was scaring her off, leaving him no choice but to hire Becca. Despite the town council's endorsement, he couldn't hire Becca until he knew what she was running from. If she'd broken the law, there was no way he'd hire her.

Flynn threw open the screen door so hard it banged against the opposite wall.

Everyone in the house paused to stare at him, even the dog.

Becca's hand was frozen midair, clutching a coffee mug she'd been about to put in the dishwasher. The skin around her eyes was tense.

Definitely cornered, ready to run.

Flynn looked away.

Grandpa Ed pinned him with a stern expression that demanded an apology.

After a moment, Flynn muttered one.

An older woman sat on the couch across from his grandfather. She was as tall as she was wide, dressed in dark blue scrubs decorated with the bodies of pro wrestlers. Her thinning, too-brown hair was helmet-short. And the frown she wore indicated the interview he'd forgotten about wasn't going well and wouldn't likely improve with his appearance.

His grandfather performed the introductions. "Miss Caldwell's come a long, long way for this interview."

"I'm sorry I'm late." Flynn came forward to shake Miss Caldwell's hand. "We had an emergency at the construction site."

"So I heard." Miss Caldwell stood, accepting his handshake with a firm one worthy of the professional wrestlers that dotted her attire. She remained standing, as if preparing to leave. "Is the position still open?"

"No," Grandpa Ed said briskly. "I've got Becca."

Flynn ignored him. "We haven't made a decision. Becca is a temporary solution."

Miss Caldwell didn't believe Flynn, nor did she sit. She glanced toward the kitchen.

Flynn followed the direction of her gaze.

Becca wore the same black exercise leggings and pink hoodie that she'd had on that morning. Her long, black hair hung in a thick, smooth braid down her back. No scrubs. No disapproving frown, although he knew she had one. Becca looked like someone's girlfriend, not a caregiver.

Flynn blinked and glanced back at Miss Caldwell, who looked as if she might want to plant at least one of her bright white sneakers on his backside.

"Well." Miss Caldwell ping-ponged looks at each of them. "Mr. Blonkowski has my résumé. I'd better be going."

Given the choice between arguing that Miss Caldwell should stay or having his caregiver—at least temporarily—be Becca, Flynn surprised himself. He thanked Miss Caldwell for coming, and escorted her as far as the front door.

Grandpa Ed turned on a rerun of *Jeopardy!* The well-known theme blared from the television.

Flynn swiped the remote from him and muted the show. "I thought we agreed to be nice."

"Miss Caldwell wouldn't have lasted a week driving an hour in good traffic, much less ninety minutes each way in bad traffic. Did you see her chin? It was soft. The first time I lost my temper she'd be out the door. I did her a favor."

"She looked capable enough to me." The term *battle-ax* came to mind.

"She's very qualified." Becca scrubbed the sink as if it deserved punishment. "I think she'd do an excellent job. She wouldn't quit in a week."

"She might last two," Grandpa Ed allowed grumpily. He lowered his voice. "Any woman who'd praise the competition is worth hiring."

Flynn took off his baseball cap and ran a hand through his hair. It was long enough to pull into a short ponytail, longer than Joey's had been the last time he'd seen him, but not as long as Joey's had been today. "You drove Miss Caldwell away."

His grandfather huffed. "I did not."

"Yes, you did." Becca wiped her hands on a dish towel, sniffed it, made a face and set it aside. "She was confused as to why I was here. We used to work at the same agency."

"Used to?" Flynn asked.

"Yes." She drew a deep breath.

Flynn had a feeling he wasn't going to like whatever she said next.

Thank God.

"We don't care about your previous employment." Grandpa Ed gave Flynn the stink eye. His back was to Becca, so she couldn't see him. "Do we, Flynn?"

"Yes, we do."

"No, we don't."

Flynn's fingers dug into the crown of his baseball cap.

"I'll tell you anyway." Becca raised her chin, as if bracing herself for a punch.

Flynn looked forward to whatever she was about to say. Her confession would most likely convince his grandfather they couldn't hire her.

"Three years ago I moved to Santa Rosa. I worked for the agency that's sending candidates out here. I was assigned to care for an elderly woman who rescued Australian shepherds." Becca walked over and knelt beside Abby, stroking her dark fur. "When Lily passed away, her son wanted to take all the dogs to the kill-shelter. I protested and eventually found homes for them all, including Abby. But I got fired because caregivers aren't supposed to get involved with their clients."

The little dog stared at Flynn with dark, accusing eyes, as if to say: *find fault with that*.

Grandpa Ed scowled at Flynn. "You did the right thing, Becca. No one's accusing you of anything."

His grandfather couldn't see Becca's features flinch, as if the right hook she'd been waiting for had been struck. Flynn felt a corresponding jab to his gut.

She was guilty. Of what, he had no idea. But if she was the only acceptable option to Grandpa Ed, he was going to find out what she was hiding.

"We'll be hiring you regardless," Grandpa Ed said. "Won't we, Flynn?"

Flynn didn't answer. He looked at Becca. Deal breakers lined up in his head like dominos—theft, blackmail, murder, angry ex-husbands searching for her. "I need to talk to Becca outside. Alone."

To her credit, Becca walked out, head high, as if she'd known all along the gallows awaited.

He led her toward the river, stopping to sit on a fallen log overlooking the steep bank that cut away to the slow-flowing water. She settled on the log a few feet away from him, brushing at the bark as if it was a crumb-littered bench seat at a restaurant.

"I'm sure you've realized my grandfather wants to hire you," Flynn began. "But there's something else you're not telling me and I won't hire you until I know what it is."

THE TRUTH PRESSED at Becca's throat.

She swallowed it back.

Took a breath.

Risked looking toward Flynn.

Beneath his black ball cap, his reddish-brown hair glinted in the afternoon sunlight, almost as blinding as the rippling river. His jaw was a hard line. She couldn't look him in the eye.

The truth pressed on her once more.

Becca swallowed it again.

She and the truth had an odd track record. Like the time her father had walked out after learning Becca's mother had stage-four cancer. Or the first time Terry had asked her to marry him. He'd walked out when she'd said she was scared and needed time to think.

Abby pranced across Becca's toes and looked down the steep, crumbling bank toward the river, her nose quivering.

"You have two choices if you want the job." Flynn's voice was as unflappable as his jaw line. "You can tell me what you're hiding or I can do a background check."

Tell him the truth? Which version? No one ever really wanted to hear the unvarnished truth. They wanted a massaged answer tailored to their expectations. Telling Flynn about the lawsuit placed her odds of landing the job near zero. But it was a definite zero if she walked away without saying anything.

"I want this job." She swallowed and re-phrased. "I need this job." To repair her rep-utation before it fell from somewhere near barely employable to no-way-in-Hades em-ployable.

"I need someone I can trust taking care of my grandfather."

Untrustworthy. Becca stiffened. She glanced over her shoulder at the driveway, even as Abby picked her way daintily to the shoreline.

"Agnes trusts you," he said softly. "And I trust Agnes. But I need a reason to believe in you."

His words drew her gaze back toward his. Gone were the hard lines, the guardedness, the at-a-distance cool. In their place was com-passion. A white-flagged truce.

If there was a chance, she had to take it. She had to speak up, without varnish or angles. On a big gust of forced air, she told him the truth. "After leaving the agency I went to work for a wonderful woman who was estranged from her son. Gary had decided twenty-some years prior that his mother didn't respect him enough, so he didn't visit. He didn't call. The most he could be troubled with was a generic card on holidays." Virginia had been heartbroken every Christmas, every birthday. "I worked for Virginia for two years, and while I was with her, she learned that I had a tremendous amount of debt."

At the mention of her money woes, Flynn's expression seemed to close off.

It seemed pointless to say more, but Becca hadn't told a soul other than her lawyer, and the story continued to bubble out. "My husband and I had bought a house in San Diego and when he died, I couldn't make the payments. Terry had life insurance, but we'd only been married a few months when he died. He hadn't changed his policy to include me." She twisted her wedding ring. "The money went to his mom. The debts went to me. I sold his truck. I sold our furniture. I traded my car for the motorhome and let the house slide into foreclosure, but we still had credit card debt." It was amazing how quickly the interest on a few purchases multiplied. "When Virginia's kidneys started to fail, she insisted on paying off the last ten thousand dollars I owed. I knew it went against the caregiver code, but by then she was more like a grandmother than a client, so I accepted."

"Ten thousand dollars." Flynn's voice was so flat. Him being a millionaire and all, ten thousand dollars was probably nothing.

To her, it'd been a fortune. "I'd been struggling for so long, I didn't want to struggle anymore. I shouldn't have taken that check." Becca rubbed her palms up and down her thighs. "I didn't ask for the money. I've never asked my clients for anything."

"I bet Virginia's son was livid."

"There's an understatement." Becca wanted to laugh but couldn't quite work up the energy. "Although he inherited close to half a million dollars, he's trying to bring a lawsuit against me."

"Trying?"

"There's a pretrial hearing in a few weeks." She rubbed her hands over her legs again. "I know accepting that money wasn't one hundred percent right, but it wasn't one hundred percent wrong, either."

He studied her face, intent blue gaze checking for any clue that she was less than truthful. "The legal system moves slowly. What've you been doing since Virginia died?"

"I spent the past nine months working for a wonderful man who passed away from heart failure a few weeks ago." She'd told Harold she couldn't deliver the ring. He'd argued, in a twiglike voice staked with death-is-coming urgency, that his daughter would think he'd had an affair if he left the ring to Agnes in his will. It'd taken Becca a week after his death to work up the courage to contact Agnes. And a week more to show her face.

Regrets? She had too many.

"And you didn't accept any money from him?"

"No." Her voice was low and husky. Her liar's voice. She prayed he wouldn't notice. She hadn't accepted money, after all. But if Harold's daughter looked for the ring...

"Why live in a motorhome? You're out of debt now, right? Why not rent an apartment?"

Why was it Flynn asked questions no one else did? Questions Becca didn't want to answer. But the job was at stake and she'd already told him so much. "I helped my mother pass on. I helped my grandmother pass on. I'm on a first-name basis with grief, but that doesn't mean that I can shoulder the cares of my client's family. During their last few days, I'm already thinking about where I'll go next. I know it's a cowardly defense mechanism, but it works for me."

It had been different when Terry was alive. The San Diego metropolitan area had all been new to her, making it easier to accept assignments in suburbs that had different characters and different landscapes.

When Flynn didn't say anything, Becca pressed on. "I like people. Your grandfather may grow fond of me. I can tell him about my case, if you like, to make sure he's still comfortable hiring me. But from what Agnes told me, you'll only need someone for a few weeks." When she was done, she might even accept another assignment in the small, quaint town.

Flynn blinked, confusion crowding his brows.

"I mean," Becca clarified, because it looked like Flynn thought Agnes had predicted Edwin's demise, "Agnes said you told her it would only be a few weeks before Edwin is up and moving around. Like his old self."

"Yes," he said vaguely, turning to stare at

the river, as if trying to figure out how to gracefully get rid of her.

Her getting the job also seemed to have drifted down river. "I'm so glad your grandfather's prognosis is good. I'd like to say goodbye to him before—"

Flynn's glance cut to her.

"—I leave." She stood and whistled for Abby, who was rooting around deep in the bushes lining the bank.

"Wait." Flynn touched her hand, sending a current of heat up her arm. He pulled away abruptly and ran his fingers against his thumb, over and over, as if she'd shocked him and his fingers needed reassurance that nothing out of the ordinary had happened.

She'd shocked herself. The jolt of awareness proved that he was a man and she a woman. If there was an awareness switch, she'd like it turned off, please.

Abby ran up the bank, dancing at Becca's feet.

"I know I'm going to regret this." Flynn was still rubbing his fingers over his thumb, staring at them in wonder. "I won't let you near my money or my grandfather's checkbook. What assurance can you give me that you won't take advantage of him? Or me?"

He was offering her the job in a roundabout way that wounded her pride.

Common sense dictated a grateful yet graceful acceptance. "Only my word. If you can't accept that, I'm sure Gerry Caldwell is available."

His brows lowered. "Grandpa Ed wants you. I know you need this job, probably for a character reference or something that'll help you with your court case."

"How did you—"

"I guessed. It's what I'd do. Keep my nose clean. Working for a millionaire without any missteps can be a powerful statement." His words were all business, even if his gaze pried and stroked where it didn't belong.

Blackberry bushes lined the path they'd taken to the river. Bees buzzed behind her, the noise vibrating against the circular realization that there was no trust here. No trust. She wanted him to have faith in her.

What she didn't want, what she couldn't afford, was the attraction between them, stoked by his intent gaze, as if he, too, was trying to figure out: *Why her?*

"This is a bad idea." She turned and started down the path back to the house.

Abby leaped ahead.

"Wait." His longer legs stretched past her, until he blocked her way. "They released my grandfather from the hospital, but his health is a delicate balance. You seem to understand him. He'll be upset if I hire someone like Gerry Caldwell."

"Your grandfather will be fine. People overcome this kind of thing all the time." She couldn't not reassure him. Who wouldn't be afraid of losing a loved one after two heart attacks and a stroke? She tried to go around him, but Flynn stepped in her way again.

"I know I can be blunt—"

She crossed her arms tightly over her chest.

Abby came to sit at her heels.

"But…" Flynn opened his mouth, closed it and opened it again. "You aren't making this easy. Not by showing up unannounced, when the only people who show up at my doorstep or call anymore are trying to scam me. And not by telling me you took money from a client."

"And?" She sensed there was more.

"And truthfully, I had something of a shock

this morning. I saw the man who calls himself my father at the job site. He's an ex-con and the reason I have zero tolerance for people who break the law."

Becca's arms loosened. "I think your grandfather saw him, too."

"He told you?"

"No. Edwin said he saw someone he knew, but he looked like he'd seen a ghost. It upset him." She stared into Flynn's clear blue eyes and lost her train of thought.

"It upset me, too. He robbed a bank when I was eight. I haven't seen him for close to twenty years. Not that it matters. He's not getting any money from me, and I don't care what he thinks of me." He paused and shifted awkwardly, as if realizing his mouth had run past the normal filter applied by his brain.

Becca saw the little hurt boy behind his eyes, and a part of her she needed solid and strong softened. Her hand twitched with the urge to reach out and comfort him. A light touch to the arm, the shoulder, his cheek.

Not helpful. So not helpful. She shoved her hands into her hoodie pockets and started walking.

He matched her pace until they nearly

bumped hips on the narrow trail, until she had to stop before they toppled on each other. This time, Abby waited ahead of them.

Becca drew a breath. "Really, I'm grateful—"

"I need help, Becca. You'll make my grandfather happy." The sincerity in his tone made her hope, that treacherous thing, whisper in Becca's ear—about happy defense attorneys and dismissed court cases. Impossible. "Are you sure you can trust me in your home every day?"

Trust me with your grandfather? With your things? With you?

Becca's gaze rested on the ground, where, presumably, she'd find her lost common sense. Instead, she saw a glint of copper, barely visible in the dirt beneath the toe of Flynn's sneakers.

It couldn't be a penny. It had to be a leaf or a rock or something.

She could feel Flynn's gaze upon her, gauging her character. "Old Virginia didn't write a will or anything?"

"I have no proof. Only my word." She tried not to sound bitter, but she was afraid she failed. "It doesn't seem like you have much faith in people." And yet, there was the penny, clearly visible when Flynn shifted his feet, an indication that she should accept.

"Since I became wealthy, my faith in my fellow man has been put to the test." Flynn tipped up the brim of his baseball cap. "However, I am good at offering second chances. Are you good at accepting them?"

Becca searched his face to see if this was some kind of cruel joke.

He wasn't joking. His blue eyes reflected a combination of sorrow and regret. He wanted to believe the best in her. Wanted, but couldn't quite. "For my grandfather, if not for me."

Her determination to refuse him wavered. If she took this job, she'd see Flynn every day. A daily opportunity for attraction to bloom and cause complications. Complications to the lawsuit, to her equilibrium, to her heart.

None of that mattered as much as it should. Edwin needed good care and she could give it to him.

As if sensing her capitulation, Flynn named a generous hourly wage.

Part of her wanted to accept the indecent sum. The sensible part of her realized it would only make her look guilty in his eyes. And others.

She snuck a glance at the penny again, at President Lincoln's wise stare.

It was official. She was nuts. "I'll take half that an hour." It was what the agency would have paid her.

Flynn started to protest, but she'd have none of it. "That's my going rate. Take it or leave it. I won't let you overpay me."

He chuckled mirthlessly. "Everyone lets me overpay them."

"Then you're a gullible fool. I can work for you until my hearing. In exchange, I want a letter of reference from your grandfather."

He cocked one burnished eyebrow. "Why not from me? I'll be the one paying you."

She shrugged, as if it didn't matter, when in fact she'd sell her wounded soul for two good references. "Okay, I'll take both." The combination was a one-two punch that could knock the lawsuit against her off its foundation.

"Let's shake on the deal." Flynn's smile didn't penetrate her armor. She was ready for it this time.

Their hands met in midair.
Becca told herself she felt nothing.
She was a horrible liar.

CHAPTER FIVE

"WE NEED TO TALK." Grandpa Ed was waiting for Flynn in his recliner. The television—off. The old man's lopsided frown—on.

Flynn felt as if he'd been caught out past curfew. Only this time, the only crime he was guilty of was ignoring his urge for self-preservation and submitting to his grandfather's wishes. "I hired Becca."

He'd hired her, giving her the impression that Grandpa Ed was going to get better. Despite the truth—that Edwin might very well die before her court hearing. Despite how worry and determination in her gaze seemed connected to his chest—the more noticeable the worry, the tighter his chest. He'd always been a sucker for people in need.

Need was not a word he wanted applied to the dark-haired, legally harried beauty.

Grandpa Ed's fingers brushed air, as if casting his concerns aside. "It was the right thing to do. That girl needs the job more than I need her."

And here he'd thought his grandfather was charmed by Becca. He'd never figure his grandfather out.

Flynn sank onto the couch.

"I saw your father today." Grandpa Ed sounded old and hollow.

Flynn nodded, grateful for Becca's heads-up. "He works for the main contractor on our winery." Flynn tried to keep his voice calm. Stress and upheaval were to be avoided with his grandfather at all costs.

Unfortunately, Joey Harris embodied stress and upheaval.

"Fire him. He's only there for your money."

It was Flynn's fear, as well. "I'm not firing him."

"Flynn—"

"It's what he'd do. Fire someone he didn't like. I'm not sinking to Joey's level." Flynn lowered his voice, tried to sound upbeat. "Letting Joey work there proves he means nothing to me."

"But what if he tries to talk to you? What if he comes here?" Panic noosed about Grandpa

Ed's words, as if the old man had something to fear from his son-in-law.

"He won't." Flynn wouldn't let him.

"But—"

"He won't dare show his face at the house." But the only way Flynn could make sure he didn't was to tell Joey he wasn't welcome here. Face-to-face. Man to man. Boss to hired help.

Flynn had every reason to expect his command would be obeyed.

If he didn't factor in things like history or experience.

BECCA HAD TO be more careful what she wished for. She'd wished for the perfect job.

The perfect job was one where she never had to care for someone who was dying, where she could earn a great character reference, where she could walk away without saying goodbye in a cemetery.

She should have specified to God and the Universe that the perfect job also entailed a No Hottie Zone.

Becca slouched into the dinette couch in her motorhome and stared at the two pictures beneath the kitchen cupboards. Terry hugging a buddy after making it through an obstacle course during training, his face striped in camouflage paint. But no amount of camouflage could disguise his grin. He'd loved the marines. He'd loved the action and the hardship and the honor. He'd loved her. If she lost the lawsuit, Terry would be disappointed.

Abby jumped into the shotgun seat of the motorhome, looked out the window and barked.

Something thumped against the door. "Becca, there's a phone call for you." It was Agnes, whose hospitality was a bright note amid the stress.

The only person Becca had given Agnes's number to was her lawyer. Her heart didn't leap with anticipation or hope. It did a slow slide toward her toes.

"I brought dinner." Agnes held a tray with two plates of chicken and vegetables. Her cordless phone was wedged in between the plates, at risk of being ambushed by the broccoli.

Becca relieved Agnes of the tray, placed it on the motorhome's dining table and picked up the cordless phone.

Agnes followed her up the stairs. Her

sweet, short self looked more fitting in the motorhome than Becca felt most days.

"I've been talking to your landlady. I hear you got a job." Hank Weinstein's pack-a-day, deliberate cadence was meant to intimidate clients and foes alike. "I want you to treat this client with kid gloves. I want more than a character reference as an exhibit. I want to put this client of yours on the stand."

Becca tried to imagine out-of-breath Edwin being cross-examined by a hostile attorney. It was easier to picture Flynn in the attorney's face, his temper as fiery as his hair. "I'm not sure he's going to be up to it."

Agnes rummaged in the kitchen drawers for cutlery.

Hank swore. "Is the old guy dying?"

"No." Becca wanted to explain, but she was very much aware of Agnes setting the table and listening. If she'd learned anything about Harmony Valley over the past few days, it was that the elderly residents loved to gossip.

"Then he'll testify. I bumped into opposing counsel in court today and they sounded too excited, like they've got something unpleasant planned."

"Really." Becca didn't like unpleasant surprises. She glanced at the ruby ring on Agnes's finger.

Hank reminded her not to take any gifts—monetary or otherwise—from clients, harped on her about her court date and then hung up.

"Problems?" Agnes asked sweetly, pouring two glasses of milk.

Becca forced a light-hearted response. "Nothing a good lawyer can't handle." After filling Abby's bowl with kibble, Becca sat across from Agnes and cut a piece of chicken. "This is sweet. But I don't expect you to make dinner for me. I'm parked in your driveway, not your guest bedroom."

"I love to cook and I hate eating alone." Agnes looked around the motorhome with undisguised curiosity as she speared broccoli. "This is cozy."

"We like it." It had everything Becca needed—kitchen, bathroom, shower, wheels to move on with. All that was missing was a laundry room.

"Is that your husband?" Agnes pointed to the picture of Terry. "He looks handsome."

The chicken suddenly seemed very dry. Becca swallowed. "He was, although how you can tell beneath all that war paint is beyond me."

"Anyone who can smile like that is handsome in my book." Agnes's gaze moved on to the other picture. "Who are the women?"

"My mom and grandmother. That was taken at Mom's college graduation." The Polaroid shot had faded, even the orange in her grandmother's dress, but their smiles still felt bright.

Abby finished her dinner and went to sit at the steps leading outside, ready for her walk.

"Feel free to park here as long as you like. It's the least I can do, along with a couple of dinners to repay you for bringing me Harold's ring." Agnes gazed at it fondly.

"He told me about your struggles." A widow who wasn't a widow and had chosen to honor her marriage vows, rather than follow her second love.

Agnes glanced furtively around, as if checking to see if anyone was listening at the windows. "No one in Harmony Valley knows. They would have said it was too soon after Manny passed away."

"Not even Rose or Mildred?"

"No one." Her gaze begged for silence.

"Not anyone in my family. Can you imagine what a tramp they'd think I was?"

"I gave my word to Harold that I'd return the ring and not tell a soul." Becca prayed she'd never have to choose between her promise to Harold and self-preservation if Virginia's son's lawyers found out about the ring.

"This ring is proof that love lasts forever." Agnes sounded so certain.

Becca didn't want to disillusion her by adding: *even if life was not.*

"I see love in the peach tree my husband and I planted in the backyard. The winding path he made through the garden for me. His fishing gear in the garage." Agnes pushed her food around her plate. "My loss is wrapped up here, entwined, like my life, to this place. But the ring reminds me that I chose to stay, that I could have gone out into the world, that I could have been…different."

Becca sat very still. She'd given up "their place," divided up Terry's personal things with his mother, split up her memories into manageable chunks. She had little things that fit into her compartmentalized life—his high school basketball jersey, a card he'd made her one Valentine's Day, his Purple Heart medal tucked in her dresser drawer.

"Do you think of him when you see a stray dime?" Agnes asked.

A grief counselor had told Becca about the comforting tradition of thinking it was Terry who placed lost coins in her path, helping reassure her of decisions, reminding her of Terry's love. "I chose pennies."

"My Manny has always been dimes, but I could think of Harold when I see pennies." Agnes gazed out the window. "Like you, I learned too young about grief. It made it hard to love again. But Harold was wonderful. He understood when I needed to be alone, to cry, to have silent conversations with Manny." She managed a brave smile for Becca. "It made it harder to give my heart back to Manny when he returned. It was years before I could trust he wouldn't disappear and leave me with the pain of loss."

Becca nodded. She'd never joined a support group. Agnes was the first widow she'd spoken to about her loss. It felt good to talk to someone who'd been through what she had, even if Agnes's husband had shown up alive a year later. "I've decided not to risk loving again. I'm comfortable with my life."

Flynn's patient expression came to mind, bright blue eyes beneath reddish-brown hair, glistening in the sunlight as he listened to her confession about Virginia's gift. Terry's penny at his feet.

"We'll always grieve. There will always be that sense of loss and emptiness because our men were a part of our hearts." Agnes tsked. "But thinking you'll never love again when you're, what? Twenty-seven? That's just asking for love to be dropped in your life."

"I won't be that foolish." Becca couldn't stand to have her heart torn apart again.

BECCA WAS A FOOL.

Yes, she needed the money this job would bring. Yes, her lawyer was pleased with fresh job-related references. Yes, Edwin needed her.

Yes, she'd had a dream about Flynn.

One of those naked dreams, where she was naked and Flynn noticed.

Becca knocked on Edwin's front door. She was a bit early for her first day at work. It was six forty-five. But she wanted to make sure Flynn saw her with her clothes on. It was one of those "expel the dream" moments by facing a dose of reality.

She knocked again. Abby put one paw on the front stoop and looked at her expectantly.

The house was silent. The wind skipped through the eucalyptus trees bordering the property along the river. The sun had risen long ago, but its rays filtered lazily through a layer of fog.

A quick glance allayed fears that Flynn had taken his grandfather to the hospital. Both Flynn's black truck and Edwin's black Cadillac were in the carport.

Becca knocked a third time.

Abby gave the door a gentle scratch.

The living-room curtain moved, just enough for Becca to catch a glimpse of Flynn in a pair of navy boxers, a toothbrush in his mouth, his wet hair hanging haphazardly around his face. The curtain dropped back, but not before Becca registered how Flynn's body was well formed and muscular.

Heat flooded her veins, filling her mind with unwanted images that had to be part of the dream she didn't remember. His arms around her. His lips working their way along her collarbone.

Becca turned away from the door, fingering her wedding band. She retreated as far as the bottom step, trying to breathe deeply, hoping to dispel the heat rushing through her cheeks. Maybe if she jumped around a bit, made it look like she'd run over from Agnes's house, he'd attribute the blush to exertion rather than…

She refused to give the cause of her blush a name.

The door opened behind her.

She whirled, expecting more of Flynn in boxers, unsure whether she wanted to see him that way or wanted him wearing an unflattering parka, snow pants and a neon orange ski mask.

He'd thrown on jeans and a wrinkled navy T-shirt. His hair still hung around his face, glints of dark copper calling to her fingers. For a moment, Becca imagined she saw a heat in his eyes that matched the temperature in her veins.

She clutched the strap of her purse. "I'm here." So lame. She might just as well have said, *"Take me."*

"I wasn't expecting you this early." The

frost in his voice cooled any misconceptions she'd made.

"I need to do a few things around the house and I…kind of half ran over here. I'm outta breath." Lame didn't get any lamer. "May I come in?" Maybe he'd changed his mind. Maybe he'd realized this was a game of fire they shouldn't be playing. Maybe—

He opened the door wider.

Abby took that as an invitation to enter, bounding inside and trotting around with her nose to the ground. She wouldn't be happy until she tracked down all the occupants in the house. Her tail wagged like a small black fan as she disappeared down the hall.

"Is Edwin up?" Becca put her purse on a hook by the door.

"Not yet."

"I'll make coffee."

He stood between her and the kitchen.

She veered to open the drapes. There was a letter on the coffee table. Still nervous, she picked it up. Totally the rude, uncivilized employee. He should fire her. "India Mentoring Program?"

Flynn walked to her and leaned over her shoulder. "They want me to go to India in

October to mentor other entrepreneurial pro-grammers."

"That's quite an honor." She stepped back with a frantic glance at her jeans and T-shirt, suddenly fearing last night's naked dream was no longer a dream. But she was dressed and so was he.

He looked at her as if she was the trouble his mother had warned him about when he was a teenager. "I like giving back, but it's a monthlong program."

"But that's four months away. Edwin should be stable by then." She edged farther toward the kitchen.

Flynn frowned. "It wouldn't feel right to leave him."

Abby trotted back to Becca, looking happy with herself.

"Did you wake up Edwin, girl?" Becca leaned over and ruffled Abby's fur. She drew a deep breath and shoved her libido back where it belonged—in hibernation. "I'll start by ironing your shirt."

He gazed down at the navy cotton. "Un-necessary."

She shook her head. "Necessary. Unless you're in college and also wear white ankle socks with your flip-flops, you need to wear a decently ironed shirt every day."

"Point taken." He started to peel off his shirt.

"Whoa. House rule number one." She expected she'd need many. "No shirt, no service." Heat creeped up her cheeks again and had her retreating toward the kitchen. "I'll start coffee and breakfast while you iron."

His deep chuckle did nothing to dispel the previous night's dreams.

CHAPTER SIX

"I TOLD YOU Becca would be perfect for the job." Slade's triumphant grin caused Flynn to grumble about good friends and loyalties.

"I thought the finish on the kitchen table was worn off." Will's golden boy grin mirrored Slade's darker version. "Turns out it was just years of grime. Look at this shine." He passed a hand over the smooth surface. "It's a wonder we didn't contract some dreaded disease eating on this thing."

"It wasn't that bad." Flynn stared at the winemaker's résumé in his hand, but the job duties seemed to be listed in Greek. He couldn't get beyond the first line of experience: *supervise the crush, pressing, settling, juice treatment and fermentation of the must.*

Huh?

His lack of translation abilities had nothing to do with Becca's presence. She was solicitous of his grandfather's needs, but insistent that the house be Hoovered and degermed to avoid infection for Grandpa Ed. Personally, Flynn figured his grandfather was immune to the house germs, having lived with them for years, but Grandpa Ed agreed to whatever Becca suggested.

Becca was everywhere, her snug jeans and bright red T-shirt a beacon, drawing his gaze. Her flowery scent a trail he couldn't block out. Becca was currently in the back, cleaning Grandpa Ed's bathroom. He'd tried to tell her to stop working once he and his business partners had returned after lunch, but she'd insisted on continuing.

Will leaned conspiratorially across the table. "Is Becca the reason you rediscovered how to iron a shirt?"

"No." Flynn pushed Will back, sparing a glance toward his napping grandfather to make sure his chest rose and fell in a regular rhythm. Alive was good.

"Are you expecting Kathy?" Slade glanced out the kitchen window at the new red sports car pulling into the driveway.

"No." It was Tuesday afternoon. What would his half sister be doing here? Had Joey contacted her?

Flynn rejected the idea almost quicker than it came to mind. Joey had given Kathy his last name, but he wasn't her father—not by blood or by action. She'd been conceived during one of his many incarcerations.

"We'll move outside," Slade said. He and Will retreated to the porch overlooking the river, taking the stack of winemaker résumés with them.

Flynn loved his younger sister. If his first eight years had been rough, her first ten had been hellish. After he'd come to stay with Grandpa Ed, she'd lived a few more nomadic years with their drug- and alcohol-addicted mother, who had no problem dropping Kathy with a just-met neighbor and disappearing on a binge.

"Grandpa Ed, Kathy's come for a visit." Flynn gently roused his grandfather from his nap in the fully extended recliner.

His grandfather blinked slowly awake. "Put me upright, will you? All the blood's rushed to my head. Did Kathy bring Truman?"

Flynn glanced out the door while operating the chair's remote. His ginger-headed nephew got out of the car with deliberate care, as if he was eighty, not eight. "Yes."

"Remember your promise," Grandpa Ed reminded him.

"Of course." He wouldn't tell Kathy their grandfather was dying. She'd hate him for it later. But it was better than wondering if he'd survived another night or would live to see tomorrow.

Abby pranced at Flynn's heels, watching his sister and nephew come up the front walk.

Flynn opened the front door and the little dog raced down the steps, circling the pair like new additions to her flock.

"Who got a dog?" Kathy wore flip-flops, jeans and a loose yellow T-shirt. She looked too young to be the mother of a seven-year-old. And at twenty-five, she was.

"Abby isn't mine. She belongs to Grandpa Ed's caregiver." He hugged Kathy. "Are you too big for a hug?" he asked Truman, who was kneeling down to pet Abby.

Truman solemnly shook his head and stood, as if accepting his punishment.

Flynn embraced him with care. The kid always seemed as if he was about to shatter. "What brings you out on a Tuesday, Kathy? Shouldn't you be working?"

She dropped her basketball-size purse on the couch. "I quit."

Flynn was suddenly glad Slade wasn't around to hear this. When Flynn became wealthy, he'd paid off his sister's condo, bought her a new car, paid off her credit card debt and generally paid for anything else she claimed to need but couldn't afford on her secretary's salary. Anything to make up for those first ten years. Slade disapproved.

"I'm assuming you have another job lined up," Flynn said.

"No." She bent to kiss Grandpa Ed's cheek. "They wouldn't give me vacation and I...need time off."

"That's nonsense. You don't just quit a job." Edwin waved Kathy back. "Where's my great-grandson?"

Kathy's face pinched, as if she was fighting off tears.

"Here," Truman said softly, coming forward to hug Edwin as if afraid he'd break the old man. "Are you done with hospitals, Grandpa Ed?"

"I hope so." Edwin clung to Truman's hand. "It's good to see you, boy."

"You, too, Grandpa." Truman looked up at

Flynn with big, blue eyes. "Can I play with Abby?"

"Sure," Flynn said.

Truman drifted down the hall with Abby, humming to himself.

"What's wrong?" Flynn demanded in a low voice so Truman wouldn't hear.

Kathy's hand drifted around her waist once, before she caught him looking. "Nothing."

"Quitting your job isn't nothing," Grandpa Ed said.

"I know." Her gaze cast about. "I need...I need...some time to myself." Kathy's voice was delicate, a thin twine about to snap. "Truman's great, but I'm crumbling and I...I need to get away for a few days."

Becca's soft tone drifted from down the hall. Flynn couldn't make out her exact words, but they were levelheaded, soothing.

He drew a deep, calming breath.

"What about Truman?" Grandpa Ed's voice rumbled with displeasure. "Why can't you get away with him?"

Kathy held up her hands. "I don't just need a break from my job. I need a break from Truman. From my life. I feel so overwhelmed."

"Why?" Flynn asked. "It's summer. There's

no homework. Truman's attending summer camp." Flynn knew all about Truman's summer camp. He'd paid for it. "I thought you liked this job."

Grandpa Ed tried to sit straighter. "In my day, people didn't up and quit their jobs."

Her normally bubbly laugh had an edge of hysteria to it, as if Kathy was on a ledge and had missed catching the rope that would've saved her. "Please don't ask me questions. I need Truman to stay with you for a while."

"Kathy," Flynn began, making sure Truman wasn't in the hall and couldn't hear him. "If you'd just tell us—"

"I'm fine." Her gaze whipped about the room again. "Or I will be soon."

Gone was his sweet-natured little sister, the one who used to ride on his handlebars and beg to go fishing. Gone was the woman who put her son first.

"You should face up to your responsibilities." Grandpa Ed was on a roll. "You need to earn your own way. And you're a mother. You need to provide stability for Truman, not just disappear for days at a time. Where are you going?"

Kathy straightened her shoulders. "I won't

tell you. I don't have to tell you." Despite her determination, tears welled in her eyes.

Flynn thought of Becca's trapped look. This was the same, but different. Kathy had moved from being trapped to doing something about it. "We won't stop you. We're just concerned. If there's anything you need—"

"A break. I need a break. I keep telling you and you don't want to listen." Kathy's chest heaved.

Fear scuttled down Flynn's spine. "Don't be like Mom," Flynn whispered. Moving on and disappearing was the only thing their mother did well. If Kathy left for longer than a few days, Truman would suffer.

"It's not like that. Please, I can't say anymore." Kathy wiped away a tear. She grasped at Flynn, her emotions as heavy and stifling as her perfume. "I just need a few days. A week, maybe."

"Okay," Flynn relented.

"Thank you, oh, thank you. Truman's bag is in the car." Kathy grabbed her keys and bolted out the door into the sunshine.

Flynn followed her at a more deliberate pace, listening to the low buzz of male voices on the deck that stopped, as if on cue, when the screen door banged. "Everything is all right, isn't it? You're not going to go off somewhere and—"

"I am not suicidal." Kathy fumbled with the key fob. "I just…made some mistakes and I need to correct them." She froze, an animal caught crossing the road at night, realizing too late there was no escaping the approaching headlights. She'd said too much.

A warm wind sent the towering eucalyptus above them swaying ominously.

Flynn kept his face carefully blank. "Kathy." Her name seemed a cold reality check.

She shuddered back to the present. "Flynn, I had Truman when I was a baby. You and Grandpa Ed convinced me to keep him. I had to drop out of college my first semester. I love him, but you owe me some space." Kathy blinked, as if surprised she'd voiced such brutal honesty. She looked away, working the keys in her hand like a stress ball. "No more questions, please."

Kathy was at the breaking point. Maybe she was right. Maybe she needed to find herself. One thing was certain. Flynn wasn't leaving her alone with his nephew until he was reassured that she was fine. "Okay."

She hugged him, a quick catch and release.

He wrestled a large suitcase out of her small trunk and lugged it into the house, aware that his friends and business partners had overheard all the drama. He was grateful Grandpa Ed couldn't hear as well as he used to.

"Baby, come say goodbye to Mama." Kathy ran up the steps after Flynn.

Truman stood in the hallway, a resigned expression on his face, as if he'd known his mother was going to leave him, as if he'd known it since the day he was born.

Why wouldn't he? It ran in the Harris genes.

FLYNN'S SISTER HAD no idea how lucky she was to have a child, much less the adorable little boy that had won over Becca's heart in less than five minutes. Children were a blessing. And blessings were hard to come by when you were a woman alone.

Becca introduced herself, trying to smooth the awkward moment. "Kathy, your son is one smart cookie. Truman just taught Abby how to jump through a hula hoop. Show your mom, Truman."

The boy edged forward, dragging a pink hula hoop that was almost as tall as he. His posture whispered of low expectations, of disappointment and dismay. He should have been bouncing with enthusiasm, energy and laughter.

A familiar ache coated Becca's throat.

She glanced at Flynn for answers, but he leaned against the doorjamb, as if he needed it to hold him up.

Edwin only had eyes for his great-grandson.

Kathy stood in the middle of the living room where the coffee table used to be, her hands limp at her sides, her face wavering between determination and tears.

Truman stood staring at his mom, as if imprinting her on his heart.

"Tell Abby what you want her to do," Becca urged. "You can do it."

"Mama." His voice so timid, so tentative, that Becca nearly rushed forward and swept him into her arms. And then Truman thrust his thin shoulders back, just like Becca had seen Edwin do. His voice strengthened, challenging his mother to leave. "Mama, watch."

Truman turned to Abby, holding out the hot-pink hula hoop. The marble racing through the pink plastic was the only sound in the room. "Jump, Abby. Jump."

Abby looked up at the little boy with her doggy smile, mouth open and delicate pink tongue hanging out.

"Jump, Abby," Truman repeated.

Without enough warning, Abby jumped through the hoop, almost landing on Kathy's toes before bounding back to Becca.

Truman giggled. "Did you see, Mama? She jumped for me." There was a breathless urgency in Truman's voice, a desperate plea for his mother's approval. Becca's heart ached for him.

"I did, baby." Kathy knelt and opened her arms. "You're so talented. I don't deserve you. Give me a hug."

"Good girl," Becca whispered to Abby. The dog sat primly at Becca's feet, surveying the crowd as if awaiting her due.

Truman submitted to Kathy's embrace. Despite Kathy's desire to leave her son, there was love on Kathy's face, and the pain of separation all mothers with hearts were supposed to feel. It was apparent in the almost tearful downturn of her eyes, the pinch of her nose and mouth.

Kathy ran a hand over the crown of Truman's ginger hair, kissed his cheek, stood and turned, her face a mask of determination.

"When are you coming back, Mama?" The timid, tentative character was back in his voice.

"I'd like to know that, too," Edwin said gruffly.

Kathy grabbed onto the screen's handle without turning. "Soon, baby, soon."

And then she left.

Flynn followed her out.

Edwin stared at the ceiling.

Truman trudged to the front window. He propped his elbows on the window sill and his chin on his fists.

"Well," Becca said as cheerfully as she could past the lump in her throat. "There's a big suitcase that needs a bedroom. How about the room your mom slept in when she lived here?"

Truman blew out a breath. "It's pink."

"But it has toys," Becca said.

"I don't need toys." He watched Kathy get in the car. "I'm going to help Grandpa Ed get better."

Becca's heart melted. "How about this? You

can sleep in your mom's bedroom and help me care for your grandfather, but you have to take breaks. It's a law. And on your breaks you can play with toys and Abby."

"Truman likes checkers." Edwin plucked at the fabric on the arm of his chair. "The checkers set is in the hall closet."

"Grandpa always beats me," Truman said glumly.

"That will change," Becca predicted. "I think you should challenge your grandfather to a game of checkers. He needs to keep his brain sharp."

Edwin made a grumbling sound of protest. "My brain is sharper than the butcher knife in the kitchen."

"We'll see," Becca injected her voice with enthusiasm.

Kathy drove away, gravel spitting a sad protest beneath her wheels.

Truman stood watching her long after she'd disappeared down the driveway, the same as his uncle.

Who stood on the front walk. Alone.

CHAPTER SEVEN

"WHAT ARE YOU DOING?" Flynn leaned against the door frame to Kathy's old room, watching Becca poke around in the closet. The room was girly pink, princess pink, too cheerfully pink for Flynn's dark mood.

It was damage control time. He'd seen Becca's slightly horrified look when Kathy left, as if she was judging his sister.

"I'm trying to figure out how to make Truman feel at home here without making him feel—" Becca lowered her voice, fingering the sequins on a black prom dress *"—abandoned."*

Flynn glanced down the hall to make sure Truman was still occupied playing checkers with Grandpa Ed before stepping in and closing the door. Will and Slade had left, deciding that family drama was a good enough reason to table reviewing résumés for a day or so. "Kathy isn't abandoning him."

There was a small picture on top of Kathy's dresser, a photo of Flynn and Kathy as small children, their red hair gleaming in the sunlight. His mother knelt behind them with the same red hair. Joey, his high-cut cheekbones prominent over his smile, wrapped his arms around them all.

Flynn rubbed at his carbon copy cheekbones, then pulled his baseball cap lower. "We didn't have an easy childhood."

"Nobody does. If people knew what they were signing up for when they got married or had sex, there'd be fewer marriages, fewer divorces and fewer babies." She rifled through the hangers. "I have a lot of respect for people who stick around. It's so much easier to disappear."

Flynn wrestled with how to answer that. "It's easy to hate someone when they bail. But no one should be penalized for needing a little breathing room." His father's face, old and wrung out, came to mind. Flynn dismissed it. "Kathy will be back soon. Next weekend at the latest."

"You're sure that's what this is?" Becca stopped inventorying the contents of Kathy's closet. Her hand clung to black chiffon. Her voice dropped to a whisper. "The last words my dad said to me were a promise to see me soon."

Flynn's heart twisted. "How old were you?"

"I was ten. My mother had just been diagnosed with fatal lung cancer." She let her hand drift along the delicate fabric to the hem. "My dad could have stayed. It wasn't easy to stay until the end."

Without realizing it, Flynn stepped forward. He put a hand on each of her shoulders.

"He could have taken me with him." Becca's voice was a mere whisper now. "Or come back to get me. I would have forgiven him if he'd come back."

"I know," Flynn said, turning her and pulling her into his arms, because he did know. He knew all too well. The wishes for a parent's return, the pep talks about how their leaving didn't matter, looking for a familiar face in the crowd at every milestone, never finding the one you both longed for and dreaded seeing.

Becca stood stiffly in his arms.

He rubbed her back. "But they don't come back, not unless they want something." Like Flynn's mother. Like Joey. "And by that time, they don't deserve anything."

Her muscles loosened, relaxed. Her hands crept around his waist.

Flynn rested his chin on top of her head. He could feel when she'd gathered herself, sense when she realized her employer was holding her.

"Flynn." She tried to pull out of his arms, but it was a token struggle, an I-shouldn't-be-hugging-my-employer moment.

"Give me a minute. Her leaving was a bad episode of déjà vu." He held on, making gentle circles on her back. Because she needed to be held as much as he did. It was a rare thing to find someone who'd been left behind. "Do you have any family left? Brothers? Sisters? Grandparents?"

She shook her head.

And her husband was gone, as well.

Her behavior with her elderly clients made sense. She was so easy to get along with. Everyone in Harmony Valley loved her right away. And she probably ate acceptance up like soft ice cream, slid into her client's family seamlessly as if she'd been born there, taking on the tough jobs of elderly care the family appreciated, with a cheerfulness they were grateful for. Yep, she'd fit right in, until accepting gifts would seem natural, although it went against professional standards. Because her clients were all the family she had. Short term.

He didn't envy her.

"House rule number two." Becca stepped back, succeeding in gaining her release. "No hugging the help, especially behind a closed door." She crossed the small room to open it.

Flynn's arms felt oddly empty.

Silence settled between them as uncomfortable as a thin blanket on a cold night.

She heaved a great sigh. "I apologize. That was unprofessional."

"I hugged you."

"You were unprofessional," she amended with a wry grin. "What are you going to do with Truman every day?"

He removed his baseball cap and ran his fingers through his hair. "I thought I'd drive Truman into Santa Rosa for summer camp every morning." An hour's drive in good traffic.

"Oh, don't do that." Becca shook her head. "He wants to help care for Edwin. He's already been cast aside by his mother—don't you send him off, as well."

Flynn settled his cap back on his head, his gaze caught by the family photo on the bureau. It was slightly comforting to think that Dane hadn't seen the resemblance between Joey and himself. "I can watch him, but not all day. Maybe Agnes can help."

"I don't mind watching him."

He should have known she'd offer to help. Becca probably stepped in wherever she was needed, regardless of her job description. Containing a smile, Flynn leaned against the door and made her an offer that was double her hourly wage.

"OMG! My lawyer would drop my case. I'm not doing this to get a raise. I'm offering to help. Don't you dare make things worse for me than they already are!"

"I hired you to take care of my grandfather, not cook and clean and babysit. I'm adding to your responsibilities. You should get a raise."

"Money won't solve your problems or mine."

He shrugged. His grandfather had said much the same thing, refusing to allow Flynn to upgrade anything in the house. "Fine. So I'll go back to cooking and cleaning."

"Like you cook." Becca crossed her arms

over her chest. "I carried out the kitchen trash today and it was filled with take-out containers."

"I didn't cook when my grandfather was in the hospital. I'm a guy."

Her eyes widened and blinked, as if she was fighting an eye-roll. "And the dust in the living room was so thick I could have written you a message on the mantel."

He thumbed his chest. "Again, guy."

Becca did roll her eyes then. "I will not accept a raise. I'll quit if you give me one."

"You won't quit. You need the references."

She scowled at him, knowing he spoke the truth.

"We'll compromise. No raises. But I can pay you overtime."

She didn't like that, either. She clomped around the room a bit, muttering and refusing his offer, for all kinds of reasons. He rather enjoyed watching her.

But after a few minutes, he'd had enough. "Come on. It could be worse. I was considering demanding you park your motorhome here."

"No!" She held up a hand as if warding him off.

He laughed. "So we have a deal? Can we shake on it?" He had a sudden theory about Becca. Every time they touched, awareness grew. Awareness of her smile and how that smile made something warm spread in his chest. A warmth he hadn't felt in an oppressively long time.

She accepted his terms with a firm handshake that sent a buzz of electricity up his arm.

She felt it, too.

From her scowl, he'd guess she didn't like it. Not at all.

But he did. And he smiled all the way down the hallway.

"YOU DON'T NEED to walk me home," Becca said as she, Slade and Flynn crossed the Harmony River bridge after dinner. Abby led the pack, pausing to listen to the frogs serenading them beneath the bridge. "Either one of you."

"I'm not walking you home." Slade chuckled. "I'm walking home in the same direction as you after having mooched a home-cooked meal."

"I'm going over to Agnes's because her toilet is running." Flynn carried a small toolbox.

"I'm not walking you home, either." But there was a lightness to his words that threatened Becca's composure.

She'd let Flynn hold her. She'd caught him smiling at her as if he'd found something dear he'd misplaced years ago. Then there'd been that innocent handshake that had shaken something deeper inside of her. Something that reminded her of whispered endearments and soft touches.

Flynn seemed to find the attraction between them amusing.

Becca was not amused.

"You're always getting called somewhere to help someone fix something." Slade laughed. "Usually toilets."

"I like taking things apart and fixing them. But I need to fix this toilet quickly, because I don't want Truman alone with Grandpa Ed for long." He'd given Truman the responsibility of watching Edwin, as well as schooling him on how to dial 911, and providing him with Agnes's phone number in case there was an emergency.

"I could have stayed with him," Becca pointed out.

"And hurt their manly pride? I had no

choice." Flynn chuckled, but Becca noticed he picked up his pace.

Abby glanced over her shoulder as Flynn gained on her, prancing a bit to catch his attention.

Slade walked backward, gesturing to a row of houses on a side street. "You could work full-time fixing everything in Harmony Valley. No one except Rose keeps their house in good repair."

"Including you. I don't see you working on your house or asking me to help." They walked down the alley behind Main Street toward town square. "Afraid of my mad fix-it skills?"

"No." The humor drained out of Slade like air out of an anchored helium balloon. He turned back around. "I'm afraid you'll make the house livable again."

"Say what?" Becca was confused. "Do you live in a shack?"

"The bridge club calls it the Death and Divorce House." Slade's voice was raw and hard. He tightened the knot of his tie.

Becca didn't know what to say.

They rounded the corner of the alley behind Main Street and stepped onto town square near Harmony Valley's only restaurant, El Rosal. Pop Latin music came out of speakers on the patio of the Mexican restaurant.

Slade bid them good-night, crossing north beneath the square's enormous oak tree toward his ill-fated house. Abby paused, sniffing and watching him leave. Then she glanced at Becca and pranced toward Agnes's house.

Becca and Flynn walked east in the middle of the street because there was no traffic.

"Flynn! Flynn!" A gangly old man waved to them from in front of a shop with a barber pole. "It's my sink. It's leaking."

Flynn sighed. "I was afraid I wouldn't make it to Agnes's without an interruption."

"It's good to be loved. I'll see you in the morning." Becca turned to go.

"Hold up." Flynn grabbed her hand with gentle urgency. It had been a long time since anyone had touched her that way. "You're leaving me?"

"I can't help you."

He hesitated only a moment before coming up with a counter argument. "If Phil's sink is fixable and an emergency, I'll need you to go back to the house. I can't leave Truman that long."

He had a point. Becca reclaimed her hand and followed him toward the old barber shop. Abby ran past so she could once more be in the lead.

Main Street was a beautiful example of old town Americana. Gas streetlamps, brick buildings, benches beneath established trees. The only thing missing was commerce. There were only two businesses open on the block—the barber shop and the Mexican restaurant.

Flynn introduced Becca to Phil. Abby sniffed out all of Phil's secrets before he brought them inside and pointed toward his shampoo bowl with a hand that shook. There was a large water stain on the wall beneath it. Not to mention, the odor of wet mold was hard to miss.

"Phil, how long has this been leaking?" Flynn asked.

"I noticed it today."

Becca suspected by Flynn's frown that it had been leaking long before that. But Flynn didn't make a smart remark or criticize. He took out a hammer, knelt next to the wall and poked it through, pulling down all the dry-wall until the pipes were exposed in a two by three hole.

Spotting a broom and dustpan in a corner, Becca swept up the debris. Flynn gave her a grateful look.

Phil sank into one of his barber chairs. "If you've got plumber's tape in that box of yours, I bet I'll be back in business faster than a cat can say meow."

"No such luck." Flynn knocked his head on the sink when he stood, nearly tipping his baseball cap off. He rubbed his head. "This needs a real plumber. The pipe's rusted through."

"It's nice of you to help people out," she said, needing to fill the silence once Flynn had promised to call the plumber and they were on their way again.

"My grandfather started prostituting me out when the winery was approved by the town council, like I was their thank-you gift." Flynn pointed out a house they passed with a short, golden lawn. "Last month I hired a gardening service to mow the weeds down on the abandoned homes. We want to bring honest, hardworking people back here. Can't do that when it looks like a good place to build a meth lab."

"I'm impressed." He was a great guy. Her first impression—the one where she thought he needed taking care of—had been wrong. Flynn could take care of himself and the rest of Harmony Valley's residents. "Most millionaires would buy a tropical island and retire."

Flynn walked her to the door of her motorhome. "That's why most millionaires go bankrupt within five years. This is a sabbatical for us. We're going to design and program another app. We've got an idea. It's in the conceptual stages now."

Becca put her key in the lock. "Good luck with that."

He stood next to her, as if waiting for a good-night kiss.

Becca stared at him. Abby stared at him. Agnes opened the door and stared at him.

Becca leaned closer, allowing a small smile. "House rule number three—good-night kisses aren't allowed."

He leaned closer, until his lips were almost brushing her ear. "Unless you're on the Harmony River bridge. Local tradition trumps house rules every time."

CHAPTER EIGHT

THE NEXT MORNING, Flynn was at the collapsed barn site earlier than anyone, including Dane, anxious to hear the revised budget and time-line for the project.

The grapevines near the river were still blanketed in fog, but tendrils were drifting upward and dissipating beneath the sun rising over the mountains. It promised to be another warm, beautiful day. And it would be as soon as Flynn got past this meeting.

He couldn't stand still. He'd worn his best blue jeans and an ironed green polo, pulling the brim of his baseball cap low, schooling himself to show no emotion, no matter what Joey said. If Joey showed up.

But it was Becca who was on his mind. The swing of her braid as she walked. Her easy smile. The way she was kind to everyone and tough on him.

That wasn't totally true. She was kind *and* tough on him.

He walked around the collapsed wing of the barn, unable to stop smiling. And then he stumbled over the barn's weathervane—a trotting, cast-iron horse.

Will walked around the far corner of the barn, just as a truck pulled into the winery entrance. It was Slade.

The three men came together on the circular drive in front of the barn. As usual, Flynn was underdressed. Both Will and Slade had on khakis, although Will had chosen a black polo. The tie Slade smoothed over his dress shirt was coffee-brown.

"That tie new?" Flynn grinned, ready to cut the tension with a familiar bit of ribbing.

"You've seen this tie before," Slade groused.

"I don't know." Will picked up the ball right where Flynn left it. "It looks new. Those ties of yours can't last more than, what? Three to four days of your worrying strokes."

Ba-da-bum.

"Hardy-har." Slade nodded at the weathervane horse. "That'd make a nice logo for the winery."

Flynn lifted it upright so they could get a

better look. "Better than a big *H* and a big *V*."
Which was all they'd come up with.

A beat-up white truck pulled between the
palms, followed by Dane's big silver-gray one.

"That's him in the white truck, isn't it?"
Will asked. "Your dad."

"Don't call him that. His name is Joey."
Flynn thrust his shoulders back and walked
toward the farmhouse.

As Dane went over the revised budget with
Slade and Will. Flynn drifted back toward the
barn, pretending to survey the soon-to-be-
demolished structure, not at all surprised to
hear booted footsteps bring Joey to his side.

"It's a shame the old girl collapsed. I bet
she's weathered many a storm." Joey's voice
rifled through his memories in a way that was
intimate and inviolate.

Flynn dug his fingernails into his palms. He
hadn't expected starting a conversation to be
so hard. What he wanted to say had no relationship whatsoever with what he'd planned
to say.

And so, he kept silent.

"But this way, the new girl will weather a
hundred more years."

Flynn's nails dug in harder.

"How've you been?"

His gaze slashed to Joey. "Since when? Since you saw me a few days ago? Or since you saw me nearly twenty years ago?"

Joey didn't so much as flinch. "That's a hard way of looking at things, son."

"Don't call me that," Flynn said, low and urgent.

Joey held up his hands. They were gnarled and scarred. "Just so you know, I've been working for Dane for several years now. I'm not following you and I don't want any of that fortune you made. I don't want any trouble, either." And then his voice grew conciliatory. "But when life puts your past in front of you, you have to face it."

"We've faced it. Now I'm moving on. I have no problem with you working here, but you stay away from me, my grandfather and our house." Flynn walked away without waiting to see if Joey agreed.

WHEN EDWIN OPENED his eyes, he could hear someone moving around in the hall outside his granddaughter's room. "Kathy?"

A small dog yipped once.

Which dog was that? They'd always had big water dogs, Labs and the like.

"Irma?" Edwin called for his wife. Had she taken in another stray?

The bedroom door opened and a pretty young woman with a long black braid smiled gently at him. A small, mostly black dog scampered over to the bed, rising up on its hind legs so it could see him.

"Good morning, Edwin." Her face, so familiar.

She wasn't one of the Harmony Valley kids. All the homegrown ones had left for college or jobs. So who was this? Her name was... "Becca."

"That's right." She crossed the room and opened the slider drapes. Weak sunlight filtered through the dual canopy of fog and eucalyptus trees. "It's a beautiful summer day. Flynn's left for the construction site. Breakfast is ready. We need to get you up and moving before the physical therapist comes."

Memories came crashing back with bomb-blasting intensity. He'd been in the hospital, poked and prodded like a science experiment. But he knew the truth. This was no experiment.

He was dying.

All his plans, all the strategies he'd set in play for his country. They'd all played out.

He was dying.

Becca kept on talking. "…Flynn home after lunch. And this afternoon you'll have a visit from the speech therapist."

The winery. Harmony Valley. A last-ditch effort to save the town that had been a shelter for so many for more than one hundred years. Flynn had promised to bring people—young, vibrant people—back to Harmony Valley. Only now Flynn was busy managing construction, dropping the ball on the people end.

Years ago, when Edwin first discovered this tiny, sheltered town, he'd written letters to people he'd read about in the newspaper. Burned-out professors whose radical ideas never got funded. Victims of unspeakable crimes, grave accidents, vendettas. The oddball persona that didn't seem to fit in. He'd been a Pied Piper, calling them here, to rebuild their lives and finally fit in.

There was work to be done. Edwin swung his legs out from under the covers and sat up.

The world spun.

He would have fallen over if not for Becca's quick, steady hands. "I've got you."

"Grandpa, I'm here to help you get up." Truman, his great-grandchild, climbed up on the bed next to Edwin. He wore pajamas with trains on them he'd grown out of. The boy had probably never been on a train.

"Where did you come from?" How could he have forgotten his great-grandchild was here?

"Mama dropped me off yesterday. Don't you remember?"

He hadn't, until Truman prompted him. He'd been so proud of Kathy taking on the responsibilities of a single parent until yesterday.

"It's okay." Becca's dark eyes soothed the panic riding roughshod through him. "I forget things all the time."

Edwin swallowed. He'd always prided himself on his memory, always relied on his brain's acumen. What more did he need to understand the end was near?

If he wanted to save Harmony Valley before he died, he'd need to do it pronto. "Would you help me write letters, Becca?"

"Certainly."

"And I want to visit my friends."

"We have a full day today. It might be better to stay at home and rest. We want you to have a quick recovery."

"Soon I'll have all the time in the world to rest." Edwin intended to add more to bring his point home, but Becca was nodding, as if she understood how important a man's last wishes were.

"AND THEN MAURICE landed in the blackberry bush and the dog got away with his hat!"

The old men in the barbershop chortled with laughter. They were exchanging stories of the good old days, when they'd been young studs, at least in their minds. But it was heartwarming to see their camaraderie.

She'd grown up in Los Angeles apartment complexes, where no one knew their neighbors, much less a whole community.

The barbershop was a narrow hole in the wall. Or, more precisely, a narrow shop with a hole in the wall beneath the sink. Flynn's plumber had yet to make an appearance. Instead of posters of good-looking men, Phil had pictures of famous sports teams on display.

Truman was outside with Abby examining the red-and-white-striped barbershop pole from different angles, trying to figure out how to open it up to fix it.

Phil's hands trembled badly. And that was when he was sitting down. Standing up, Phil had an exaggerated swagger that made his hands shake worse.

"Phil, what are your grandchildren doing?" Edwin was brave to trust Phil not to trim part of an ear along with his hair.

Phil rattled off names and occupations. All of them seemed settled far away from Harmony Valley.

Edwin swiveled the red barbershop chair. "And Felix, where did yours end up?"

While the retired fireman filled Edwin in on his family, Truman opened the heavy glass door and came inside, narrowly missing getting whacked on the behind by the swinging door's recoil. He plopped on the folding chair next to Becca and whispered, "How much longer?"

"Not too long. Your grandfather needs lunch." They had to take his blood sugar level and inject him with insulin. "Maybe you should wheel his walker next to him so he gets the hint."

Truman was across the room in six steps,

Abby at his heels. The little dog was in love with the boy. And their relationship seemed to bolster Truman's careful nature.

It was bittersweet to see Abby so happy and engaged. Much of Becca's work involved Abby being inactive for long hours. And there was evidence that service dogs led shorter lives due to the stress of worrying about those they assisted and the more intense situation they were put in—city sidewalks, doctors' offices, hospitals.

Edwin was in the middle of a speech that caused Felix's and Phil's expressions to glaze over. She'd heard his speech a few times already today. "And that's why it's important that we ask our families to return."

"My grandkids won't come back here until I die." Phil stared down his nose at Edwin as if he'd suggested he move to the moon. "And that's only if I leave them my house on the condition they don't sell."

Edwin seriously considered the idea for several seconds. Then he waved it aside. "That won't work, Phil, you're going to live forever."

The men guffawed some more.

Edwin noticed Truman and his walker. "What's this?"

"It's time to head back to the house," Becca said briskly. "Blood sugar test, lunch and your meds." Along with a nap with his feet elevated before his speech therapist arrived.

"I have one more stop to make." He'd already had Becca drive the Cadillac to the houses of some of his friends.

How successful was his campaign to increase Harmony Valley's population? Not at all.

"We'll go this afternoon," Becca bartered with more urgency now. Either the lighting was bad in Phil's shop or Edwin's skin was turning pale everywhere but his fingers, which were still tinged a light blue. "Or we'll call and have your friends come over."

Truman positioned the walker in front of the barber chair Edwin was in and set the brakes as Becca had shown him. Abby sat out of the way watching the two of them.

"All right," Edwin relented. He stood and disengaged the brakes. "I can see when I'm outnumbered. But I want to buy a newspaper before we go back."

"You can have mine." Phil handed the newspaper to Truman. "Giants won last night."

"I'm not interested in sports scores." Edwin

lumbered in Truman's wake. "I'm writing letters."

Truman held the glass door open

Phil and Felix shared a look that gave Becca a split second of unease before she followed Edwin out the door.

What was wrong with a man writing letters?

"WHERE HAVE YOU BEEN?" Flynn demanded when Becca parked the Cadillac in front of the house.

Becca wasn't sure who he was upset with—her or his grandfather.

"I needed some air." Edwin opened his car door slowly.

Truman and Abby tumbled out of the car and ran into the house.

"I called the hospital." Flynn's voice had a taut, astringent quality, as if too-tart lemonade had left his mouth parched.

"There was no need to do that," Edwin grumbled. "I'm not dying, as you can see."

Flynn couldn't see. He was in a state, his hair sticking out stiffly from beneath his ball cap as if he'd been worrying the ends.

"I'm sorry." Becca retrieved the walker from the trunk. "We should have left a note."

"You think?" The look Flynn gave her was absent of any of the flirting, friendly quality from the night before.

"Don't fuss, Flynn. I had enough of that in the hospital." Edwin struggled to stand, then gave up with a defeated sigh. "Why don't you help me out of the car and up the steps?"

Flynn did as asked. The exertion of standing combined with the physical demands of walking forced Edwin to sit on his walker halfway up the front path.

"We learned a lot about limits today, didn't we?" Becca tried to lighten everyone's mood, but she knew she shouldn't have let their excursion last so long. She chalked it up to the lessons learned the first week on the job.

While Flynn and Truman settled Edwin into his recliner and checked Edwin's blood sugar, Becca put lunch together. She couldn't see the entire living room when she stood at the sink, only the foyer.

"Do you want the TV on your game shows?" Truman asked.

"No," Edwin said. "I want to read the paper. You can watch whatever you want."

Flynn came into the kitchen, anchored his

hands on either side of the sink, and hung his head.

"He may look tired, but it was a great mental exercise for him." Becca reached over and squeezed Flynn's hand. It was cold, or she would have released it immediately. "We know his limits now. He'll get his second wind around dinner time."

"I came home and you were all gone. I thought...I called..." His voice was barely above a whisper.

"We'll leave a note next time."

"There won't be a next time. He shouldn't be going out at all." Flynn turned to her. The ache, the sadness, the fear were all reflected in his eyes. Flynn knew he'd lose his grandfather one day, but he, like so many others, prayed their loved ones would live forever.

"He needs to build up his strength." Selfishly, Becca pictured Edwin stronger and able to get to the witness stand. "He wanted to go out. You shouldn't treat him like he's dying."

Flynn closed his eyes, turning his hand so he held hers.

She should have pulled away, but his concern for his grandfather touched her. And it had been so long since anyone under the age of seventy had held her hand.

Gradually, Flynn's hand warmed around hers. "He's all I have."

Becca had no answer to that.

Edwin rattled his newspaper. "Truman, the message machine is blinking. Hit the replay button for your great-grandpa."

You have...three...messages.

"Hi, Edwin. It's Richmond. Glad you're back home. I hear Flynn knows his way around a car engine. If he has a minute, send him by my place, will you?"

Beep.

"Edwin, you old coot. Mike Mionetti. Zenobia tells me Flynn's going to fix her computer. I've been having trouble with my TV antennae and the missus says I shouldn't go up on the ladder. Ask him if he can climb up there before the next episode of *Dancing with the Stars*."

Beep.

"I knew those doctors couldn't keep you locked up forever. Have Flynn go by Mae Gardner's house. I noticed she had a couple of shingles loose on the south side."

Edwin cleared his throat and raised his

voice. "Flynn, do you have time today to make the rounds after lunch?"

"I was going to spend the afternoon with you." Flynn's eyes met Becca's. His were filled with a resolute sadness, as if he was being rejected.

"I raised you to help your neighbors." Edwin ran out of air, coughed several times, then drew a deep breath that rattled his lungs. "Besides, I've got speech therapy this afternoon. It won't take long. And I bet Truman would like to help you."

"Don't go," Becca whispered to Flynn. "I bet he'd be just as happy if you stayed here."

Flynn shook his head slowly.

"I'm a good helper," Truman piped in.

"Of course you are," Edwin agreed. "And when you're done you ask your uncle Flynn to take you by El Rosal for ice cream. Hard work deserves a reward."

The urge to enfold Flynn in her arms was strong. She patted his hand with her free one instead. "I'll make sure he's waiting for you when you get back."

Becca knew she shouldn't promise.

But Flynn needed something to hold on to.

CHAPTER NINE

"UNCLE FLYNN, CAN you teach me how to fix things?"

"Sure." Flynn drove down Main Street toward Richmond's house on the east side of town.

His grandfather looked like death in a Dixie cup. All he wanted to do was sit with Grandpa Ed and talk, but his grandfather was always sending him on some errand. And whenever Flynn was home they were both exhausted.

Truman gazed out the window. He had one arm flung around Abby, who shared the luxury truck's bucket seat with the small boy. He'd become more animated and less deliberate in the past few days than Flynn had ever seen him. "I want people to call my house and ask me to do stuff, like they do you. And then I can fix things for my mom and she'll be happy."

Flynn remembered thinking the exact same

thing when he was a kid. He wanted to be indispensible. An insurance policy for any kid who felt disposable.

He needed to talk to Kathy. His phone calls so far had rolled directly to voice mail, as if her phone was turned off or she was ignoring him. Just like their mother. "I bet you already help your mom around the house in lots of ways."

"I do. I put her to bed and get her up in the morning in time for work." Truman kicked his feet out. "But if I had a dog, like Abby, I could help a lot more. Abby could fetch the newspaper and bring in a firelog and find the remote when Mom can't."

"Abby's a good dog," Flynn allowed, thinking how heartbroken Truman would be when Kathy returned to get him or Becca moved on. Maybe Flynn would get him a dog of his own. "But Abby will never be as good of a helper as you are."

Truman's chest swelled with pride.

At Richmond's house they—Flynn— quickly discovered that the retired postal worker had left his car lights on and run his battery down. Flynn got out his jumper cables.

On to Mike Mionetti's house, where Abby

and Truman played in the front yard with Shep, Mike's old sheep dog, while Flynn climbed up on the roof and adjusted the old school antennae.

Finally, they stopped by Mae Gardner's house, where Flynn had Truman count how many of her black asphalt shingles were missing. Mae gave Truman ten peppermints, one for each missing shingle.

"I don't really need an ice cream," Truman said quietly as they drove back toward the one small grocery store in town. "I didn't do any work."

"You're my wingman." There was no way Flynn wasn't making a big deal out of their afternoon together. "You talked to my customers and kept them happy."

Truman brightened slightly. "But if they were customers, how come we didn't get paid?"

"Because we're neighbors. And neighbors take care of each other."

"Not where we live," Truman said glumly.

"HERE'S THE LETTER I want you to type." Edwin handed Becca a yellowed sheet of paper a few hours after Flynn and Truman left on their fix-it rounds. "And here are the people I want to write to." This page, equally aged, was filled with chicken scratch names.

A breeze fluttered through the curtains and murmured through the trees outside. Becca couldn't remember ever being anywhere that was so quiet. Unwilling to disturb the peace, she almost hadn't vacuumed earlier.

Edwin worked the buttons of his recliner into a full horizontal position, wriggling a bit to get comfy.

Becca scanned his letter first. *"I'd like to invite you to set aside the cares of the outside world and explore the small community of Harmony Valley."* She didn't try to disguise the shock she felt as she stared down at him. "Are you asking all these people to move here?"

"Don't quibble." Edwin's voice carried more than a trace of indignation, as if he wasn't used to his commands being questioned. "It's worked before."

So this was what raised the eyebrows of Felix and Phil.

Becca perused the second sheet. "There must be thirty names on this list. A fallen politician, a retired wrestler, a woman who was mugged for her iPhone, a fired sheriff. I've seen these people in the news."

His eyes drifted closed. "Yes. They all could use a respite from the outside world, don't you agree?"

"Well maybe." These people were going to toss his letters in the trash. Or worse— they'd show up here looking to move in with Edwin. Becca's lawyer would have a heart attack if she helped him write these letters and she couldn't very well blame him. "As long as none of these people are serial killers."

"Don't be negative." Edwin didn't open his eyes.

Becca set the letters aside and covered him with the green afghan. She studied her work and added a throw pillow beneath each hand to try and combat his poor circulation. "At least let's get you a post office box or send these from the address of a real estate agent. You don't want strangers showing up on your doorstep."

"Why not? You did." That lopsided grin was endearing even with his eyes closed. "I have a typewriter in my room. Feel free to use it."

"A typewriter? What about a computer?"

Becca had never used a typewriter in her life. She didn't know how to correct her typos on one. "I think I'll wait until Flynn gets back. I'd much rather type this up on a computer." And see what Flynn had to say about the letters. She was hoping he'd give them a big veto.

"It's not up to him." Edwin puffed up indignantly, dragging his eyes open. Apparently, a Herculean effort, as they shuttered closed almost immediately. "I want to continue our town visits tomorrow. Someone has to have relatives who want to move back here."

"I don't want to be a killjoy…" *Liar.* "But don't you need jobs to attract nonretirees?"

"Not necessarily. We could be a bedroom community. People could commute."

Edwin's heart may not have been at full capacity, but his brain was sharp as a tack. "This from the man who told a caretaker applicant it was too far to drive from Santa Rosa every day."

The right side of Edwin's mouth tilted upwards. "That's entirely different. She and I would have butted heads all day long. Whereas you—"

"Seem unable to control you." Becca gestured in exasperation.

"We're back!" Truman burst into the house, followed by a panting Abby, who went right for the water bowl. "Uncle Flynn bought me a missile popsicle. It was awesome."

"I see he did." Becca smiled.

Truman's hands and shirt were stained orange, pink and yellow.

"Let's get you cleaned up and then you can tell your great-grandpa all about your afternoon."

Truman struggled out of his shirt as he ran down the hall. Then he ran back, his arm stuck in the too small shirt. "Help."

Becca laughed, easing him out of the shirt.

Truman watched Flynn come in the door. He rubbed his colorful hands up and down his bare chest. "We did good today, didn't we, Uncle Flynn?"

"Yep. But you're breaking house rule number one." Flynn grinned at Becca in a way that had her heart leapfrogging where it didn't belong. "You've got to wear a shirt outside of your bedroom."

Truman scampered down the hall, giggling.

Flynn held Becca's gaze just a little too long before he settled into the couch. "How're you feeling, old man?"

"Old," Edwin replied. "Is all right with the world?"

"In this corner, at least."

"That's all we can ask for." They grinned at each other.

Becca missed moments like that—inside jokes, light banter, love.

She missed it, but not enough to risk another heartbreak.

WHATEVER BECCA WAS cooking smelled really good. His grandfather and Truman dozed in the living room, worn out by the day's activities. Flynn was pretty worn out himself, but having tried getting in touch with Kathy again today, his eyes were busy staring at the ceiling and wondering when he should call the police. Seven days had come and gone, and there was still no word from Kathy.

"Dinner's almost ready." Becca peeked around the corner of the kitchen. "Flynn, can you come help me?"

Flynn was hungry, and for more than food. He rounded the kitchen arch and almost ran into Becca, who was waving some papers.

"Your grandfather asked me to write a letter to all these people." Becca handed him his grandfather's notes. She kept her voice down.

Flynn scanned the letter and then the list of people his grandfather wanted to send it to. "This will either be brilliant or make Harmony Valley the laughingstock of the nation. I'll talk to him."

"I'm torn because he so clearly wants to help the town, but I'm not sure he's going about it the right way." She hesitated before adding, "And frankly, I can't be a part of it. My lawyer…"

"I made him a promise that I'd bring people here. It's my fault he's taking it into his own hands and coming up with these letters. Maybe there's no harm in sending them. He's addressed this one in care of the WWE Corporate Headquarters in Stamford, Connecticut. That's probably not enough of a complete address to deliver it."

Becca's lips twisted with doubt. "Be gentle. I don't want him to feel like I'm laughing at him. I'm primarily concerned for his safety, particularly if he insists on putting his address on the letters."

"I'll take care of it. Thanks." His gaze caught on hers. There was an awkward moment where he'd swear she was thinking what he was thinking: *they both needed a hug.*

But the moment passed, and she stepped back.

Becca gestured toward the stove and the steady tick of the egg timer. "I made turkey meat loaf, roasted vegetables and salad. The rolls are in the oven. I feel obligated to warn you that it's all low salt. The smell promises more flavor than it delivers."

"As long as it's good for Grandpa Ed, I'll eat it."

She patted his shoulder as she went toward the door. "He'll get better every day. Just you wait and see."

Flynn reached for her arm, stopping her. "Becca." It wasn't fair that she didn't know the truth. She was taking care of his grandfather and if she pushed him too hard for the sake of a recovery that would never happen, she'd never forgive herself.

On the other hand, she said she made it a habit of moving on after her patients died. And that she wanted a client who was going to get better for a change. He couldn't tell her.

She stared up at him, concern clouding her features. "Hey. It's all right." She reached up and touched his cheek. The warmth of her hand spread through him. "It's okay to worry."

"Is it?" And then Flynn swept her into his arms and held her close. He buried his nose in her dark hair, breathing in the scent of fresh flowers.

He needed this. He needed someone to hold him and to hold someone in return. The tension inside his chest burst and settled lower, attempting to turn into desire.

Her arms held on to him loosely. A friendly hug. A neutral hug. He wanted more. His hand drifted down to the small of her back and pulled her even closer. He nuzzled her ear, exhaling a gentle puff of air.

"House rule number two—no employee hugs allowed. Remember?" Her voice was businesslike, but he could feel her tremble against him.

Reluctantly, he let her go.

Her cheeks were aflame, highly satisfying to Flynn's male ego. "I should be going. When the timer goes off, take the bread out and serve dinner." Her gaze caught on something at his feet. "Did you drop a penny?"

"No." He would have reached for her again,

but Truman came around the corner from the living room, rubbing sleep from his eyes.

"You can stay for dinner, Becca." Truman hugged her leg.

She turned her slender back on Flynn, and bent to give Truman a hug. "No, sweetie. Agnes is expecting me."

"Will you come back tomorrow?"

"Yes. And I'll make breakfast again. Maybe tomorrow morning we'll make something your great-grandpa will like."

"I like pancakes better than cereal." Truman grinned sleepily.

"Everyone likes the sweet stuff," Flynn said, just to get a rise out of her.

The timer went off.

Becca walked into the living room without so much as a backward glance. "House rule number four—only one treat a day." Becca gathered up her purse and Abby's leash. "Good night, Edwin. I'll see you in the morning."

Grandpa Ed roused himself with a start. "You're not spending the night?"

"No," Becca said with too much emphasis. And then she disappeared.

Truman blinked at the front door and then

turned to Flynn. "I like her. You should keep her."

"From the mouths of babes." Grandpa Ed chuckled, operating the remote to bring his recliner to a sitting position and then the slow boost to standing.

"From the mouths of babes," Flynn echoed. He picked up the penny at his feet and started to smile.

CHAPTER TEN

"I USED TO think the most amusing part of living here was our elderly residents. I mean, who can't find humor in creative taxidermy, one-woman musicals and feuds over naked yoga?" Slade sat on a warped plastic chair on the winery's farmhouse porch with Flynn and Will, stroking his blue tie and grinning while they watched the construction crew prepare to demo the barn. "I've changed my mind. Flynn has become the most amusing part of my day."

Will tipped the ladder-back chair he'd brought from home on two legs and peeled a strip of old paint off the porch wall. There was already a small pile of paint strips at his feet. "Totally with you on that one. Flynn's a regular three-ring circus."

Ignoring the friends who'd bookended him onto a milk crate on the porch, Flynn reviewed the supply list Dane had given him for cost approval. He had more serious things to worry about, like how his grandfather didn't seem to be getting any stronger. The trip he hoped to take with him seemed inconceivable.

Across the driveway, Dane's crews had finished taking out windows, carefully salvaging exterior boards, iron hinges and latches, until only the barn's skeleton and tin roof remained. Dust kicked up from scurrying workers, blown lazily by the light breeze off the river. Chains ran from the center ceiling beam through a hole in the tin, draping down to attach to two yellow backhoes, ready to pull the barn on top of the already flattened wing.

Leaning in for maximum torment, Slade's grin widened. "Hiding from Joey. Circling your grandfather's pretty caregiver."

"Hovering over Edwin until he snaps," Will added.

Flynn held on to his temper with a slippery grip. "Since when is it a crime to worry about your grandfather?"

"I like how he avoids the other two accusations," Slade said.

"Okay, all right. I admit…" Flynn lowered his voice. "I've been *avoiding* Joey. And maybe I have been *circling* Becca." She was like a familiar puzzle he couldn't remember the key to. One minute they were on the same path to solving it, and the next, she was backing away and touting a house rule.

He was coming to hate house rules.

"Becca's a sweetheart, but she has definite boundaries." Will seemed to read Flynn's mind.

"And yet, the girl has guts. She doesn't let Edwin push her around." Now that Flynn had admitted his foibles, Slade leaned back. "Or you."

"That's part of the problem." Will nodded. "Flynn can't direct Becca the way he conducts the symphony before us today."

Becca had successfully avoided being alone with Flynn for days. Flynn liked to think he let her. But he'd been busy monitoring the demolition prep and helping elderly residents. At the same time, a communications tower was going up on Parish Hill, sending the town into this century with cell phone and internet service.

"Head count!" Dane shouted, gesturing for the crew to move back from the barn. "Every man report to your foreman *outside* the barn."

"I can't believe we're finally taking it

down." Flynn took a picture of the barn with his cell phone.

The legs of Will's chair landed on the porch with a thud. "Rose cried when I told her. Emma helped me convince her grandmother it was for the best."

And it was for the best. Nearly all the remaining old beams had cracked under the pressure of the wing collapsing. They'd had no choice but to bring it all down and start over.

Flynn glanced over toward Jefferson Street.

A caravan of cars were parked along the street. His grandfather's black Caddy. Agnes's green Buick. Old Fords and Hondas. Trucks and SUVs. It seemed like everyone in town had come out to see the end of an era.

Agnes, Mildred and Rose stood by the Buick with their binoculars. Truman and Abby leaned out the back window of the Caddy.

"All clear?" Dane called.

"All clear!" Joey answered, sparing a glance toward Flynn as he flicked his gray ponytail over his shoulder. And then he blended into the crowd of construction workers.

"Let's take her down!" Dane waved at the backhoe operators.

The big yellow rigs started up with a loud rumble, sending bursts of black smoke into the air. The backhoes lurched forward. The chains attached to the center beam lost their slack. Wood groaned.

Flynn stood and leaned on the porch railing. Slade and Will joined him a moment later.

The groans twisted into high pitched creaks as the backhoes inched forward, accented by the pop-snap-pop of mooring bolts giving way and the high-pitched metal protests of the bending tin roof. Amazingly, the barn's beams held.

"She's not going without a fight," Flynn murmured, privately rooting for the barn. He valued roots and history, all except his parents' section of the family tree.

And then there was a cascade of snapping wood and the barn gave way, beams bouncing into the ground, sending clouds of dust into the air.

The construction crew cheered.

No such cheers came from the audience along Jefferson Street.

"I hope we're doing the right thing," Will said as reverently as if they were in church.

"Kind of late for doubts." Slade smoothed

his tie. "What's for dinner at your house, Flynn?"

"Mooch off Will for once," Flynn countered, grateful for the change in mood, but knowing he'd set another place for dinner.

"AGNES! AGNES!" FROM the back of the Cadillac, Truman waved Agnes over. She'd parked her Buick behind them. "Wasn't that awesome?"

Becca's diminutive host came over to Truman, resting her right hand on the open rear window. "My heart's pounding."

While Truman recounted the collapse, despite Agnes having seen it, Becca noticed Agnes wasn't smiling. And she wasn't wearing her ruby ring.

The muggy heat that had been building during the morning, that had been building in the Cadillac, built in Becca, until she burst open her car door and glared at Agnes across the roof of the car. At least, she glared at Agnes's forehead. The older woman was so short, not much of her face was visible above Truman's window.

"Where are you going?" Edwin hadn't said much during the demolition. He'd stared out the window, rarely blinking, as if his mind was occupied elsewhere.

"I thought I'd help Agnes get Mildred and her walker back in the car." Drawing on a drained store of patience, Becca walked back to assist Mildred, making sure that Rose buckled herself in the backseat.

The grass alongside the road had been freshly cut, compliments, no doubt, of Flynn. The air smelled green with a frosting of diesel fuel.

Becca pushed the candy apple–red walker around to the Buick's trunk. "Agnes, can you open the trunk?"

Agnes said goodbye to Truman and walked back slowly. Given the car was what the residents liked to call "a classic," the trunk wasn't automatic. Agnes had to insert a key into the lock.

Although she kept her voice down, Becca wasted no time in subtleties. "What happened to Harold's ring?"

Agnes rubbed a hand over the bare fingers of her right hand. "People were starting to ask questions."

"Harold wanted you to have that ring." Becca's hands plopped on her hips. She'd risked a lot to bring Agnes the ring. If Agnes didn't appreciate it, it had been a foolish risk.

"I can't tell people who gave me the ring," Agnes said in a hushed tone of voice. "If I did, I'd have to explain everything."

Becca opened her mouth to argue, but Agnes wasn't finished.

"And I can't make something up. Don't you dare ask me to lie." Agnes gasped and bent to pick something up. She held up the small copper disk and whispered, "Harold."

Becca scanned the ground beneath her feet. Nothing.

"What are you two whispering about?" Rose craned her gracefully wrinkled neck out the window.

"I'm making sure Becca isn't allergic to shellfish," Agnes lied smoothly, fisting the penny in her hand. "I want to make shrimp for dinner."

And this from a woman who professed not to want to lie. Penny or not, Becca rolled her eyes.

"You were going to have shrimp and not invite me?" Rose pouted.

"What does it mean?" Agnes was pale, her

gaze darting about the ground as if she suspected Harold's ghost lurked at her ankles.

"Harold would be disappointed," Becca
whispered as she walked away. She knew
that she was.

But that didn't mean Becca couldn't understand where Agnes was coming from.

Secrets were hard enough to keep without
announcing you had one by waving a ring on
your finger.

AN HOUR AFTER demolition, the construction
crew swarmed the debris. Dane's plan was to
salvage sections of the tin roof and as many
beams as they could. He'd been right about
the market for old barn parts. They had no
trouble finding buyers.

The audience on Jefferson Street had long
gone, as had Will, off to another meeting with
their legal team to sign the agreements they'd
made with Mayor Larry, who was trying to
stall once more.

An old man rode his three-wheeled bicycle
down the gravel driveway toward the barn.

Joey stopped the cyclist where the driveway
branched. The two men had a short conversation and then Joey pointed out Flynn, without

looking around, as if he knew exactly where Flynn was.

Flynn tamped down his annoyance. He always knew where Joey was, too.

Smiling broadly, Slade followed Flynn off the front porch to greet their visitor.

As the bike rider pedaled closer, Flynn realized it was Snarky Sam. His was one of the few remaining shops in town. It was part antique shop and part pawn shop. The small, spritely man wore a green-checkered flannel shirt and a scowl. "Flynn, I hear you've got some skill as a handyman."

"Some," Flynn allowed, aware that Joey hadn't returned to the job site, but was listening in twenty feet away.

"I'd appreciate you stopping by the store." Sam studied the wreckage that had been the barn. "Shame, that. Progress comes at too high a price."

Flynn ignored Sam's disapproval. "What's the problem?"

"I've got no electricity in my storage room. Dang near tripped over a stack of fans last night."

"Are you sure it isn't a bulb that needs replacing?" Slade barely suppressed a grin.

"My conversation is with Flynn." Sam bristled. "You get me? And I just replaced the bulbs in that fixture last week."

"We'll come by in a couple of days," Flynn reassured him. "In the meantime, don't walk in there after dark."

"I'd appreciate it. And while you're visiting, you might look at my storage shelves. Seems like they might take a tumble." Sam pedaled his bike in a meticulous circle and then just as slowly pedaled back to the main road.

"We'll come by?" Slade chuckled. "You and Truman?"

"Me and you, buddy. You've got nothing better to do." Flynn flipped Slade's tie. "And you've been dying for me to ask you to help. Admit it."

Slade stepped back, one hand protectively over his tie. "I'm good with a hammer. I think I proved that when we built a float for the spring festival."

"Even Truman can swing a hammer. For this job we need my electronic wiring skill." Flynn was a hardware engineer by trade, able to design and program intelligence on computer chips, or figure out code to work on certain kinds of computer chips. "Once that plumber fixes the leak at Phil's barbershop, we'll need someone with drywall experience to patch it up. Have any experience with plaster board?"

"I'm not skilled labor." Slade smirked. "But I've watched a lot of do-it-yourself shows this past year and I can steady the ladder for you."

"Then you've got enough experience to help me and Truman."

"I know I'm going to regret this," Slade said with a shake of his head.

"You won't." Flynn thumped him on the back.

"I'll help you." Joey walked over. "I know how to drywall and paint, and I know the basics of electricity."

Flynn held his ground. "We're not going to hotwire a car." The last thing he needed was to be working side-by-side with Joey.

Joey's face reddened. But before Flynn could turn away, he blurted, "You don't want to be responsible if the place burns down, do you? And harm comes to the old man?"

Flynn and Slade exchanged worried glances. While Flynn was comfortable rewiring a computer, a building was another story. And Slade was probably only comfortable plugging in his headphone wires to his phone.

Flynn understood the trapped look on Joey's face all those years ago and on Becca's face when she'd first arrived. He imagined Slade was seeing the same look on his face now.

CHAPTER ELEVEN

"WHY IS THE message light flashing on the answering machine?" Becca asked Truman the morning after the barn came down.

She was a little late because she'd talked to her lawyer on Agnes's house phone. Hank still didn't know what opposing counsel was up to, and was glad to hear everything in Harmony Valley was going well. His definition of well being that Edwin was alive and hadn't given her any gifts. "Where were you last night that none of you could answer the phone? Did you drive into Cloverdale for ice cream?"

"Grandpa Ed said not to answer because Flynn and I were too tired and busy to accept more work. Uncle Slade joined our crew, but we're still not caught up." Truman's little face beamed. He loved being on Flynn's repair crew. And he seemed to love being here.

Becca couldn't associate the boy she'd first met with this one.

Edwin wheeled his walker around the corner of the kitchen slowly and carefully took his seat at the table. "Are we having pancakes for breakfast?"

"You're having oatmeal." Becca put a steaming bowl in front of him and added a dollop of nonfat milk. "With a bowl of fruit."

"Not even strawberries with sugar?" Edwin's face fell. "According to my doctor, my heart won't get any better. Seems a shame to waste it on oatmeal." He looked up at her hopefully. "How about a strip of bacon?"

Truman was giggling over his pancake.

"If you eat your oatmeal, tomorrow we'll have turkey bacon," Becca promised. "Now, about the messages on the machine."

"Word's gotten out. Free repairs." Edwin's voice began with annoyance and transitioned to pride. "I raised that boy right. Flynn can't pass a motorist without stopping to help. You'll be the same way, Truman." Edwin stirred his oatmeal once and then pushed the bowl away. "What else is there to eat?"

"Oatmeal is part of a heart-healthy diet." Becca pushed his bowl back toward Edwin. "Why doesn't Flynn listen to the messages?"

"We didn't tell him," Truman piped up. "He

fell asleep on the couch last night. Grandpa
Ed put the phone ringer on silent. The only
way we knew there was a call was because
the machine would start talking." Truman did
his best robot impersonation. *"We can't come
to the phone right now."*

"I almost had another heart attack when
Felix Libby's voice came on the loudspeaker
about some broken cat contraption." Edwin
chuckled. "I made Truman put the entire thing
on mute."

Becca turned on the phone ringer in case
Flynn tried to call. "Did Flynn take your
blood sugar this morning?"

"Yes, before he left an hour ago. I took my
insulin, too. Flynn was mumbling something
about Mildred's clogged bathroom sink."

It was official. Flynn was a saint. And
saints didn't appreciate people who withheld
the truth, no matter how well intentioned. It
was a good thing to remember when the naked
dreams plagued her in the middle of the night.

"First business of the day, Truman. I want
you to listen to all the messages and write
down all the names and telephone numbers,
and whatever needs fixing." Becca realized
that at age seven, Truman might not be the

best speller, but she was sure if he didn't take good notes, someone would call back.

Edwin played with his oatmeal some more before pushing the bowl away again. "Second business of the day is a trip to Cloverdale. I realize the world has advanced beyond the typewriter, but I couldn't wait for Flynn to loan you his computer any longer. I typed up the letters and envelopes last night. All I need is postage."

Becca scrambled for a delay tactic, something to postpone the mailing until she could reach Flynn. Flat tire? Hot day? Busy schedule? Yes, their schedule. "We can't go into Cloverdale, you have therapy this morning."

"I called and cancelled. This is more important."

"Edwin!"

He looked up at her, a wry half grin on his face. "I'm an adult. I make my own decisions."

But how the court viewed his decisions and what Becca did to help or hinder them was another thing entirely. One that could cost her her career.

"This guy looks like he's ready to subpoena somebody," Slade said.

Flynn and Dane looked up.

They were expecting the building inspector to review their cleanup on the demolition. They couldn't start new construction until they passed inspection.

The man who got out of the nondescript minivan immediately set Flynn's teeth on edge. He wore a cheap, rumpled suit and tie, but accessorized it with a calculating smile, as if he was assessing the net worth of everyone he saw. "I'm looking for Flynn Harris." But he looked right at Flynn.

"That's me." Out of the corner of his eye, Flynn saw Joey amble closer. He flashed Joey a shutter-quick frown meant to convey the eavesdropping and meddling needed to stop.

Joey ignored him and came closer still, his nose twitching like Abby's when she evaluated a stranger.

"I'm Wes Webber." The suit pulled out his business card and handed it to Flynn. "Private investigator. Can I talk to you alone?"

If anything, Joey got twitchier.

Something wasn't right. Flynn led the man over to the far curve of the driveway, leaving Joey, Slade and Dane huddling together like gossipy old women.

"What's this about?" Flynn demanded. But Flynn could guess. It was Joey. He'd stolen something.

"Rebecca MacKenzie." Webber paused, cataloging Flynn's reaction.

Flynn didn't disappoint. He took a step back, needing to shore up his equilibrium. "Becca?"

The rumpled suit nodded. "She worked for my client's grandmother. There's a question of missing funds."

Flynn felt his protective hackles rise, but he said nothing. Because to say anything was to admit he knew something. He wasn't Joey Harris's kid for nothing.

Webber studied Flynn as if he was an outdated display at the Tech Museum. "I went by your house just now, but there was no one home."

Flynn looked quickly around the driveway, as if expecting to see his grandfather's Caddy, but it wasn't there and hadn't been. He'd told Becca not to take his grandfather out. He'd told her to let him know when they had to go out. He'd told her, and she hadn't listened.

Unless she'd taken him to the hospital.

Flynn ground his teeth together tight enough to pop a filling.

"Ten thousand dollars in missing funds," Webber was saying. "I'm building a case against her."

"What does this have to do with me?" There was no way Flynn should be upset with this man. He was only doing his job. It was Becca who'd put herself into the position of being accused. She'd probably accepted the money under the stress of impending loss and the feeling of being part of the old woman's family. Flynn should be mad at her. Instead, he wanted to deck Webber.

"I hear she's taking care of your grandfather."

Flynn wasn't going to make it easy on the guy. "Meaning…"

Webber held up his hands and looked at Flynn as if he was a sucker about to get his palm read at the local fair. "I don't imply anything. I seek out the facts to back up crimes. And I'm good at my job. Rebecca's case is going to pretrial in a few weeks and I'm going to collect as much evidence and testimony as I can against her. She's a master manipulator.

Everyone she's worked for thinks she really cares about people."

"She does care. She cares too much. Don't come by my house. Ever. Again." The accusations alone would give his grandfather a heart attack.

Flynn handed Webber his card, but the private investigator stepped away and laughed.

He laughed as if he knew something Flynn didn't. "Keep it. You're going to need it."

BECCA SLIPPED OUT the screen door with Abby when she heard Flynn's truck parking in the driveway. The midday sun glared off Flynn's windshield. She held up a hand to shade her eyes, but still couldn't see his face.

She heard Flynn get out of his truck, blinked at him when he came closer, still in a haze of sunlight and whispered, "They're napping. Your lunch is on the back porch." And then she turned to go back inside, intending to change Edwin's sheets.

Flynn had other plans. He captured her hand and led her along the wraparound porch.

"Flynn, I—"

He shushed her and walked faster, pulling her along. "House rule number five—don't wake those in your care." Anger vibrated through his words, vibrated through the heat of his hand, vibrated up her arm as she tried to tug herself free.

He must have found out about their road trip to the Cloverdale post office this morning.

"Flynn, look, I'm sorry about this morning. I would have called you if cell service was up."

He stopped in the middle of the back porch, in front of the table with the sandwich she'd made and covered, in front of a spectacular view of the river. The bramble of blackberry bushes on the slope beneath them was covered in sweet white blossoms being romanced by busy bees. Abby sniffed at them through the slats and moved farther down the porch to sit.

Flynn didn't let go of her hand. How could he have known they'd left?

Someone must have seen them drive out of town and told Flynn. Once Harmony Valley got internet, she'd bet good money there'd be a lot less gossip going on. They'd be too busy watching kitten videos online.

"Edwin outmaneuvered me. I was going to tell you after lunch."

After Flynn had a chance to unwind a little.

"Tell me what?"

He didn't know? She'd dug herself an unnecessary hole. "We must not be talking about the same thing. I took Edwin to Cloverdale this morning."

Flynn's grip on her hand convulsed. "I specifically told you not to take him anywhere." He wasn't looking at her. He wasn't looking at his sandwich. He was looking at the river.

Intuition reverberated in her ears, murmuring a warning. A warning about what?

"Edwin typed his letters. Addressed them. Stuffed them in envelopes. What was I supposed to do? I told him we shouldn't go, but he'd already canceled his physical therapy." Becca spoke with freight train speed, words tumbling practically on top of each other. "I drove everyone to the post office in Cloverdale. I had Abby and Truman sit with Edwin in the car in the shade while I bought stamps—your grandfather gave me cash. And then we drove straight back here. I put the change and the receipt on his dresser. We were gone less than ninety minutes."

"And yet, my grandfather's exhausted. Why else would he be sleeping at lunchtime?" Flynn gave her a sideways look. It was the same look he'd given her the day they'd met. Probing, piercing, heartbreaking.

It said without a word he didn't trust her.

The noise in her ears was nearly deafening. She hadn't realized how much Flynn's good opinion meant to her. This wasn't about letters of reference. It was more personal, and therefore more disappointing.

Becca tugged on her hand, but Flynn wouldn't let go. "Edwin spends most of the day napping. It's why he's so lucid when he's awake." She put her hand over his, the one that gripped hers so tight. "Tell me what's happened."

Flynn stared at their hands, blinking as if he hadn't noticed he'd been holding hers. And then he released her. Stepped away. Put the railing at his back.

"I had a visit from a private investigator this morning." His blue eyes pinned her in place. He was unaware she couldn't breathe enough to escape, even if she'd wanted to. "He's investigating you. He said he came by the house this morning. You were gone."

"I'm so sorry." For too much. "When the investigator didn't find us here, I bet you didn't know if I'd rushed Edwin to the hospital or taken him out around town on an errand." She dragged in a breath. "Of course, I'll leave. You don't have to ask me."

He looked perplexed. "Why?"

"I don't want Edwin upset if that investigator comes here again."

"I told him to stay away from the house," Flynn said, submitting her once more to his probing gaze. "I put my reputation on the line for you."

She wanted to scream. That ring. She'd known she shouldn't honor Harold's last request. "You shouldn't have done that, Flynn. I'll leave."

She didn't want to, but she didn't want her mistakes to reflect on Flynn. And to prove it, she took the first step.

Flynn blocked her before she could take another. He held on to her arms. "Don't run. Don't quit. Whatever it is you're guilty of besides taking the money, if you run it'll only make them look that much harder for something."

She opened her mouth to deny she was guilty of anything else, but all that came out was a half gasp.

Since Terry died, no one had stuck up for

her. No one. Becca wanted to lean against Flynn's chest and let him shoulder her burdens, but she couldn't. She'd made a promise to Harold and to Agnes. She couldn't tell him.

Becca lifted her gaze to Flynn's.

His lips thinned. "You're not a very good liar."

"I haven't lied to you." Her deep I'm-not-telling-the truth voice.

"You haven't told me everything." His fingers dug into her arms. "I can get you a lawyer."

"No! I have a lawyer. There's nothing to worry about." Not unless they discovered Harold's ring. Her voice pitched low enough to sing bass in a boy band. "I'll have your character reference and others. My lawyer would be overjoyed if he could get your grandfather on the stand. Can you see it? Edwin telling the courtroom Gary's accusations are nonsense?" She tried to laugh, but it got caught in her throat and sounded more like a sob. She pieced together a smile. "Not that I'd let Edwin get up there."

"He can't testify." Flynn's grip faltered. "The legal system is a tangled web. Whatever lawyer you've hired can't be the caliber of someone I can afford."

"If I let you hire me an attorney, I'll look even more guilty." She reached for his hands, removing them gently from her arms. She gave them a slight shake, a thrill going through her when he gripped her hands tighter. "You have enough to worry about without taking on my burdens. I'll be fine."

"That's just it. I can't. I can't stop worrying about you. I can't stop wondering why you live a nomadic life, why you don't have any friends, why you aren't a stay-at-home mom with a houseful of kids. You don't have to do this alone." He stared at her lips in the same way a parched man stares at a glass of water.

Intuition reverberated again, this time with a very clear warning—*move or accept his kiss!*

A kiss would ruin everything.

What a way to go.

Wisely, she ignored that thought and the pound of her pulse, and forced her feet to move a solid step sideways. "Flynn, you worry about everyone in Harmony Valley. You don't need to add me to that list."

Still holding her hands, he turned with her,

as if they were doing a slow country reel. "Becca, I can't explain this, but—"

"Flynn." She managed to get her hands free. "House rules, remember? You can't hold my hand. Or hug me." She wouldn't add the *K* word to the list. He ought to know kissing was out. "I have to do this by myself and be aboveboard in everything I do."

"Alone in everything? Aboveboard in everything?" His hand cupped her cheek and for the life of her, she couldn't keep herself from resting her cheek against his palm. His gaze burned with the promise of heat, of kisses and soft whispers across pillows. "Promise me you won't quit. My grandfather needs you."

She shouldn't. She couldn't.

But in the end, she did.

NEARLY KISSING BECCA was becoming a habit that made Flynn's brain a mess.

Manual labor didn't help. Idle conversation didn't help. Days went by, time passed. It didn't help.

Webber had warned him Becca bonded quickly with her clients in order to sucker them in, but the private investigator didn't know her. Becca truly cared about people. If only Webber could see Becca with Truman or his grandfather, he'd realize she wasn't a thief. But that might upset Grandpa Ed, and was a risk Flynn wasn't willing to take.

Becca was genuine when it came to her feelings. She was loyal. Offering to quit when she needed a reference was just one of many check marks in her favor. Refusing to accept a pay raise when she began watching Truman was another.

And then there was the soft feel of Becca's skin, the ripe promise of her lips, the trapped look in her eyes. Flynn had to figure out a way to help her, even if he never kissed her.

That was the hardest thought of all to move on from. Kissing Becca.

Until he saw Joey on Sunday.

Flynn was finishing up fixing a cat kennel in Felix Libby's side yard when he saw Joey slowly drive by. Slade was two houses over, fixing Maurice Ingleton's loose screen door.

He knew Becca was a good person inside, just as he knew Joey wasn't. The way a man treated his kids said a lot about him.

Flynn shied away from putting his sister Kathy in the same box. She'd call. Soon.

Truman and Abby were playing in Felix's

front yard. Felix rescued cats, so the backyard was off-limits to them. Fulfilling his role as Flynn's wingman, Truman handed him things he needed whenever Flynn asked—water, a new box of nails, a screwdriver.

The white truck backed up and into Felix's driveway.

Truman watched Joey pull in.

Before Flynn realized what was happening, Joey got out and introduced himself to Truman.

By the time Flynn made it to the driveway, Truman and Abby had made a new friend.

Joey threw Abby's tennis ball across the yard. His T-shirt sleeves were rolled up. His tattoos showing. He looked at Flynn. "He yours?" There was hope in Joey's voice.

Flynn wanted to tell him to get lost. Instead, he gritted his teeth. "Kathy's."

Joey's face fell. "He's got your mother's eyes."

"What do you care?"

"I loved your mother. And you." He met Flynn's gaze squarely. "And when I was on the good side of the barbed wire, I was good to Kathy."

Flynn couldn't argue with that.

Truman and Abby ran around the yard, taking the ball away from each other.

Flynn swallowed his pride and decades of crushed hopes. "Is that why you never tried to contact me? Because you loved me so very much?"

Joey's eyes turned cold. "He didn't tell you, did he?" He shook his head. "You'd think now, when he's dying, that the old man wouldn't lie to you."

"He's not dying." Becca wasn't the only one keeping secrets.

"I've seen men die." Joey's gaze flickered to a distant point on the horizon, before flickering back to Flynn. "I saw Edwin the day the barn collapsed. You can lie to others, if that's the kind of man you've become, but don't lie to yourself."

Flynn didn't want to ask. He didn't. He clenched his fists. "My grandfather isn't a liar."

"Isn't he?" Joey laughed bitterly. "He lied about everything. Your mother. Me. The money."

Flynn waited. He wouldn't give Joey the satisfaction of asking for details.

"He paid me to stay away." Joey jutted his

jaw, so like Flynn's. "Paid me well, even in prison. Paid your mother, too, I expect."

Flynn's world spun on its axis. His parents had chosen to leave him. His parents considered him a mistake, unloveable, a castoff. Hurt churned in his gut, rejecting what Joey said, rejecting and doubting his grandfather, the man he couldn't confront about this without getting upset, raising his blood pressure and potentially ruining his old ticker permanently. It was safer to reject Joey's words. "I don't believe you."

Joey shrugged. "I'm not the one about to die with lies weighing on his soul."

"Grandpa Ed isn't about to die." Flynn had been lying for weeks about his grandfather's condition. How long had his grandfather been lying about Flynn's parents?

"Don't kid yourself. He looks like he has one flag staked in the grave already." Joey backed toward his truck. "You ask him. You ask him about me and your mother. I'll see you tomorrow at Sam's." He waved to Truman. "Nice to meet you."

So confident. So self-assured. Flynn felt none of those things as he watched Joey drive away.

"Are you done with the cat cage? My tummy tells me it's snack time. And at snack time Becca makes yummies." When Flynn didn't answer, Truman tugged on his hand. "Uncle Flynn? Are you okay?"

He wasn't. He was seeing his mother's hand clutching a small piece of paper the day she'd left him in Harmony Valley. Had Grandpa Ed given her a check? Or had Joey's suggestion put the image there when it hadn't been there before?

Flynn scrubbed a hand over his face. "Let's load up the truck."

CHAPTER TWELVE

"WE'RE HOME!" TRUMAN ran up the front steps and inside. "We need a snack."

Flynn trudged across the lawn behind him. Joey had to be lying. His grandfather couldn't have paid Joey to stay away all this time. He couldn't be that cruel.

Flynn stood in the doorway. His grandfather's face was hidden behind a newspaper.

Becca was in the kitchen, setting the microwave to cook popcorn for Truman. She glanced at him over her shoulder and immediately turned. "What's wrong? What's happened?"

Flynn held up a hand, a numb, cold hand.

"Grandpa Ed." Flynn walked over and sat on the floor at his grandfather's feet, like a child waiting for a story. "Joey came by while I was working. He asked about Truman. He wanted to know…if Truman was mine."

His grandfather set aside his newspaper, his

chest heaving as if it was suddenly hard for him to breathe. He rubbed his chest. Coughed. "You talked to him? I told you not to talk to him."

Flynn nodded. "And he told me... He accused... Did you pay Joey to stay away from me?" He prayed the answer was no. If it wasn't, all the years of pining for his father, walking with his head held high when his friends had their dads at ball games and karate lessons, all the years of alibis he'd told himself about not caring that he never saw Joey Harris again, would be a sad, unnecessary fairy tale.

Becca talked quietly with Truman in the kitchen. Flynn was grateful she was keeping him occupied. He was often grateful to her for her thoughtfulness and stability. He'd be more grateful if she'd wrap her arms around him and make him forget the idea Joey had put in his head.

His grandfather couldn't be that cruel.

But his grandfather had yet to speak.

Grandpa Ed struggled to hold his composure. His lopsided expression wavered and wobbled. And then it crumpled, destroying what little hope Flynn had left.

"Do you remember those months after your father went to prison? The squalor? The gunshots, both day and night? Drug dealers for neighbors?" Edwin lisped. "I died every time I came to visit, begging your mother to come home." Edwin's breathing was ragged, scaring Flynn as much as his words, but he wouldn't stop him, not until he knew the truth. "But your mother didn't want to come here. Harmony Valley lacked the things she craved—drugs, money, men. Do you remember the men?"

Flynn did. He didn't want to. They'd come and go. Watching movies in his mother's room, she'd say. Even at eight he knew better. But the few times he'd protested, he'd earned a slap and harsh words. She'd tell him to take Kathy outside. They'd huddle in the bushes at the bottom of the stairs until her movie visitor was gone, until she was sober enough to remember her children weren't at home.

Flynn fists dug into his thighs.

Becca's and Truman's voices. Abby lapping up water in the kitchen. The scene so normal. His life so surreal.

"Kids shouldn't be raised that way. She gave you up first and disappeared. Took me nearly three years to find her and Kathy." Grandpa Ed touched the brim of Flynn's ball cap. Sighed when Flynn said nothing, and continued. "Joey wanted to take you away from me when he got out. He was hoping to be released early on good behavior. I couldn't trust him to stay within the bounds of the law, not a third time. So I paid him. I gave him money until you graduated high school." His voice rose high and tight. "What was I supposed to do? How was I supposed to protect my grandchildren?"

"You could have told me." Flynn's voice sounded like he was eight years old again, clingy and fragile as he watched his mother drive away. "I would have liked to have some say in it."

Abby walked over and laid down next to Flynn. He rested a hand at the base of her small head.

"I suppose I could have told you sometime in the past eight or nine years. You could have sought Joey out and seen for yourself what he was like. But he's here now, isn't he? Looking for money. I'm sure he blew every dime I gave him on drugs and women when he was released four years ago." Grandpa Ed reached a hand toward Flynn. His fingers brushed Flynn's baseball cap.

Flynn ducked away. He wasn't ready to forgive. His hat ended up in Grandpa Ed's shaking hand.

After a moment, his grandfather put the ball cap on his own head. "I've been worrying about how to tell you. The longer you keep a secret the harder it is to let loose."

Flynn's gaze drifted to Becca. She stood in the archway separating the kitchen from the living room, a hand over her mouth. Her gaze softly pleaded for Flynn to forgive.

He couldn't.

Truman came to sit in Flynn's lap with a bowl of popcorn. "Grandpa Ed, did you know someone has a zoo-ful of cats in town? He has all different sizes and colors of cats. They didn't like Abby, but they liked me. I like this town. Everyone here likes me." Truman opened his mouth to say more, and then decided he'd rather fill it with a handful of popcorn. He slouched against Flynn's chest, smelling of sticky, sweaty boy. "But I miss Mama. When is she coming back?"

Flynn could feel the boy's conflicted emotions in every breath—there was the desire for his mother versus the desire to stay where he'd found happiness. His chest felt heavy.

Grandpa Ed managed to reach a hand far enough to rest on the top of Truman's ginger mop. But his gaze was on Flynn's. "Harmony Valley is the best place for little boys. You can dream big here, no matter if you want to be president or a millionaire."

Flynn knew it was true.

No matter how he wished he'd learned about it differently.

"HEY." BECCA FOUND Flynn on the back porch where the combination of shade from the roof and surrounding trees and the cool breeze off the river did little to cool Flynn's burning sense of betrayal, if she could judge anything by the way he looked.

Shoulders hunched, head lowered. He ignored the serene view of the river, choosing instead to study the blackberry vines that reached for the rail at his feet.

She handed him a beer. "I thought you could use this."

Flynn twisted off the cap and took a long pull, continuing his perusal of the brambles on the slope below. "What I could use is a memory wipe. I don't suppose you have that in a kitchen cupboard."

What she really thought was that Flynn could use a vacation—someplace warm and sunny where he could lie on the beach and just be. He overbooked every day, was on the move from sunup to sundown, fulfilling his responsibilities to the winery partnership, helping people in the community with honey-do repairs. He barely managed to eke out time with his grandfather and Truman. When did he ever take a moment for himself? Never.

"No memory wipes. No do-overs, either." She put the house rules on pause and brushed his hair away from his forehead, smoothing his long locks on either side behind his ears. "I suppose now's not a good time to tell you about hat-hair."

Edwin still wore Flynn's hat.

"No." He didn't smile. He barely looked at her.

Becca clutched the railing, her body wavering restlessly as if she was moored there during trouble waters, waiting for him to say something. Flynn was always saying something. "Well, I guess I should get back inside." She didn't raise anchor. She waited.

He sipped his beer and said nothing.

Flynn without words was extremely troublesome. She tapped the railing. Studied the profile that had been half-hidden by a baseball cap 99 percent of the time she'd seen him.

The hat made him look young. The long hair made him look young. The torment in his eyes aged him.

"Your cheekbones are more prominent without the hat." They'd never overwhelm the intensity of his blue eyes, though.

Flynn grunted and swigged more beer.

She tossed her braid over her shoulder. "Makes me wonder what you'd look like with a haircut." Made her want to run her fingers through his hair.

He sighed and slid an arm around her waist, cinching her against him. "Could we just… maybe…not talk for a minute?"

Becca forgot to breathe. Her left arm was trapped between them. To move it around his waist was to disregard the house rules that had bound her status as an employee. She stood stiffly, listening to a bird singing nearby, debating what to do.

He mumbled a curse, set his beer on the railing, then reached behind and between them to drag her hand up and around his waist. "Becca."

She wasn't sure if he was chastising himself or her.

He reclaimed his beer with one hand, with the other he rested his fingers over her hip. "Becca," he murmured again.

This time the note was clear. He'd been chastising her. Maybe she deserved to be chastised. She'd missed the feel of a hard body holding hers. She'd missed holding hands and long walks. She'd missed shared confidences and slow kisses.

Becca stole a glance at Flynn. They fit together standing like this. His arm in the small of her back. Her face so near his that all he had to do was lower his chin to kiss her.

Flynn didn't take advantage, seemingly content just to hold her.

She let a small sigh slip past disappointed lips, and leaned more deeply against him.

This was what he needed. This would have to do.

"Grandpa Ed raised me when he didn't have to," Flynn said after they'd been standing silently for several minutes.

"Points for that. You seem to have turned out okay."

"He told me not to write my father in prison." There was pain in Flynn's words, balled up, crumpled tight. "He told me he'd let me know when Joey was released so I could prepare myself." Flynn scoffed. "So I could prepare myself for the truth? That my father did want me and my grandfather lied about it?"

"It sounds bad when you put it that way."

Flynn's fingers clenched on the beer bottle, clenched on her hip. "Why didn't he tell me? Why couldn't he tell me?"

"Maybe they made a deal." Becca slid a hand over his at her waist, her touch smoothing the curl to his fingers. "Sometimes you give your word not to tell anyone and you keep it, no matter who it hurts and no matter how badly you want to tell someone." She wanted to tell Flynn about the ring. She did. But if she told him, there'd be no more hand holding, no more hugs and definitely no kisses.

He'd asked for the whole truth. He'd told her not to withhold anything. She had.

He'd hate her. Look how hard he was taking his grandfather's confession.

"Careful, Becca. Or I might think you aren't telling me something."

What she wasn't telling him was that she didn't want to take his final paycheck in a few weeks—she didn't want to move on. And she was dying for a kiss.

She pulled him toward her, lifted up on her toes and kissed him. A quick buss of lips. There was no locking. No exchange of saliva. Lift, kiss, back away.

Her heart pounded as if she'd just done a sprint to the main road and back. Her pulse beat out a warning at her temple, turning her brain back on. Her impulsiveness required a new house rule. "House rule number six—a chaste kiss on a boo-boo makes it all better. Hope you feel better soon." She took another step back, fully intending to retreat.

"Not so fast." Flynn tugged her back into his arms. Her body pressed against hard muscle and emotionally distraught man. "I challenge that house rule."

"On what grounds?" Her hands rested on his chest, same as her gaze.

She knew she should go. She knew she wouldn't.

It was as if she'd discovered a list Flynn made. A honey-do list.

Honey—do let your arms shelter me.

Honey—do let your lips make it better.

Honey—do let your heart heal mine.

He smoothed her hair, mimicking the way she'd touched him earlier, stray strands tucked behind her ears. His hand caught her braid, using it gently to tilt her face up to his. His blue eyes had darkened and targeted her lips. "Your line of reasoning is unsound."

"How so?"

"I hurt everywhere when you're not kissing me." And then he crushed her to him, his lips claiming hers.

Becca's hands slid up his chest and over his shoulders until her fingers speared through his hair. His kiss was sultry and blistering, burning away the tension that had been knotting inside her for weeks, until she felt relaxed and renewed and pent up, all at the same time.

A bell went off inside her head. Ringing and ringing and ringing.

She hadn't set a timer. She hadn't set an alarm. Although heaven knew she probably should have.

"Becca? Should I answer the phone?" Truman's voice.

Becca stumbled back, dazed. Flynn steadied her, but the look in his eyes was anything but steadying. It said more. It said now.

The phone rang again.

"Becca?" Truman called with the weary impatience of a child.

"Yes, please." She took a steadying breath, rationalization and regret preparing arguments against sensation and emotion.

"Yes, please," Flynn murmured, pulling her closer.

"Uncle Flynn! It's Mama!"

"We'll talk about this later."

Flynn released her and hurried inside so quickly, he couldn't have heard Becca whisper, "No, we won't."

Rationalization and regret won.

"I KEPT GETTING the machine," Kathy said when Truman handed the phone to Flynn.

Despite the immense relief in hearing Kathy's voice, Flynn couldn't banish the feel of Becca's lips on his or her fingers running through his hair. But he could form simple syllables. "Uh-huh."

"She's not coming home yet." Truman crumpled at Flynn's feet, deflated by Kathy's news.

"I hate to disappoint him. He's okay, right?"

Flynn's brain finally slid into a gear that could communicate intelligently. "Kathy, where are you? What's this all about?"

Becca slipped into the living room. Her black hair was mussed over one ear. Her lips were swollen from his kisses. She walked toward him, and for a moment he thought she was going to wrap her arms around him again. Instead, she knelt next to Truman and, with Abby's help, encouraged him to get up. The trio went down the hallway.

"Can't tell you," Kathy was saying.

"I've tried to call your home and cell." Flynn's grip on the phone tightened against nearly two weeks of helplessness. The wonder, the worry, the demoralizing what-if scenarios. "Why aren't you answering?"

Grandpa Ed was still wearing Flynn's black Giants cap. It made his nose more obtrusive. "Tell her it doesn't matter what she's done. We'll forgive her."

Kathy huffed into his ear.

Gesturing to his grandfather to keep quiet,

Flynn tried again. "What if something happened to Truman? How would I get in touch with you?"

"You can't. I thought I'd be done with this in a week, but…I need more time."

Flynn swallowed back his frustration. "More time for what?"

Someone spoke in the background. A man. Deep voice. Assertive.

"I have to go." No arguments. No bargaining. Complete acquiescence.

The bitter taste of fear lined the back of his throat. She was disappearing, as their mother so often did. "Wait. Kathy."

But she'd already hung up on him.

Flynn tapped the disconnect buttons in the cradle, but all he got was a dial tone.

"Where is she?" Grandpa Ed demanded. "Can you go pick her up?"

Flynn shook his head. It was his mother all over again. Except…

He gave his grandfather a hard look. "You didn't pay Kathy to leave Truman here, did you?"

"No!" His reaction was so strong and so immediate that Flynn believed him.

"Uncle Flynn?" Truman stood in the hall,

Becca's hands on his shoulders, Abby at his feet.

Flynn shook his head.

Truman bolted across the living room and into Flynn's arms. "I'm scared. I put Mama to bed at night. I get her up in the morning. Whose gonna take care of her?"

Becca's gaze questioned. Flynn wasn't about to admit he'd heard a man's voice in the background.

"Your mom is fine. She's extending her vacation is all." Flynn stroked Truman's ginger hair, just like he'd stroked Kathy's when they were kids.

Truman broke away and bolted for his bedroom.

Where was his sister? Who was she with? Why wasn't she coming back?

Flynn had the private investigator's card. He could have Webber find Kathy. And while he was at it, he could have him look into his father's past. Or Becca's.

There wouldn't be any more secrets.

There wouldn't be any respect, either.

Flynn's cell phone started to beep and vibrate in his pocket. He pulled it out and laughed. Finally, something was going right.

"The communications tower is up and running."

"Cell phones? Internet?" Edwin stared at the pictures on the walls. "That'll rattle these old birds in their cages more than any earthquake."

"TRUMAN?" BECCA KNOCKED on Truman's bedroom door. It wasn't fully closed all the way, and Abby nosed her way in.

"What is it?" Truman lay facedown on the bed, as if he couldn't stand to face his mother's absence.

Abby hopped up with him, laying her head on his back and looking at Becca as if to say: *help him.*

Becca sat down on the bed near Truman's feet. She'd taken down the pink curtains and replaced them with beach towels. She'd switched out the pink ruffled bedspread and replaced it with a blue and brown prairie quilt she'd found in the hall closet. She'd had Flynn move Kathy's dresses and shoes up to the attic. It felt more like Truman's room now.

She rubbed his back. "Abby needs to go for a walk. Want to come with me?"

He shook his head.

Becca rubbed his little back some more. "Sometimes it's tough being a kid, isn't it?"

He moved his head in a way that she took as assent.

"It's not fair that you have to watch out for your mom all the time and now your grandpa, too."

He half turned, his knobby knees bumping into her hip, his arm gathering Abby to him like a teddy bear. "What happens if my mom doesn't come back? She's out there all alone and she's scared. I could hear it in her voice."

No little boy should recognize fear in an adult's voice. "She might have been more worried about you. That's what you could have heard."

"But if she doesn't come back, what's going to happen to me?"

"Truman, she's coming back." Becca hoped, for his sake.

He didn't look so sure. "I suppose I'd live here. But there's no school. I asked. What am I going to do?"

He was such an old soul. She smiled. "Your Uncle Flynn is building the winery so they can reopen things, like the school and the ice cream parlor."

"But Becca." He sat up, worry furrowing his little brow, "if they open the ice cream parlor, Juan will be unhappy."

Abby sat up, too. She licked his cheek.

"Who's Juan?"

"He owns El Rosal. The Mexican restaurant? That's where people in town buy ice cream now."

"If more people move here, more people will eat lunch and dinner at El Rosal. Juan will be happier than if he just sold ice cream." Although it was a restaurant, El Rosal also sold the bare essentials, like bread, milk and ice cream.

"Oh." Truman hugged Abby again. "Does Abby really need to go for a walk?"

"Abby always needs to go for a walk. Or learn a new trick. Or meet new friends."

"Me, too." Truman scooted into Becca's lap, cuddling into her arms as if he'd been born there.

Becca's throat threatened to close. She'd given up on having children, but these days being with Truman had shown her how rewarding motherhood was and what she'd be missing. "You know, when I was a kid and the world seemed like it would swallow up my loved ones—" which it had. She prayed it wouldn't do that to Kathy "—I used to sit in my special place and sing."

He cocked his head, clearly engaged. "What song made you feel better?"

She launched into a silly tune, gyrating kookily and shaking him along with her.

He giggled, as she'd meant him to. It was a song her grandmother had sung to her when Becca was in a funk.

"Really. You laugh, but by the time I get done singing that song, I feel better. Want to sing with me?"

Flynn poked his head in the doorway. "Ready to go fix some stuff? We've still got a long list."

Truman squirmed out of her lap. "No time to sing, Becca. Gotta go help the neighbors." He ran past Flynn, Abby close behind him.

Flynn's stare was smoldering. "We'll talk later."

"House rule number seven—never, ever talk about a mistake."

He frowned, but left her when Truman called him.

Which was a relief. Wasn't it?

CHAPTER THIRTEEN

"Good night, Agnes." Becca closed the front door behind Abby and turned toward the driveway and her motorhome.

Daylight was fading in the valley, but one thing was clear. There was a man leaning against her motorhome door. A man without a hat.

"You didn't answer my text." Flynn waved his phone at her.

"I haven't turned my cell on in more than a week. It's in the motorhome." She came closer, trying to think of a good house rule.

"That explains why you haven't accepted my friend request on Facebook."

"It's been a long time since anyone's sent me a friend request."

"Then I'm glad I sent you one." His smile had too much of what her grandmother would have called vinegar, raising her suspicions. "Turn your phone on. I'll wait."

"You want me to go inside, turn my cell phone on and read your text? Accept your friend request? Why can't you tell me what you sent? Or show me on your phone?" She was close enough to make a graceful grab at it.

"Check your text messages." Flynn slid his phone into his pocket. "Some texts need to be read in private."

Okay. She was intrigued. "Wait out here."

"At least leave Abby with me. I'll throw her ball."

Who could turn down a deal like that?

It took a few minutes for Becca's outdated phone to boot up.

The motorhome was hot after being closed up all day. She used the time while the phone did its start up routine to open the windows.

There was only one message.

Walk with me so I can apologize.

Becca opened the motorhome door. "Apologize?" For their kiss? She wasn't sure if she was touched or offended.

Even in the fading light, she could see

Flynn's eyes danced with promise. "Walk with me, Becs, and I'll tell you."

She was tempted.

"Flynn, what are you doing out here?" Agnes opened the door, a purple chenille bathrobe cinched at her waist.

"Nothing." He sounded as innocent as a boy caught stealing another boy's candy. "I'm walking Abby."

After a moment, Agnes nodded. "Would you come by tomorrow and show me how to connect to the internet? I want to join The Facebook."

Flynn kept a straight face at her misnomer of the popular social website. "I sure will. We ordered a USB antennae for every resident. It should get most of you online."

Agnes looked confused, but she thanked him and said good-night.

"I got one for you, too," Flynn said, holding out his hand to help Becca down the motorhome steps.

"I don't have a laptop." She couldn't afford a roaming internet connection. "All I've got is this phone."

Abby bounded up to them, spun and sat on

Becca's feet, as if giving the opinion that she shouldn't go.

He curled his fingers back and forth in the universal *come to me* wave.

Becca sighed and took his hand. Abby bounded back down the stairs. Becca followed. "I don't think an apology is necessary. Let's go by house rule number seven and not talk about it."

"Remind me." He tucked her hand into the crook of his elbow and started walking toward town square. "What did the text say?"

"Walk with me so I can apologize?"

"We're walking. Don't rush me."

Harmony Valley was beautiful as the sun set. The wind picked up, rustling the leaves in the trees with more enthusiasm. The air began cooling off.

They walked in the middle of the street, it being close to or past most residents' bedtimes and there being no traffic. The carpets rolled up around eight in Harmony Valley, with lights out for many around nine.

Two night owls were having drinks on El Rosal's patio. Flynn and Becca waved. Abby ran over to greet them with a quick sniff and tail wag.

Flynn led her into the back alley toward the Harmony River bridge, on the other side of which was Edwin's driveway. The gentle gurgle of the river and the frog symphony greeted them as they came closer.

Becca stole a glance at Flynn. "Are we going back to the house? Is something wrong?"

Flynn stopped in the middle of the bridge. "Look at that sunset."

It was beautiful. Pinks, oranges, blues. Being from Los Angeles, she hadn't seen many sunsets like it, even when she'd lived in San Diego. The smog was too thick in Southern California.

They leaned on the bridge and watched. Abby got restless and went to investigate the frog song coming from the far bank.

"Did you patch things up with Edwin?"

"No. He won't give me my hat back, either."

She gazed at his long locks. There was something different about him tonight. "Did Kathy call again?"

"No."

Something had to be bothering him. "Is Truman okay?"

"Set aside your caregiver role for a minute

and watch the sunset." He turned her face toward the west. The intense colors were fading. An inevitable turning, a regular loss, like the cycle of life, like the cycle of her life.

She sighed, wishing that things were different. That she was different.

"What is it?" Flynn spoke softly, as if afraid to disrupt the sunset's show.

Becca turned her head toward him. "Maybe we should talk about what happened earlier."

"House rule number seven—no talking while watching the sunset." Again, he took her chin and turned it toward the retreating sun.

She decided not to tell him about her own house rule number seven. "But—"

He shushed her. "If you watch a sunset in Harmony Valley in silence it washes your cares away."

"That's a bunch of—"

He shushed her again.

Grinning, Becca complied. How could a sunset, no matter how beautiful, wash away her cares? She'd kissed her employer. What if Flynn was subpoenaed? What if they asked him under oath if she'd ever done anything...

well…out of bounds while he was her employer?

Flynn draped his arm over her shoulders.

Becca tensed and started to turn toward him, but he drew her against him and shushed her.

"You're thinking when you should be watching," he said.

Really, she had no choice but to watch the sunset. In silence. With Flynn.

She didn't want to be anywhere else.

The sun dipped behind the mountains to the soft passage of the river and the throaty burst of frog song.

Becca had no idea why she was out here or what Flynn was going to apologize for. It seemed more appropriate for her to apologize to him.

She turned to do so.

He was looking at her, grinning.

And then he kissed her.

She hadn't seen that one coming.

But she didn't resist. Becca liked kissing him. He was sweet and hot at the same time.

She smiled against his mouth.

He paused, smiling back at her. "Are you laughing at me?"

"I'm laughing at me. But now that I'm allowed to speak, we should stop."

He swooped in to kiss the column of her neck, working his way up to nibble on her earlobe.

The river gurgled and giggled beneath them, as happy as a silly schoolgirl.

"Flynn, really—"

His mouth captured hers again. She had to give him credit. He tackled making out with the same thoroughness that he tackled any other challenge—with dedication, passion and intensity.

She found herself balancing in his arms as she bent over backward like the famous World War II photo.

She giggled. "Stop."

He obeyed, at least when it came to lavishing his lips on her. Instead, he pulled her up against him until it seemed like there wasn't an inch of her front that wasn't touching his.

She tapped his shoulder. "This is not operating under the guidelines of at least three of the house rules." No hugging. No good night kisses. No talking during sunsets.

"Have you ever considered that you have too many house rules?" He kissed the tip of her nose. "If it weren't for house rules, you could just enjoy my kisses."

This time when he swooped in she was ready, deflecting his lips, which detoured to nibble along her chin to her ear again. "We're going to stop." As soon as he reached her ear. Or maybe after he kissed his way back to her mouth.

"Anything you say." His hands slid down to the small of her back.

Becca was awash in sensation, and he was holding her so tight she could barely breathe. In short, he was big trouble on an old bridge.

"Stop," she panted.

"Gotcha." He didn't. Why should he? She'd been crying wolf the first two times. He seemed to be memorizing her curves. His hands left a trail of heat across and around her body. He couldn't have done a more effective job if he'd been applying suntan lotion on her for a hot day at the beach.

"Wow. Whoa. Stop." She captured his clever, pleasing hands, because somebody had to remember what was at stake.

Flynn laced his fingers with hers and brought his forehead down for a meeting of the minds.

She wanted to laugh some more. Instead, she remembered—finally—that she needed to keep her head for a few more weeks. She shoved him back, albeit, not as firmly as she might have done had he not made her lose her resolve.

Becca shook her finger at him, the way she'd seen Edwin do countless times. "I am not amused." Clearly a lie, she used her lower-than-low voice.

He grinned. "I sincerely apologize for having such a wonderful, hot, awesome time with you on the Harmony River bridge."

"You what?" She squeaked like a mouse caught in a trap. "This was your plan all along? Kiss me and apologize?"

"Here's the thing, Becs." His shortening of her name gave her a small thrill. "If you live with someone sixty or so years older than you, you tend to hear a lot of clichés. One of my personal favorites is, *it's easier to ask for forgiveness than to ask for permission.*"

"I'm going to slug you." She started walking home, whistling for Abby, who came racing up and past her. She stopped walking at the base of the bridge. "Wait a minute. This is *the* bridge."

Flynn's grin dared her to wipe it off.

"The bridge where couples kiss good-night?"

"So you've heard of it. Maybe the apology wasn't necessary."

"Are you saying that I knew? That I realized? That I'd jeopardize everything for a kiss?" She whirled and would have tripped over Abby if he hadn't caught her. She leaped ahead, mumbling, "Stupid, stupid, stupid. What would Harold say? Or Virginia?" Or Hank, her lawyer?

Flynn was next to her again. Annoying that, how he could catch up to her without breaking a sweat. She should have been taller or leggier or smarter. Any of the three would have gotten her out of this situation more quickly.

"I'm sorry." But Flynn was laughing when he said it. "Do you want another apology?"

"No." They were walking so fast Abby barked in front of her. The little dog always seemed to have boundless energy, but she was in it for the long haul. Short bursts wore her out. "Suck it up, girl."

"Now, Becs, be reasonable. It was nice, wasn't it?"

"I can't afford nice. I can't afford anything

at all." She stopped and knocked on his noggin with her knuckles—a wake up call, not a pounding. "Do you not get it? I'm your employee for the next few weeks. That's it. That's all I can be."

"Okay, got it. Two weeks. It's a date." He tried to capture her hand.

"No, no, no. No dates. No plans. No nothing. If you can't think of me as your employee, think of me as one of the guys."

He frowned. Turned and pointed back toward the bridge, frustration jerking his movements. "That sunset is imprinted on my brain. And it didn't happen with Will or Slade. You are not, and never will be, one of the guys."

Okay, he was getting riled now. This could be a good thing.

Becca hurried around the corner of El Rosal and entered town square. The restaurant's patio was empty. Town square deserted.

"It's not like you're a local. I don't expect you to know about our traditions, like ice cream with your friends on that bench over there, or marriage proposals under the town square oak tree. But I do expect you to be civil and accept an apology when it's given." Flynn didn't sound apologetic or flirty.

Definitely riled.

"You weren't sincere."

"Neither were you. You aren't sorry we kissed. You're sorry we didn't kiss two weeks from now when your court hearing is over."

The hardest part of his tirade was realizing he was right.

Becca slowed, glancing up toward the sprinkling of stars just starting to come out.

Terry, give me strength.

It probably wasn't wise to ask her departed husband for advice when she'd just been thoroughly kissed. The good news was lightning didn't strike her down. The bad news was Terry didn't whisper sage words of advice in her ear or show up in plasmic form to kick Flynn to the curb.

She stopped and glanced at the ground. Of course, there was a penny.

Refusing to pick it up, Becca spun her wedding ring on her right hand. "From the moment I saw you tonight, leaning against the motorhome, I didn't give Terry a thought. What kind of widow am I?"

"The kind who loves him so much, she can't take the symbol of his love off completely. The kind who did the best she could to hold her head high and clear up the debts you made together. The kind who knows that at some point, Terry would want you to move on." Flynn didn't touch her. He didn't have to. His words enveloped her in a way his arms couldn't.

Her hand drifted to her stomach, covering the butterfly sensations that made her nervous. "Why are you always right?"

"I'm brilliant."

She laughed. How like Flynn to make a joke out of it.

She picked up the penny. "Thank you. The walk was…interesting."

"Do it again tomorrow?"

"Nice try." She pushed his shoulder. "Now, get on home before someone sees us together and talks."

"Too late." He pointed to the opposite corner of town square, where a woman in a flowered housecoat and bunny slippers was walking a Saint Bernard.

CHAPTER FOURTEEN

IF CHAOS LIVED somewhere, it was Harmony Valley.

Flynn was trying not to think about Becca while working on the electrical in Sam's back room when Agnes, Rose and Mildred descended upon him.

"You're a hard man to track down," Agnes said, holding the door open for Mildred and her walker.

"We're here for our progress report," Rose adjusted the coattails of the Sherlock Holmes jacket hanging on a stuffed skunk Sam had on display. Then she admired the mounted deer head on the wall, complete with toupee and tie. "And to see if Sam has anything new on display."

Mildred flipped the seat down on her walker and sat on it. "It's been days since we've talked. We attended a gallery opening in Santa Rosa and a matinee performance of

The Book of Mormon in San Francisco. We had to get caught up on laundry before we got caught up on you."

"Hold that door." Becca escorted Flynn's grandfather into the store. She looked like his kind of candy in snug jeans and a bubble gum–pink T-shirt that complemented the blush in her cheeks.

In the back room, Abby barked and came racing to the front. Becca leaned down to pet her. Then Abby did her wiggly greeting to each person, before returning to the back room and Truman.

Grandpa Ed saw Mildred sitting and promptly took a similar seat on his own walker.

"What are you doing here?" Flynn forgot Becca and kisses. "I thought we all agreed you were to stay at home."

Becca shrugged. "There was a rebellion."

"I told you I didn't want a jailer," Grandpa Ed grumped.

"And Truman could use a snack." Becca held up a plastic bag filled with apple slices.

"Are all you people parked out in front of my store?" Sam said from his seat behind the glass display counter. He'd stopped reading a

Superman comic book. "Where are my customers supposed to park?"

Everyone started giving Sam excuses at the same time. Becca stepped forward and introduced herself.

"Nobody is staying very long if you're not working on my problem, unless you have commerce with me. You get me?"

Becca paused to admire a display of Depression glass. "This is beautiful. Is it for sale?"

Sam warmed up a smidgeon, while Flynn placated the ladies of the town council. "We had to remove the old foundation." Like they needed another delay. "We're pouring the new foundation tomorrow. Beams will go up next week."

"What about the farmhouse?" Agnes's right hand was clenched against her chest, as if she held something she was afraid of losing. "What's happening with it?"

"They're gutting most of it."

Mildred gasped. "But the antique buffet—"

"Will remain as a key feature behind the tasting room counter," Flynn reassured them. "We're trying to save as much as we can. I promise."

The ladies finally left. Voices drifted out from the back room. Truman's. Becca's.

Flynn turned to his grandfather, who still wore Flynn's ball cap. "I thought we agreed you should stay at home."

"I live my life on my own terms. I'm here to visit Sam." Edwin stood and wheeled himself closer to the glass display counter, sitting across from his comic-reading friend. "If I die today, then I'll die a happy man. I've decided I don't want to go tethered to that fancy recliner you bought me."

"Those game shows will be crushed." Flynn leaned on the counter, reluctant to leave his grandfather alone. And he didn't want Grandpa Ed to see Joey working in the back.

THE STOREROOM AT Snarky Sam's was crowded with junk. And that was a nice description.

A concrete-frosted wheelbarrow was parked in one corner with two bread makers stacked in it. A brandy cask had been rolled into another and was topped with several toasters. An artificial Christmas tree crowded the door. Several square fans were lined up around the tree. There was barely room for Slade and the older man up on the ladder, who poked beneath the light fixture that was rumored not to work.

"Becca!" Truman ran to greet her, hugging her leg and snatching the apple slices. "This is the greatest place ever. Sam said I could have a toaster to take apart. And Uncle Flynn said I could use his tools as long as I didn't plug it in."

Becca added that to her mental monitoring list. Wouldn't do to have a curious boy in her charge electrocute himself.

The man on the ladder turned to her with a smile so familiar, it distracted. "Are we getting another pair of hands?"

"That's Joey." Truman spoke through a mouth full of apple slice. "Doesn't he look like Uncle Flynn?"

"He does," Becca said. The high cheekbones. The strong, wiry body. The intense gaze that seemed to see everything. The resemblance was so strong she could see why Flynn hid his face beneath a baseball cap.

But the smile was also the same. It said

I'm sweet, and loveable and trustworthy. No agendas.

Just like Flynn.

"He's Flynn's dad, which means we're related."

"He's your grandfather?" Becca didn't mean to be rude, but she hadn't expected the man Flynn despised to look so friendly.

"There's been some debate about that." Slade handed Joey a pair of wire cutters.

"I'm Kathy's stepfather." Joey clipped something through a hole in the ceiling.

"But his picture is on my dresser. He's hugging my grandmama." Cheeks as stuffed as a chipmunk's, Truman was clearly enjoying the debate. "Which means he's my grandfather."

Joey handed the wire cutters back to Slade. "By marriage."

"Although Truman doesn't seem to care." There was contained laughter in Slade's voice.

Joey shrugged, as if having little boys show up and love him was nothing. But his smile never faded.

"I like this town," Truman said. "I have lots of uncles. I found a new grandpa. And I have neighbors who help each other. I'm going to ask Mama if we can move here." And then he fell silent, as if remembering that no one knew where his mother was or when she was coming home.

FLYNN WALKED BECCA and his grandfather out to the black Caddy parked at the curb. It was a slow walk in the heat with long shadows cast upon the pavement.

When Flynn opened the car door, heat rose up off the leather seats even though they'd left the windows down. "I wish you'd let me buy you a decent car with air-conditioning."

"Too late for that. It is what it is. My car. My life." Grandpa Ed grunted. He set the walker to one side and grabbed onto Becca's hand to steady himself. "I wish I'd told you about Joey sooner. But that won't change the fact that I didn't."

"No, it won't," Flynn allowed, staring at his grandfather until the old man looked up at him. "You did what you thought was best."

Grandpa Ed nodded once, a curt we-don't-do-emotion admission that something important had just occurred. If not forgiveness, then acceptance.

"Can I have my hat back?" Flynn wasn't like Slade and his ties. He didn't have a hat for every day of the week multiplied times his different moods. He had one hat. It fit his head perfectly.

"No." The old man closed the door, with a chuckle that deteriorated into a dry cough.

Becca had the trunk open. She studied his face intently as he brought the walker back. "You hate that you look like Joey, don't you? That's why you hide beneath the ball cap."

Trust her to get right to the point.

Flynn stared longingly at the back of his baseball hat. "I thought if I didn't look so much like him that she'd come back." No need to explain who she was. His mother.

"When I saw Joey, I saw the resemblance right away," Becca said.

Nineteen years of hiding beneath a ball cap had gotten him nowhere. "That's it. I'm going to cut it off." He set off down Main Street toward Phil's barbershop.

"Wait. Don't be too hasty," Becca called after him. "I saw the resemblance, but I also saw the differences."

He heard her get into the Caddy and start it up. She pulled up next to him as he marched resolutely toward the nearest pair of scissors.

"What's going on?" Grandpa Ed coughed some more. "Where are you going?"

"To get a haircut."

It was one of the few times in recent history his grandfather had nothing to say.

"But not at Phil's," Becca said. "Right? You're going home to get your truck. We'll give you a ride. You can drive down to Cloverdale."

"Why wouldn't he let Phil cut his hair?" Grandpa Ed's wheeze was barely audible over the Cadillac's rumbling engine.

"Come on, Edwin." Becca pounded the steering wheel. "His hands shake like maracas on a dance floor."

"Nonsense, Phil cut my hair the other day."

"Yes, and I was afraid he might take your ear off!"

"Take my grandfather home," Flynn said through gritted teeth. The breeze buffeted his shoulder-length locks.

"Now look here," Grandpa Ed huffed. "I've been taking care of myself for years without your help. If I want to watch you get a haircut, I'll watch you get a haircut."

Flynn stopped and put his hands on his knees so he was level with them. "Fine. Park the car and meet me inside. If Phil clips my ear off, you can drive me to urgent care in Cloverdale."

He marched across the street after they passed. Becca had to circle town square to come around and park in front of Phil's. Flynn helped his grandfather out of the car, to his walker and into the barbershop.

The broken barber pole taunted him. That should be next on his fix-it list.

Phil sat in his barber chair. He peered at them from around the newspaper he held with quaking hands, as if people who walked through his door were a distraction, not potential customers. "Flynn, the plumber came today. We have new pipes."

Flynn nodded. "I've got someone to patch that hole. But first, I'd like a haircut."

"You don't say." Phil crumpled the paper on his lap. "I never cut your hair. Not since Edwin stopped bringing you in here for crew cuts."

It was true. Flynn had become handy with a pair of scissors. And his hands didn't shake.

Phil's did. So much so he could barely fold his newspaper.

Flynn was starting to have second thoughts.

Unacceptable. He walked over to the second barber chair.

"Don't," Phil stood and stopped him.

"You won't cut my hair?" Flynn was confused.

"It's a sign." Becca's wide-eyed stare further challenged his resolve. "Are you sure you want to do this?"

"There is no sign," Phil snapped. "No need. Everyone knows that chair is broken. The missing hardware is in the drawer over there. Every time something falls off, I put it in there. My lumbago keeps me from leaning over to fix it."

Flynn caught sight of himself in the mirror. Instead of his face, he saw Joey's. All he needed was a rubber band, gray hair and a goatee. He claimed Phil's chair. "Do it."

Phil covered him with a plastic drape. "I'm not going to have to promise you a sucker to keep you still, am I?" He chuckled, struggling to get the snaps fastened in back. "I haven't had a kid in this chair in more than six years."

Flynn's Adam's apple bobbed. He clung to his resolve.

He broke out in a sweat as the snip-snip of scissors hovered too close to his ears.

With each lock that fell to the floor, Flynn felt more like himself. Once the big pieces were cut off, Phil took the shears to his head, giving him a close cut that looked nothing like an old ex-con would get. It was more like Slade's neatly cut, Wall Street style.

"He looks like a man." Edwin tugged the ball cap lower, but not before Flynn saw the unshed tears in his eyes.

"Very handsome," Becca agreed, her smile as warm as her gaze, until she caught him looking. "We need house rule number eight."

"No, we don't." He was done with house rules.

Flynn did look different. But he imagined that if he stood next to Joey, people would still say they were related.

"Whoa," Slade said when Flynn returned to Snarky Sam's stuffy back room. "You look like Flynn Harris, but your shirt is ironed and your hair is cut."

Joey stopped twisting wires on the light fixture. "You thinking about joining the military? Or the police?"

"Which worries you the most?" Flynn countered.

"I don't much like the idea of you getting shot up." Joey went back to his wiring. "I'd rather think of you eating junk food and getting fat while you program your computer games."

Flynn was speechless. He'd expected a more cutting comment.

"Funny." Slade gave him a once-over. "That's how I imagined him aging, too. I might have to change my impression."

Flynn scowled. "Are you almost finished? There's some work that needs to be done at the barbershop. The pole's broken, one of the barber chairs is a hazard and there's a hole in the drywall under the shampoo bowl."

Truman tugged on Flynn's shirt, his blue eyes puppy dog large and hard to resist. "I can fix a barber chair."

"I'll help you," Slade offered with just the right amount of enthusiasm to please a child. Slade was a natural with Truman, reminding Flynn that Slade was an absentee father, not by choice. His ex-wife was hoarding her precious meal tickets, as if she suspected after a visit to Harmony Valley his twin girls would never want to return to New York.

"Awesome." Truman grinned.

"Why don't you flip that switch and see if this is working proper?" Joey held the light fixture, which turned on as planned. "We're done here. I set a couple of mousetraps in the attic. They shouldn't be gnawing on Sam's wires anymore. Might tell him to get a cat."

That was nice. Flynn didn't want Joey to be nice. It went against years of childhood and, okay, he'd admit it, adult angst.

They moved their vehicles down the street and descended upon Phil's barbershop. Slade and Truman went inside to fix the broken barber chair.

Joey began removing the barber pole from the wall.

Since Flynn was no drywall guy, he stayed out on the street with Joey. Besides, he'd had too many unanswered questions for too many years. "Why'd you do it? Why'd you take the money?"

Joey didn't so much as spare Flynn a glance. "For one thing, Edwin's never liked me. And the idea of sticking it to him appealed." His chuckle didn't touch Flynn's funny bone.

"You never thought about me?" Flynn fiddled with a screwdriver. "About how I'd feel?"

"I mostly figured I wouldn't get out until

you were in college and I didn't want you coming to visit. The clientele in the prison visitor's center isn't exactly the same as the Cloverdale bingo hall. Not a place I wanted my kid hanging around."

That made Flynn feel a little better.

"I did write you, but since I promised the old man I wouldn't, I kept them in a box. I can give them to you, if you like."

He'd written. He'd been man enough to honor a promise. The tension in his shoulders eased, but not enough to accept the letters just yet. "Did Mom visit you?"

"Nope. Got a Dear Joey letter about three months in. I don't blame her. She was a woman with needs."

Flynn threw up his hands. "Stop right there. That's the last thing I need to hear about." He knew far too much himself.

"I meant she had money needs and drug needs. I granted her the divorce." Joey pulled the wires for the pole out. "Here's the problem. It's a loose connection. Happens sometimes in these old buildings after an earthquake. Shakes things loose."

Flynn was feeling shaken loose himself.

A long-lost father coming into his life at

a time when he was losing the man who raised him?

Flynn wanted to find his footing. He wanted to steady himself in Becca's embrace.

For now, he had to be content finding his footing alone.

Although maybe he wasn't as alone as he thought. He glanced at Joey, who squinted at the wires behind the barber pole.

Maybe this man, the man who was his father, could help.

CHAPTER FIFTEEN

"I LIKE FABRIZIO. He's got years of winemaking experience and his name is fun to pronounce." Flynn was only half joking.

They'd gone back to their résumé review to fill key jobs at the winery, the most pressing of which was winemaker.

Flynn slumped in a wicker chair on the back porch and tossed a stack of résumés on the table beside him. "Who am I kidding? I don't know anything about making wine."

"Or about women." Slade's sharp grin needled. "You and Becca have been circling each other since she got here. I'm starting to get dizzy."

Will nodded, but didn't look up from squinting at a résumé.

"Just what I need." Flynn rubbed his hands over his too-short hair. "Advice from the peanut gallery. I don't see you dating anyone, Slade."

"Dating implies I'm settled. And I'm not settling here." Slade smoothed his teal pin-stripe tie. Figuring out his tie color code was the equivalent of having a temperature gauge on Slade's moods. Today was an upbeat day. Slade may have been smiling, but he wasn't joking. Both his mother and his father had died in his childhood home. For Slade, Harmony Valley was a place full of bad memories. "The only thing keeping me in town is you two and this money-sucking winery."

Will dropped his stack of résumés onto his lap. "This shouldn't be so hard. The head-hunter we hired screened candidates. And yet, there are still too many."

"Maybe we should focus on those who make the wine types we grow." Slade picked up Fabrizio's résumé from the table between him and Flynn. "Look at the wines Fabrizio makes—chardonnay and cabernet sauvignon. We grow both of those grapes."

"I don't drink wine. You choose." Flynn stood and went to the section of railing where he and Becca first kissed. How could she kiss him like that—twice—and then refuse to be alone with him?

Becca was inside, cajoling his grandfather

into some physical therapy with the help of Truman and Abby. Flynn wished he was in there, but his grandfather was always pushing him away.

"This is a partnership. Just like you brought me up to speed on programming, we'll bring each other up to speed on wine. Here's what I know. Chardonnay is a white wine." Slade, the methodical partner.

"Although the chardonnay grapes I see on our vines are green." Will, the comedic partner.

"And cabernet is a red wine." Slade, now the annoying partner.

"And the grape is red, although it isn't yet on the vines we've been told are cab." Will looked from one to the other, taking on the role of worried partner. "Should we be worried?"

Flynn shrugged.

"And now we're all on the same page. Still worried and clueless." Slade dropped Fabrizio's résumé back on the table.

Flynn turned and slumped against the railing. "My grandfather was a beer guy. My father was a beer guy. We're beer guys. Knowing what color the grapes are doesn't help us much." In hindsight, starting a winery was a rather naive endeavor if you weren't a wine lover. "I can sort candidates by years of experience."

"We need to call in reinforcements." Will got out his cell phone. "I'm calling Emma. She and Rose drink wine. Maybe she'll recognize some of the wineries these guys work for."

"I have a better idea." Slade stood and gathered the résumés. "Why don't we take a drive to the nearest wine shop and buy a bottle of every cab and chard each of these candidates make?"

Flynn straightened. Will put his cell phone down.

"We'll invite the town council for a wine and cheese party tonight." Slade fiddled with the bottom of his tie.

"Sounds good to me." Flynn grinned. It would keep the old ladies happy and hopefully out of his hair. "Let's make some calls." And while they were in town, he'd stop by the private investigator's office. And while he was there, if Wes Webber didn't make his skin crawl like he had before, he'd ask him to track down Kathy.

Three hours later, Flynn parked his truck in

front of a small office building in Santa Rosa. The cinderblock building was divided into two smaller spaces fronted with large plate glass windows. One, Boyd's Surveillance Equipment, had the glass window painted completely black, no doubt, trying to reassure clients of their own privacy. The other, Webber Investigations, was so grimy Flynn had a hard time making out anything inside.

"This guy was blowing smoke up your butt." Slade looked disdainfully upon Flynn's destination. "Is that a bullet hole?"

Flynn looked closer at Webber's plate glass. "Yep."

"You want to ask this guy to find Kathy?" Will was similarly unimpressed.

"Yep." Flynn wasn't to be dissuaded. His sister had been gone nearly three weeks. "You guys wait in the car."

There was no receptionist, only an empty desk next to a lumpy leather couch. Flynn tracked the trajectory of the bullet hole and decided it would have struck whoever was sitting behind the front desk. That explained why it lacked an office chair. It'd probably been covered in blood. Although the desktop seemed free of any life-ending stains.

Wes watched him from behind a desk in the rear office. "I knew you'd be in touch. What has Ms. MacKenzie done? Accepted a generous gift of a car? More cash? A diamond ring?" He flashed that too-slick smile. "I know. You popped the question and had second thoughts, didn't you?"

"No." Flynn's scowl was so deep-rooted, it twisted his hands into fists. "I didn't come because of Becca."

"No?" Webber tapped a folder. "I spoke with the daughter of her last client. She said Becca didn't turn in her house keys when she asked. She found Becca in her father's house, acting nervous. She's going to go through his valuables and see if anything's missing."

Flynn's insides felt like he'd been wound up tighter than a rubber-band airplane ready to launch. At Webber. "Becca wouldn't steal anything." He wasn't convincing, even to himself.

For once, Webber didn't press the point. "What can I help you with?"

Flynn retrieved a folded piece of paper from his back pocket. "I want you to find my sister. She came by the house more than two weeks ago and left her son with me. Last Sunday she called, but wouldn't tell me where she was or when she's coming back. Here's all her information." Flynn slid a photo of him and Kathy from two Christmases ago from his wallet, placing it on the desk. "And here's a picture of her."

"Abandoned her kid?" Webber scanned the folded sheet of paper. "Smart girl, leaving him with a millionaire."

"This was a mistake." Flynn reached for his things.

"Do you want her found or not?" Webber swept them out of reach, smiling like they were having a schoolyard argument involving the word *Mine!*

"I'm worried about her," Flynn ground out.

Webber took out what looked to be a contract. He filled out the client information for Flynn, including his name, address and cell phone number. Annoying, that he apparently knew it by heart. He filled in a daily rate and flipped the contract around for Flynn to sign.

"You're overcharging me." Flynn didn't know how he knew, he just knew. He could hear Becca in his head, telling him he was a sucker for always overpaying. He wanted his sister found, but if this guy was the one to find her, he wouldn't get a penny more than he earned.

Webber smiled, but it was the kind of smile you bestowed on backstabbing officemates. "That's the millionaire rate."

Flynn pushed the contract back to Webber's side of the desk. "Funny thing you probably didn't realize about me. I'm a programmer. I could hack you in less than five minutes. Another five and I'd have your website and IP address registered as a spammer's in all fifty states. Set aside the fact that email as a form of communication for your business would be shut down or that I could point your web address to online videos of toddlers shoving food up their noses." Now Flynn was just being kind. "Imagine what I could do with an hour."

Webber took a moment to chew on that before crossing out the exorbitant hourly rate and writing something much, much lower. He slid the contract across the desk.

Flynn initialed the changed rate and signed on the dotted line. "You can call my cell now. We've got service in Harmony Valley."

"Yeah, I know. I'll update you in a few days."

Flynn turned to go.

"Mr. Harris?"

Flynn turned back around.

"Since you're a client now, when I find out what Ms. MacKenzie stole from Harold Epstein, I'll let you know before I send the cops out to arrest her. What you do with that information is up to you."

Flynn didn't waste energy arguing over Becca's innocence. She was guilty of something. But a thief? Flynn found that hard to believe.

He didn't say much to his friends as they drove back to Harmony Valley. He was too busy formulating ways to ask Becca what was going on.

And contingency plans to protect her.

WHEN AGNES ARRIVED at Edwin's for the wine tasting, she not only brought Mildred, but four bottles of wine. Her hands trembled a bit as she carried them in. From nerves, not old age. It took chutzpah to bring her granddaughter's wine to a wine tasting where the outcome would decide which winemakers Flynn and his friends would interview.

She was walking more than one tightrope

this evening—Agnes had been unable to convince Christine to apply for the job. Her granddaughter had every excuse in the book. She was too stressed to apply for a new job. She didn't want to go from one high end, high maintenance employer to another. Her dad wanted her to take a job at a different winery.

Kids nowadays. She included her son-in-law, Christine's father, in that statement. The vineyards manager was always jumping ship from one job to the next. She hated that he was trying to impart his ways on Christine.

Christine was unhappy. She hadn't grown up in Harmony Valley. She had no idea how much this place needed someone like her. Or how much Agnes needed someone like her. When Becca moved on to her next client, as she kept insisting she'd do, Agnes was going to be alone once more. And no ring, no peach tree, no cherished memory would fill her dinner table the way Becca had.

She expected Edwin knew something about loneliness.

Since Irma died, Edwin's house had been a somber, masculine place, even when Flynn and Kathy lived there as children. Tonight, she could see purple and pink hydrangea bouquets through the rarely opened windows—one on a coffee table and the other on the kitchen table. The welcome mat had been hosed off, so you could actually read the word *Welcome*.

Abby greeted Agnes and Mildred at the door. She sniffed Mildred's walker before prancing on her hind legs for Agnes.

"I didn't bring you any treats," Agnes whispered. Becca didn't know she sneaked the little dog snacks when Becca wasn't looking. It was a pleasure to have people and dogs around the house again.

Mildred wheeled over to sit on the couch across from Edwin.

Pale skin, haggard eyes. Edwin looked like he was ready to hail a cab to heaven.

Agnes paused in the foyer. He didn't look like a man on the road to recovery. "Edwin, you look tired. Should we do this another day?" As soon as the words left her lips, Agnes regretted them.

"I've been tired since I turned sixty," Edwin snapped, defending his masculine ego. Agnes should have known better. "I've got the best seat in the house for this function. Don't worry about me."

"Were we supposed to bring wine?" Rose

peered around her granddaughter, Emma, who was arranging cheese and crackers on a serving tray. "I thought the men were bringing it."

"My granddaughter, Christine, made these." Agnes set the clanking cloth bag with the wine on the counter. She twisted the ruby ring.

Emma's gaze was drawn to her fingers. "That's a pretty ring. Is it new?"

"No." Agnes put her hand behind her back.

"She won't tell us where she got it," Rose grumbled, smoothing her black pencil skirt over her nonexistent curves. At eighty, Rose still had the body of a ballerina. "I figure it's from an ex-lover."

"Rose," Agnes scolded, exchanging a look with Becca, who was at the sink drying wineglasses.

"See what I mean?" Rose grumbled. "Won't say a word."

Agnes spun the ring until the ruby lay in her palm. She clenched her fingers and put her hand over her heart.

Truman sat on the far side of Edwin's recliner near the wall. He peeked out at the newcomers and then went back to playing with his action figures.

"Hello, Truman." Agnes drifted closer. "Whose house did you work on today?"

"We took a vacation day today." His smile was almost woeful.

"I hear Mae Gardner's fence needs fixing," Agnes said.

Truman perked up. "That's awesome. I get to hammer on fences."

"Agnes." Mildred pushed her walker to one side of the couch and produced a stack of paper from her voluminous purse. "I printed out the rating sheets from garden club's last wine tasting fundraiser." She looked abashed. "At least I hope that's what I printed out." Hard to tell when she had trouble seeing.

Agnes scanned them, confirming they were, indeed, what they needed.

"Pens and pencils are on the counter in the kitchen." Edwin waved a hand at Becca, who promptly took Mildred's rating sheets from Agnes and went to get the writing utensils.

A black truck pulled up and the men piled out.

Becca stopped counting pens and pencils to watch Flynn get out of the truck. She kept watching as they unloaded box after box of wine from the back.

Agnes had seen the way Flynn looked at Becca. Why the girl didn't snatch that catch up was beyond her. He was a gem who was shining brighter since he'd cut that mop of red hair.

A more immediate concern was Christine's wine. Would they agree to include it in the tasting?

Rose pressed her nose to the front window like a kid on a mission to spot the Easter Bunny. "That's a lot of wine. We're going to need spit cups."

Truman slipped next to Rose, quiet as a church mouse. After a moment, he pressed his face against the glass, too.

Without taking her nose off the glass, Rose gave Truman a thumbs-up and received a grin in return. "Edwin, do you have any plastic cups? Your young men probably have had a party or two where they needed them."

"Those red ones you throw away? No. But Flynn has a collection of plastic cups from a fast food restaurant. They have superheroes on them."

Agnes could barely hear the men outside

over the pounding of her heart. Did she have the nerve to go through with this?

Rose patted Truman on the head and headed for the kitchen, where she hunted around in the cupboards until she found cups. "These'll do. Superheroes in capes and tights. We're going old school, aren't we, Agnes? Nothing mechanical or robotic."

Agnes paced the archway separating the kitchen from the living room. "Save that last one for me. There's nothing sexier than a man in green tights."

Flynn came in with the first case of wine, followed by Slade, and Will, who stopped to give his fiancé, Emma, a quick kiss over the top of his box.

This was it. Agnes backed into the corner of the kitchen. Butterflies dive bombed her stomach. She'd never gambled in a casino, never played the lottery. Manny used to say she lacked the nerve.

"This wine wasn't on our list." Flynn picked up a bottle of chardonnay Agnes had brought, then a cabernet.

Agnes's mouth was almost too dry to form words. "My granddaughter made those wines. She's a winemaker in Napa."

"Do we have her résumé?" Flynn asked, while Will craned his neck to look at the label over Flynn's shoulder.

"No. She missed the submission deadline," Agnes fibbed, sending a few more butterflies on a kamikaze mission. "I thought her wines could be her résumé."

Slade relieved Flynn of the bottle of cabernet, frowning. Of the three men, he was always the most severe, the most intimidating.

"I vote we try Christine's wine," Edwin said. The house was small enough that all conversations could be heard. "Although she never lived here, her mother did. She's a perfect candidate for relocation."

"She could live with me." Agnes gripped the counter, unable to believe they were going to taste the wine.

Rose rubbed Agnes's back. "It's nice having someone else in the house. Isn't it Emma?"

"Yes, it is," Emma shared a secret smile with Will.

The warmth of their young love washed over Agnes. She brushed her thumb over the ruby cradled in her palm.

Flynn whispered something to Becca, but she shook her head. He frowned.

"So." Will rubbed his hands together. "Who's running this show?"

Agnes stepped forward. "I'll assign codes for each wine, put the codes on the score sheets and brown bag everything, so no one knows which wine is which."

"I'd like a bit more impartiality." Slade crossed his arms over his chest. "No offense, Agnes."

"None taken." But really, there was. She wiped her sweaty palms on the back of her denim capris. She had to make sure Christine's wine won. Her wine was good, but there were some high-end winemakers in the mix.

"Becca will do the honors. She told me earlier she wasn't going to taste." Slade guided Becca to the cluster of wine bottles on the counter. "Everyone who isn't opening wine bottles out of the kitchen."

"I'll help." Flynn hovered closely behind Becca. "I need to discuss something with her anyway. We can talk and prepare wine at the same time."

Becca carefully didn't look his way.

"No," Slade shut down the would-be Romeo. "You can make those tight circles later."

Agnes grinned. "Becca, you'll want to strip off the neck wraps before you brown bag them. Oh, and write the codes on a master list before you bag the wine."

"Thank you for the advice." Slade swept one arm toward the living room, dismissing Agnes, who exchanged one last, pleading glance with Becca.

Not that she was asking her to cheat.

THERE WAS NO mistaking the look on Agnes's face.

She was asking Becca to cheat.

Agnes was after the wrong person, since Becca had never been to a blind wine tasting before, much less an organized one. She wouldn't know how to fix the results.

But still, what was up with that?

And then there was Flynn, who said he needed to talk with her alone. Agnes kept making those I-know-what-you-did-on-the-bridge looks at Becca every time Flynn was around, every time his name was mentioned. Why weren't people understanding the concept of keeping Becca's nose clean? *It's an employer-employee relationship, people.*

Becca sealed the top of each paper bag

around the lip of the wine bottle with blue masking tape, then used a thin permanent marker to code the bag. There were nearly forty bottles of wine, two of each winery's type. While she wrestled with bags and tape, the conversations in the living room filled her with a surprising sense of longing.

"When's the wedding?" Agnes asked. Becca imagined her keeping the ruby ring carefully concealed in her palm, perhaps over her heart. She'd worn the ring every day since they'd argued about it and found that penny near Agnes's trunk.

"We're getting married next spring. After the winery is open." Becca imagined Emma lit up the room with her red batik print skirt and her happily-ever-after smile.

"I've always thought these walkers should come with a cup holder and a sound system." Mildred had been a race car driver and still loved her automotive accessories.

"Walkers aren't cars," Edwin rumbled, but his voice seemed weak and muted. He gave a little wheezy cough. "They're like adult strollers."

"After we decide on a winemaker, we'll

need to begin staffing the other positions." Will spoke in a deep, I-never-panic tone.

"The winemaker will want some say in who else we hire." She could just picture Slade smoothing his ever-present tie.

Becca smiled. This was what family was like, extended or otherwise. This was what was permanently missing in her own life. Not that she'd ever belong in the living room. As a caregiver, she'd always be an outsider at gatherings like this. She'd been fine with that for years. She planned to be fine with that forever.

"Becca's done a wonderful job with the house," Flynn was saying. "We bachelors aren't very good at cooking or cleaning or stocking up on toilet paper."

Hearing Flynn's voice, Becca's longing to belong increased. He was the carrot she happily, and sometimes unwittingly, plodded toward. But even if they explored their feelings for each other after her lawsuit was dismissed—crossing fingers, knocking on wood—it might not amount to anything.

Truman peeked around the corner. "Can I help?"

Becca didn't want Truman handling the wine. "You can pass out the rating sheets and pens. Give each person a magazine to use as a clipboard."

Truman scampered off.

She set up the wines all around the U-shaped kitchen counter and tucked the key to the codes in her back pocket.

Soon the tasting was in full swing. Only Edwin, Becca and, of course, Truman abstained.

Becca made sure people had water. She made sure people had spit cups. She made sure to stay away from Flynn.

As the tasting went on, the testers' voices increased in volume, as if the more wine they drank, the louder they had to speak. The more they laughed and smiled, the more left out Becca felt, no matter how much she told herself she didn't belong. She had to consider herself a servant, a member of the staff. But she couldn't. She wanted to belong too badly.

She slipped out the kitchen door and followed the porch around to the rear of the house where it overlooked the Harmony River. The lights from the house barely illuminated the blackberry bushes below the railing. The murmur of laughter and warm voices drowned out the gurgle of the river and the deep bass of the frogs.

On nights like this she missed having someone. Mom. Gram. Terry.

Her evenings with Agnes were precious, as Agnes treated Becca like a granddaughter. But it was all short term. Agnes. Flynn. Harmony Valley.

The front door opened. Footsteps rounded the porch.

She knew who it was before he appeared.

Flynn. A glass of wine in his hand.

She drank him in, the short hair that made him look so handsome, his wiry frame, blue jeans and a rumpled T-shirt with red wine stains on the front. She fought a grin. Flynn wasn't Slade and didn't care much about appearances. He cared about people. About his friends. About his grandfather and his nephew.

And her. He cared about her.

Becca hadn't thought about his feelings before. He was like Abby, rushing around, tending his flock. She was one of many he watched out for.

If Becca told herself she was one of many, she might not dream about him tonight. If she told herself she was content living alone, she might not feel a stab of longing when their eyes met. If she told herself he'd kissed her because she was the only available woman under the age of sixty-five in town, she might not relive the urgent press of his lips on hers.

She told herself none of those things.

They stood looking at each other long enough to pick out china patterns and silver sets.

Becca wet her lips and dragged her gaze away from his. She should return to the kitchen, pick up empty bottles, check on Edwin.

Not one tootsie in her tennis shoes budged.

"I saw that private detective today." Flynn walked to the center of the porch and rested his forearms on the railing next to her. "He said there's a family, the family of whoever you worked for last, that's taking inventory of his valuables."

Becca reached out to steady herself on a porch post. *That ring.* She never should have taken it. It was less than two weeks until her hearing. Two weeks! Would Harold's daughter, Diane, discover the ring missing by then? Could she take the chance?

Flynn sipped his wine casually, as if he wasn't studying her out of the corner of his eye. "I asked you about taking money. I didn't ask you about taking other things."

She felt the tension in his accusation in every pulse-pound at her temples.

He knows.

She had to swallow twice before she could speak. "Are you firing me?" The question fell between them, opening a chasm Becca knew she couldn't cross by walking around the truth.

Laughter built inside the house. Faded.

He angled toward her, his hip against the railing, his gaze carefully schooled. Interested. Inquisitive. Like a teacher suspicious that a favorite student was cheating, a teacher wanting to give said student the benefit of the doubt with a surprise pop quiz.

Her pulse pounded harder. She tried to smile, but her lips felt like an oak leaf come fall, dry and brittle. She'd never been good at tests.

Flynn switched tactics. "What was he like? Your husband?"

She didn't want to talk about Terry. She wanted to talk about her job and Flynn's letter of reference. She wanted to explain and apologize. Based on whatever Flynn knew.

What did he know?

"He was a soldier?" Flynn prompted, when she didn't immediately answer.

"A marine. He came from a long line of marines." But he was the first in his family to die in combat.

"You must have been very proud of him." Flynn's voice, so sure, so steady, so ready to be disappointed in her.

"I *am* very proud of him." But would Terry be proud of her? Becca was desperate to run back into the house, to find Agnes, to return the ring. And yet, she couldn't do any of those things until she passed Flynn's test. "And you? No special women?"

"Couldn't catch one with all those millions." Sometime during their conversation he'd moved closer to her. "You know how it is. You have to kiss a lot of frogs…"

He was trying to get a rise out of her, a confession. Becca's grip on the post tightened. She could still fix this. Somehow. In a way that didn't involve disappointing Flynn with the truth.

"My circumstances are unique. How do I

know if a woman wants me or my millions?" Flynn seemed to be looking out on the water, but she had the distinct impression that he was also looking at her, sizing up her weaknesses. "But you…you, Becca… Some man will want to make an honest woman out of you again."

"I can't." Her voice was low, but she wasn't lying. "I mean, I won't. I had my chance at love. When you've lost as many people as I have, you realize that love doesn't come with guarantees."

He tsked, the sound as quiet and soothing as the distant sound of frogs down by the river.

She didn't want to have this conversation. "I like being alone. I like my life." Or she had, until Harold swore her to secrecy about the ruby ring.

"You don't." He gestured toward her with his wineglass. He was close enough that the tulip-shaped rim grazed her arm. "You keep yourself apart from everyone who would call you friend. Or family."

"I have Abby. She's all the family I'm looking for."

He took a half step closer. His feet were almost touching hers. "Love will find you, whether you want it to or not."

Becca frowned and told him what she'd been telling herself for three years. "I'm not willing to risk my heart again."

He pulled back. "Never?"

Relieved, she shook her head. "I'm scared." Scared that she'd made a muck of her life by taking Virginia's money and Harold's ring. Scared that if she told Flynn the truth he'd ask her to leave. Scared that if she kept her silence he'd still send her away.

"What if love happened to walk by, Becs?" His fingers strolled up her arm.

She couldn't stop him. She knew she should stop him. This wasn't about proving her good intentions or keeping her heart safe. It was about wanting to be held. Wanting to be reassured. Wanting to know that someone in the world, other than her lawyer, believed Becca was a good person.

His fingers reached her shoulder, hesitated. "If love happened to walk by…" His fingers slid up the slope of her neck, slid around to cup her head. He searched for something to say, but then his gaze dropped to her lips.

And he kissed her.

Yes. Her heart whispered, accepting his

heat and the tannic taste of red wine on her lips.

No. Her head whispered, but too weak to be of any use.

Because Flynn knew how to kiss. He knew how to tempt her with caresses and coax her with a gentle intensity that muddled her brain.

It was a simple, physical reacquainting. Their bodies were a careful distance apart. But heat ignited in her belly, radiating outward, making her want, making her want to be closer, making her want to forget widowhood and lawsuits.

Flynn must have read her mind because the hand that did the walking slid down her back and drew her close.

Desire held sway of her body and mind, reminded her how good living in the moment could feel.

"That's my girl," Flynn whispered against her lips.

But she wasn't Flynn's girl. As soon as he found out she'd lied to him by not telling him about the ring, whatever feelings he had for her would slip away.

"Don't kiss me. Please don't kiss me." She

was trembling as she broke away from his embrace. "I asked you not to kiss me."

"I didn't… I mean, I did." He grinned. "I'd like to again. Wouldn't you?"

What a mess. She couldn't say it, but her brain was stuck on a loop: *what a mess, what a mess, what a mess.*

"I'll take your silence as a yes. You do want another kiss." He reached for her again.

She swatted his hand away. "Flynn! I told you there can't be so much as a hint of impropriety between us."

"Hey, I didn't mean to kiss you." He held up his hands. "I just came out here and there were your lips, just waiting for mine."

"There were my…" She slugged him in the shoulder, although not as hard as she might have liked to. "I just told you I wasn't looking for anyone. Including you!"

"It was just a kiss." He scowled, rubbing the spot she'd hit. "What would you rather have happened? Have me ask you about whatever gift you got from your last client? Or what you sto—"

"Don't say it. I didn't *steal* anything."

He sighed and rubbed a hand over his short hair, his hand pausing at the nape of his neck as if missing the long locks. "I can't have you here if you're a thief. I can't let you take care of my grandfather if you're a thief. I can't… kiss you if you're a thief."

She felt hollow inside, like the time she learned her mother was dying and there was nothing anyone could do about it. "I get it." She would have liked to put more heart into the statement, but she couldn't feel her heart at the moment.

"I put my trust in you." His voice hardened. "I vouched for you when someone told me not to. I took your words at face value and looked into your eyes knowing you weren't telling me the entire truth. But I didn't question you. I didn't turn you away." The expression on Flynn's face was the same she'd seen the day he'd admitted his father was in prison. The day he said he didn't care what his father thought. "I didn't think you were like Joey."

"Flynn, I'm not—"

"Don't, Becca." He moved away from her. "Don't say anything you can't back up. Your word isn't good enough anymore."

And then he was gone.

Becca felt ill.

When had Flynn's opinion become so important to her? They'd only known each other a few weeks. His loss of faith shouldn't have hurt so much.

But it did. And Becca knew there was only one way to make it right.

CHAPTER SIXTEEN

"I THINK YOU'VE had enough," Slade said, taking away Flynn's wineglass as soon as he came through the front door. He guided him to the couch.

"I didn't rate them all," Flynn mumbled, listening to Becca come into the kitchen through the back. He was an idiot for kissing her. She kept telling him to stay away and he kept bulldozing her defenses. But now he had no more excuses to kiss her.

Becca was a thief.

She'd denied it with her mouth, but her eyes—those incredibly expressive dark eyes—couldn't deny a thing. He should have trusted his instincts the first day he'd met her. She'd scammed him. And for what? A letter of recommendation.

"You've rated enough wine for one day." Slade turned back to the group, who weren't paying any attention to Flynn.

Yeah, Flynn had swallowed more wine than he should have.

But Becca was a thief.

There was no other explanation for her non-answers. He couldn't look at her, but he was aware of her every movement in the house. Her light tread on the kitchen floor, talking to Emma, washing something in the kitchen sink.

As if that kiss and nonconfession hadn't shifted her world ninety-degrees to the left.

As if she hadn't taken something from her last employer, something that wasn't left to her in a will.

Becca was a thief.

No better than Joey, who'd done time. More than once.

Flynn wanted to vomit. Flynn wanted to shake her. Flynn wanted to hire a damn good lawyer to protect Becca from herself.

Because she probably had a good reason for whatever she did, whatever she'd taken. But this wasn't a cheesy movie where a repentant apology was the equivalent of a get-out-of-jail-free card.

"Is your head spinning?" Slade sat next

to him, peering into his eyes. "You look like your head's spinning."

Flynn glared at him. "My head is none of your concern."

"Becca, what time are you coming tomorrow?" Truman popped up from behind Grandpa Ed's recliner.

Becca came out of the kitchen and put her hands on her knees so that she was at eye level with Truman. "You ask like you want me earlier or later. Which is it and why?"

She was good with Truman. She'd make a wonderful mother someday, if she'd ever realize love wasn't something to be scared of. Private investigators. Police. Them she should fear.

"I thought I'd make Grandpa Ed coffee. I like the coffeemaker. It's like a robot. You can come later and make breakfast." Truman was drawing a circle in the carpet with his toe.

"Let's check with the boss." Becca straightened, hesitating a moment before turning to Flynn. "What time do you want me tomorrow?"

Double entendres were a turn-on.

But Becca was a thief.

Flynn couldn't get his mouth to work. He'd

let a thief care for his grandfather. He could still taste her on his lips.

"What time do you want her tomorrow?" Slade murmured. "Let's not circle this issue too long."

Flynn elbowed him and turned to face Becca, fully expecting to see the word GUILTY written in black marker across her forehead. He'd sworn he'd never deal with crooks.

It couldn't be true.

Who was he kidding? It had to be true. Just look at the apologetic flare in her eyes.

"We're meeting with Dane at seven-thirty to review the budget," Slade said helpfully. "And then doing the repair rounds. Followed by Happy Hour with Mayor Larry."

"We're going to smooth out our differences with Larry tomorrow." Will slung his arm around Rose's thin shoulders. "After all, we settled our differences, didn't we, Rose?"

"Young man, as your future grandmother-in-law, I think you've had too much to drink." Rose glanced down at the coffee table. "Your spit cup is empty."

"Guilty as charged." Will gave Emma a loopy grin.

"So, you need me first thing?" Becca's voice was sweet as a rose bloom, but her past had thorns. "Flynn?" she prompted.

"At seven," he said crisply, unable to look her in the eye.

She retreated to the kitchen.

He'd be fully ironed and dressed when she arrived for work tomorrow. There would be no more interactions. No strolling past the oak tree. No viewing sunsets. No…

Flynn stood. The room barely spun.

He followed her into the kitchen, not because he wanted to, but because he was thirsty.

In the living room, Agnes was calling for ballots. They were alone.

Everything in his life was in turmoil. His grandfather so accepting of an end so near, the appearance of a father he hadn't seen in nearly twenty years, and now this— confirmation that he'd been wrong about Becca. Flynn felt his composure crack, his center shift, his equilibrium waver.

The frustration he'd held at bay for hours or days or weeks swept through his body in a cold, black wave, roiling and pounding into anger. He wanted to run, to drive too fast, to yell at someone. He wanted to scramble up into karma's face, yowl his frustration, wail his disappointment.

Flynn commanded his body to turn toward the door, but Becca's familiar brown eyes penetrated his internal rant. He reached for her, fingers sinking into soft flesh. Squeezed.

She. *She*. Everything was fine until she showed up here with her trapped eyes, widow sainthood and her happy dog.

"Flynn." Becca's voice. Peace in a tumultuous ocean.

Becca's torso was tense in his hands. He hadn't been this angry since Carl Quedoba sucker punched him in high school. Becca's cheeks were pale. Her eyes swimming with concern.

He should let her go.

He should hold her tight.

More than anything, he wanted the truth.

More than anything he wanted to hear her tell him she'd done nothing wrong, truth or not.

Flynn caught sight of his reflection in the kitchen window. Joey's unapologetic eyes stared back at him. They were the eyes of a man who'd do anything to get what he wanted.

"I'm okay," Flynn said, feeling anything

but. He wanted Becca. Enough to compromise his beliefs? Never.

He didn't let go of Becca.

Crap.

"Flynn?" she whispered, moving closer to him. "I didn't steal anything. I promise."

How could he trust her? Flynn couldn't breathe. How could he hold on to her until he decided what he was going to do?

Agnes rounded the corner with the stack of score sheets. She hesitated when she saw them so close to each other, but only for a moment. "Becca, where is the key?"

"Yes, Becca." Slade appeared behind Agnes, a grin suddenly splitting his face at the sight of Flynn's hands on Becca. "Where is the paper that says which wines are which? Agnes and I are here to help you, our impartial judge, tally up the scores."

No one seemed to see Joey in Flynn's eyes. No one seemed worried that he was holding on to Becca as if he couldn't decide whether to shake her or kiss her.

Such faith. He hoped it wasn't misplaced.

If Becca, sweet, loveable, trustworthy Becca, could be drawn to the dark side, what hope did he have for himself?

Flynn released Becca and backed to the opposite counter so he could watch her.

If he hadn't been watching Becca, he wouldn't have seen her exchange a glance with Agnes, wouldn't have seen Agnes worry a ring on her finger and Becca quickly look away.

Something ominous and bitter milked its way up his throat.

"Agnes, I never asked." Flynn forced the question out. "How did you meet Becca?" Agnes had said they'd only known each other a few days. He'd assumed Becca was just passing through and fell prey to the charm of the town councilwoman.

Agnes faced him, hiding the ring behind her back. "How did we meet?"

"She delivered something." Rose came around the corner. Her slender white brows puckered. "Never did hear what she delivered."

Becca busied herself with the ballots.

Slade spared Flynn a brief glance and a frown.

Flynn was no longer floundering. He was on a straight path to the truth. "Something you ordered? Something your family sent you?"

He held Agnes still with his gaze—a small, old doe caught in his headlights. "A gift *from* someone?"

The paper Becca was holding slid to the black-and-white checked linoleum.

Rose picked it up. "This was mine."

"Flynn, we're almost done counting." Slade's half-tossed scowl clearly spoke of not messing with old ladies or women you wanted to kiss until he'd determined who the winner was.

Flynn thrust his hands into his back pockets to keep from hauling Becca outside. He wanted to know why she stole the ring. Why she'd given it to Agnes. And why Agnes had accepted.

A debt? A distant relative? A lover?

None of them seemed plausible.

"There's a tie for the top two red wines." Becca slid her tally over to Slade.

"Christine's cab." Agnes did little claps, more interested in the score than in Flynn's revelation.

"And Fabrizio's cabernet," Slade said. "Dang if the sexy-named man didn't make some good wine."

"And the top two white wines." Becca slid the second tally to Slade.

"I need some coffee." Flynn started making a pot. He needed to be sober when he confronted Becca.

Slade and Agnes leaned over the summary sheet.

"Christine again!" Agnes was clearly on cloud nine. And as soon as Grandpa Ed heard, he'd be hounding Flynn and his partners to hire her. In his grandfather's eyes, having roots in Harmony Valley was almost as good as having grown up here.

"And Charles Montclair." Slade frowned as he rummaged around for the bottle corresponding to the results. "His label is the one with a wet dog, a skunk and a zeppelin. No clue what that means." He turned it so Flynn could see, realized Flynn wasn't in the mood and showed it to Rose, who seemed the only one in the kitchen who cared.

"Does this mean you'll hire Christine?" Agnes was nearly beside herself. She clutched Slade's arm.

"That means we'll consider her." Slade coolly removed her fingers.

It seemed logical that Christine was the

front-runner in the interview process. Stupid, really, to act any differently.

Flynn stared at Becca.

Stupid. That's how he acted around her.

He couldn't stop watching Becca's lips move as she talked to Slade and Agnes.

He couldn't stop thinking that for a few minutes out there on the porch, stupid was worth it.

"AGNES, I KNOW the ring makes you uncomfortable." Becca had pulled Agnes down the hallway and away from the others at the wine tasting. "It's making me uncomfortable. I think we should return it to Harold's daughter."

Agnes's back was to the living room, so she couldn't see the angry glare Flynn was giving them. "I don't know, Becca. Do you think Harold would be hurt if I just put it in my jewelry box?" She twisted the ring and cast her gaze about their feet.

"You won't find any pennies on the carpet. If you were embracing the ring and telling people about it, I'd never ask you to give it back." Becca had to work to keep panic from spreading from her limbs to her voice. "But you hide it. You don't even tell your closest friends about it."

"It makes me feel alive," Agnes murmured. "Do you know what that's like? To feel useless and at odds with the world?"

"I do. When my husband died I felt like my life was over. Who was I if not Terry's wife? It was part of my identity."

Agnes nodded.

"But then I found other interests. I moved away."

"You found Flynn." Agnes smiled meekly.

"That's not... He's not." Becca sighed. "It's not like that between us. I'm never going to find someone like Terry. He believed in me."

"As I recall, the dance of love wasn't a smooth, boring waltz." Agnes cradled her hand with the ring over her heart. "It's more like a passionate tango with unexpected twists and turns."

"Flynn and I aren't dancing. We aren't walking." Or holding hands or kissing. Not anymore. The thought was more demoralizing than Becca wanted to admit.

"Not even on the Harmony River bridge?"

"No, Agnes. Can we get back to the ring?"

"I'll think about it."

Edwin started coughing.

Both women looked at him.

"He's so pale," Agnes said. "My husband was pale like that at the end. And the dry cough…" She looked at Becca. "But Flynn said he was going to recover, right? You've seen his progress these past few weeks. Haven't you?"

Becca's gaze flew to Flynn's face. He'd knelt at Edwin's side when the coughing fit started. Flynn lifted his gaze to hers and she saw what she'd been denying since the day she arrived.

Edwin wasn't going to recover. He was dying.

And Flynn was lying to everyone about it. Perhaps even Edwin.

CHAPTER SEVENTEEN

AFTER THE WINE bottles had been emptied and bagged up, and the wineglasses washed and dried, after Truman had gone to bed, after the elderly town council and Flynn's business partners departed. Becca led Flynn outside onto the front porch. She sat down on the top step.

And confronted Flynn. "You should have told me."

"Right back at you." He settled across from her, patting Abby, who'd followed them outside. "Do you want to tell me about the ring now? Or should I ask that private investigator the next time he shows up?"

Becca's heart nearly stopped beating.

Abby trotted off to make her rounds of the front yard.

"Flynn, please, forget the ring. Tell me how long Edwin has. Tell me it's months." Tell her she was wrong and that Edwin had years ahead of him. The poor circulation. The occasional disorientation. The dry cough. The weakness. Being out of breath.

She'd seen what Flynn wanted her to see.

He scoffed at her. "It'd be nice to have one of your clients be alive for the court case or when you move on."

Days? Edwin only had days and she'd been pushing him to build up endurance when he could die at any time? She hugged her knees. "If you would have told me, I could have prepared myself."

He gazed up at the stars just starting to come out. "I promised him I wouldn't tell people, not even Kathy."

"Truman will be crushed." She remembered how hard it was to be a kid and lose someone. "He shouldn't be here when it happens."

"You stole that ring and I don't want you to be here."

Something inside Becca unraveled. He'd never see her as sweet and loveable and trustworthy again. If he ever had in the first place.

"But I can't fire you." Flynn's voice welled with bitterness. "My grandfather wants you here."

"I'll help him, I swear. And about the ring…
I made a promise. Just, please, trust me when
I say it belongs to Agnes."

"Trust has to be earned." Flynn didn't take
his eyes off the stars. "Give the ring back,
Becca. They're going to get you for taking
the money or taking the ring or both. It's inevitable."

She knew. But she had Agnes's wishes to
consider. It was time to change the topic of
conversation. "How can I make this time easier on you and Edwin?"

"You can't." Two words, wrought with pain.

That wasn't acceptable. "I won't take him
places anymore. I'll make him call or invite
the friends he wants to see to the house."

"You can't stop him, Becca. He wants to do
things on his terms. Much as I'd like to make
his life longer, he doesn't want that."

"It's hard to let go. I'm sorry, Flynn, so
sorry."

"Sometimes sorry isn't enough."

She knew he was talking about more than
losing his grandfather.

"I'VE GOT SOMETHING for you, Becca," Edwin
said after breakfast the next day. He was out

of breath from pushing his walker from his bedroom into the kitchen.

"Is this a thank-you for making you pancakes for breakfast instead of oatmeal?" Becca came to stand next to him, drying her hands on a dish towel.

Abby and Truman were out in front playing with a tennis ball.

"No." Edwin fumbled in his shirt pocket. "Now where did I put it?"

"Why don't you sit down and tell me what you're looking for?"

"I don't want to sit down." He wheezed. "I want to give this to you without feeling like I'm an invalid." He wheezed some more and gave her a lopsided smile. His hand dug into his other shirt pocket. "Here it is." He held out a shaky, blue-tinged hand that still bore water weight from the inefficiency of his heart.

At least now she understood why no amount of raising his arms and legs above his heart reduced the swelling.

He dropped a tarnished silver chain with a pendant into her hand.

"What's this?"

"It was Irma's." Now that Edwin had completed his mission, he wheeled to his recliner, landing with more force than usual.

After she'd established he was fine, Becca unraveled the chain and held it up so she could see the pendant. "It's the one Irma wore on your wedding day." Two hearts, joined together. It was lovely.

"That pendant separates into two hearts." Edwin was still trying to catch his breath. "Irma gave me half of it the day I left for the Foreign Service. She kept the other half and told me I'd always be a part of her heart, whether I fell out of love or didn't come back to her." He drew a few more breaths. "When I came back to marry her, we joined the pendants, and she wore it on our wedding day."

Edwin reached up and touched Becca's wedding ring. "It was her way of pledging her love. A love I still have with me. If I'd have fallen in love again, I'm sure she'd have understood, just like your man."

"It's a lovely sentiment, but I'm not looking for love." She handed the necklace back. "It's inappropriate for you to give this to me."

"You don't understand. I'm giving you the pendant. Irma would have wanted you and Flynn to have it."

Becca blushed and lowered her voice in case Truman came in. "I don't know what you're talking about."

"I saw you two last night. On the porch." He gasped, waving her off when she indicated he should slow down. "I went to the bathroom and saw you kissing Flynn."

Clearly, he hadn't seen them argue afterward. "I can't accept this. You should give it to Kathy. It'll mean more to her."

"Kathy." Edwin grumbled and jerked himself around in the chair as he tried to get comfortable. "She needs to grow up and get her act together."

"Don't say things like that." Becca turned to make sure Truman was still in the front yard. "Truman might hear you."

"Fine." He waved a hand. "Give it to Kathy if you like *after* Flynn marries you."

"Setting aside the fact that this isn't a conversation I want to have with my employer, Flynn isn't going to marry me."

"Setting aside the fact that I'm not paying your salary, I know my grandson. He can't keep his eyes off you."

"Whatever. I can't accept this." She tried handing him the necklace again.

"Wear it, just like you wear your man's ring. Don't give up hope on love, Becca. Give Flynn a chance, give the necklace a chance." He panted after such a long speech.

She loved the story behind the pendant.

Maybe Flynn will forgive me.

But Gary's lawyers would see things differently.

"You can talk all you want, Edwin, but Flynn will have the last word. If you can convince him that I should have it, I'll accept your gift. If not, you'll be giving it to Kathy."

He squinted at her. "Those terms are acceptable to me if you wear the necklace until Flynn gets home. It's what I want, last wish and all."

"Yeah, well, the wishes of old men have gotten me in trouble before."

"Not this time." He coughed like a fish out of water, struggling for air. It took him more than a few moments to add, "This time you're going to trust that I know a thing or two about love."

If Edwin was going to meddle, what she really needed was for him to know a thing or two about the law.

He gestured toward the necklace. "Now, put it on."

"Not until Flynn approves."

"Between that dog of yours and my great-grandson, that necklace could disappear before Flynn gets back. It would give me great pleasure to see it on you." He squirmed in the chair, thrusting his hand into a pocket. "What is sliding out of my pockets?"

He produced four pennies. "I don't remember putting these in here." He handed them to Becca. "I used to put pennies in my pocket when I took Flynn and Kathy to Cloverdale for pizza. Back then a penny was worth something—a gumball or a small toy from a machine."

Edwin could have experienced a moment of confusion, drifting back to the past, and taken the change off his dresser. But...

Becca spared a glance heavenward.

Really, Terry?

"I'm dying and you know it," Edwin said heavily. "Please don't refuse me this one thing."

With a put-upon sigh, Becca slipped the necklace on. She felt it all morning, brushing across her skin as she cleaned and cooked and kept Edwin company. As she laughed and played with Abby and Truman.

It was almost as if Irma was with her, lifting her spirits, clearing out the cobwebs around her heart as she prepared to love again.

Which was as ridiculous as thinking your husband put pennies in your path.

Wasn't it?

"WHAT ARE YOU doing here?" Flynn asked Joey as he pounded new asphalt shingles onto Mae Gardner's roof. He'd hoped each hammer stroke would chip away at his fascination with Becca.

It didn't.

Joey climbed up the ladder. "I thought this might go quicker if you had another hammer. You being so set on charity in this town and us waiting for the inspector to show up before we can put in the electrical. I'd rather not waste gas driving back to Santa Rosa."

Flynn grunted. He'd much rather be alone swinging at his thoughts about Becca. Joey brought a whole new set of baggage with him. Flynn had erected walls against his father years ago, but he hadn't known Grandpa Ed had paid to keep Joey away. That changed some things, but not the fact that Joey had been a lying, thieving criminal.

They worked in silence for several minutes, finishing up the patchwork quicker than Flynn would have done alone.

"Where's your sidekick?" Joey asked.

"He's Slade's sidekick today since he couldn't help with the roof."

"Nice view." Joey looked at Parish Hill, the granite face towering over them, and then over at the bend in the river as it drifted past Grandpa Ed's house. "This isn't exactly the projects."

Was Flynn supposed to reboot his childhood memories? Erase the scars? Reprogram his opinion of the man next to him after a few weeks? Not without more information. "Why didn't you refuse Grandpa Ed's money? There has to be more to it than just making the old man pay."

"Because your grandfather was right." Joey tipped his head up toward the sky, which was a clear blue that promised a hot afternoon. "I was a screwup and you would have been in foster care if I'd have taken you back."

"I suppose I should thank you." The words dragged out of him.

"I don't expect that." He stared Flynn in the eyes. "I turned my life around, but not soon enough to benefit you. Got clean. Got me a nice house. Dane busts my butt, but it's a good job." He looked around Mae's yard. "I realize you probably don't care about that, but for a guy like me, it's important. No one's gonna convince me to do something stupid or tempt me into breaking the law again."

"What brought about this change?" It sure as heck wasn't wanting to prove he was worthy of his son.

"I was lucky. I found the love of a good woman. She plants flowers and helped me find peace." He looked back over the valley. "She made me realize what was important in life."

"You never went back to a life of crime?"

"No. Anytime things get tough or I see some spoiled kid's left the latest electronic gadget unattended on a lawn, I think of her and I know I'll make the right choice." His grin was sly. "I stole for you and your mother. Things made her happy. Money made her happy." He shrugged. "Love makes me happy now. That woman who's taking care of Edwin…you think she could make you happy?"

Flynn headed for the ladder.

Joey laughed. "Hit a nerve, did I? Whether you think it's too soon or too late, it doesn't matter. At the end of the day, it's how she makes you feel as a man that counts. The rest works itself out."

With effort, Flynn kept from admitting what Becca had done. Most likely, Joey would think taking a ring and giving it to someone was small potatoes.

"Any other fix-it chores on your list today?" Joey waited for him to reach the bottom before climbing down. "Dane hasn't texted me about the inspector. I'll help out until he comes."

"Olly Bingmire's garage door won't open," Flynn surprised himself by admitting.

Joey leaped the last few feet to the ground. "Don't know much about garage doors. I did take apart the mechanism of a jail cell door once." Joey held up his hand when Flynn sputtered. "Not that I was escaping. I worked in the mechanics shop at prison. You'd be proud of your old man. I had privileges."

And what was Flynn supposed to say to that?

"Come on, son. It's getting hot out here and I'd like to get a beer when we're done."

Flynn found himself smiling as he folded the ladder and carried it to his truck.

CHAPTER EIGHTEEN

"HEY, NANA." A TALL, slender blonde stood in Agnes's front doorway. She wore high fashion Napa—skinny jeans, high heels, a clingy sweater with just a hint of cleavage. Her sleek hair was in an elegant French braid.

"Christine!" Agnes rushed to hug her, needing to reach up on her toes to do so, and still only meeting her halfway. "I was worried you wouldn't get here in time."

Her granddaughter glanced at her cell phone. "There's still an hour before dinner. Do you need help cooking?"

"No. I thought we could meet some people at El Rosal before dinner." She hustled Christine out the door and then dragged her along the sidewalk toward town square.

The afternoon breeze was hot. The sun was hot. The sidewalk was hot.

"Who are we meeting?"

Agnes cursed herself. She was flustered by

the opportunity to casually introduce Christine so soon after the wine tasting. She'd wanted it to be more of a surprise meeting, but as the clock ticked on, her patience fled. "I'd like you to meet the men who're building a winery here. Hurry up now. You should have chosen more appropriate shoes."

Those heels of Christine's had her walking on her toes. That had to be uncomfortable. She moved slower than Mildred and her walker.

"I told you I had a meeting in Santa Rosa this afternoon. I don't spend all of my time in the vineyards and wine cellars. I have to class it up for my boss and his investors." Christine didn't increase her pace. "You told me about the winery before. I'm not interested. In fact, I'm considering a career change, at least then I'd have control over the wine I make."

Agnes almost stopped, but Happy Hour ended soon. She dragged her granddaughter behind her. "Christine, you played mad scientist with different flavors of lemonade when you were two years old. Why would you want to change your career?"

"I might want to be a chef." Christine looked unhappy.

This time, Agnes stopped on the corner and looked at her granddaughter, taking in the somber eyes and pale skin. "You hate to cook. What's going on? Have you been sick?"

"No, Nana. It's nothing I can't fix." But she worried the lipstick off her bottom lip.

"You need a change."

"That's what Dad says. He keeps hounding me about leaving Ippolito Cellars, but he doesn't understand they've become like family to me. Leaving would feel like a betrayal."

Betrayal seemed to be on everyone's mind lately. Flynn thought Becca betrayed him by not telling her about the ring. Becca thought Agnes was betraying Harold by not wearing the ring.

Christine looked at Agnes's hand on her arm. "Where'd you get that ring? It's beautiful."

In the excitement of waiting for Christine to arrive, Agnes had forgotten to take it off. "You've never seen this ring? Not in all the times you played in my jewelry box?"

"No."

"It must have been tucked into a corner." Agnes hated lying to her granddaughter about the ring more than she did about the reason for inviting her for dinner tonight.

They crossed the square toward El Rosal, Agnes tugging Christine all the way.

Will, Slade and Flynn were sitting on the patio, along with Emma and Mayor Larry.

Good, good, good. Agnes headed full-speed for their outdoor table.

Christine dragged anchor.

"Look who stopped by," Agnes said, hailing her targets. "It's Christine."

Agnes made the introductions.

Slade, the oldest of the winery men, was about Christine's age and said he remembered seeing her around town during her occasional visits.

Flynn stared so hard at the ruby ring that Agnes tucked her hand in her pocket.

"You make some fabulous wine," Emma said, shading her gaze. "We had it the other night and really enjoyed it."

Christine graciously thanked them.

Slade produced a business card. "Can you send me your résumé? We're hiring someone with vision to help us make our winery a reality."

Christine took his card.

"We plan to give our winemaker carte blanche," Flynn said coolly. "Since we know nothing about wine."

"And include our winemaker in hiring the rest of the staff." Will sweetened the deal.

Christine shot Agnes with a glance.

Anyone else looking at Christine would have seen a careful smile.

But Agnes knew she was in trouble. Big, big trouble. Christine didn't appreciate being maneuvered. And her father would probably want to weigh in on the offer, drat the man.

"I have to say, we don't stand on ceremony here." Flynn tugged at the collar of his T-shirt. "Except for Slade. We can't break him of the tie habit."

The group turned their attention to Slade, who smoothed his sunny-yellow tie and smiled. "Sue me. I have style."

Christine tapped the card against her finger-tips. She opened her mouth to say something, most likely rejecting the offer to interview.

Agnes knew she was going to ruin this op-portunity. "We've got to go. Christine has to drive back to Napa this evening and I've got a roast in the oven." Agnes hustled Christine toward the house. "Well, what do you think?"

"I think I'm going to kill you. How could you do that to me? Who sets their granddaughter up like that?"

"Christine, you're unhappy. You have been for months."

"I agree, but you can't just make decisions for me about where to live and work."

"Why not? Your father does."

Christine stared at her for a moment and then shook her head. "You're incorrigible."

"Yes, but did you like them?"

Christine didn't answer.

Not then. Not during dinner. Not even when Agnes bid her good-night.

IT WAS OFFICIAL. Mayor Larry was a mooch.

It wasn't good enough that they bought him drinks. They had to buy him dinner at El Rosal, as well.

Flynn had texted Becca. Don't hold dinner for me.

She'd sent him a succinct reply. OK.

He sat there on the patio of El Rosal, the breeze teasing his too-short hair, staring at his cell phone, wanting a longer reply.

Mayor Larry recounted one of his favorite stories, one Flynn had heard a hundred times. The one about how he and his wife had produced so many tie-dyed T-shirts for some seventies rock band tour that their hands were black and the local doctor thought they might have a circulatory disease requiring amputation.

Flynn laughed at the obligatory high points and texted Becca. How is G.E.?

Becca's reply was quick. Wheezy, but good.

Flynn rubbed his hand over his forehead. He wanted to know how her day had been. He'd bet she hadn't found the time to talk to Agnes about returning the ring. If she'd give it back, he could trust Becca. He could be the man who kept her on the right side of the law, like Joey's significant other.

"Flynn?" Emma tapped his shoulder. "Do you want to bowl tonight? Amy's coming."

Amy was Will's sister and Emma's best friend. Flynn had forgotten it was bowling night. They bowled against Larry's team once a week. Emma had been taking Flynn's place these past few weeks so that he could spend every night at home with Grandpa Ed. "You go ahead." She was a better bowler than he was anyway.

Flynn nodded at Slade. "I'll get the check."

The group quickly disbanded.

Flynn sat thinking. About Joey. About Becca. About the values he'd lived by since he'd come to Harmony Valley.

Becca needed prodding to do the right thing.

He signed the bill, leaving a generous tip, and headed toward Agnes's house.

She was surprised to see him at her door. "If you're looking for Christine, she's already left."

"I came to talk about the ring." He noticed she'd taken if off.

Agnes didn't ask which ring. She blushed and ushered him inside. Her house was small, but the living room looked like a man cave, with a big flat screen, an overstuffed couch and a leather recliner. Agnes had tried to claim it for her own with a quilt over the couch back, doilies on the leather and pink throw pillows.

"Becca's in trouble." Flynn sat on the couch and explained about Becca's acceptance of money to get her out of debt. "I don't know why she gave you the ring, but I know that once what's-his-name's—"

"Harold." Agnes sank into the recliner, looking small and lost.

"When Harold's family finds out about it, they'll tell the private investigator and Becca will suffer for it."

Agnes's face turned the ashen color of her short hair. She told him the history of the ring, trying to swear him to secrecy.

It was a touching story, no doubt about it. Flynn could understand why Becca had brought the ring to her. But it didn't change the fact that it put Becca in jeopardy. "Agnes, if the police get brought into this, everyone will know the story behind the ring."

"You think I'm being selfish."

"Little bit, yeah."

"My husband wasn't a romantic man. He was practical. My days revolved around his needs and the needs of our children and grandchildren." She worried her finger where the ring had been. "Now he's gone. My children don't need me. If my grandchildren think of me, it's because it's a holiday or an afterthought. Having Harold's ring reminds me that I was once a young, vibrant woman with the entire world at my feet. Not some responsible old lady with nothing to show for her years but a clean house and a nicely kept yard."

Flynn wasn't expecting such emotion. He wasn't particularly comfortable with it. "It's a symbol of you when you were younger."

"Symbols are important. That's why we cherish wedding rings and family heirlooms." Her delicate chin jutted out. "They remind us of love, of what's honorable in the world, and how we've made our mark on it."

Flynn tried a different tack. "You're a vital part of this community, Agnes."

"I'd lost track of that until Becca brought me the ring."

"And you're willing to keep it, even if it puts Becca's reputation and livelihood at risk?"

"I…" Her determination deflated.

"Come with me to the house. Talk to her about it. Please."

After a moment, Agnes nodded. "But only if you listen to me. About Becca. About loving a widow."

Boundaries overstepped. Flynn held up a hand. "Please don't go there."

"Posh! Forget your fragile male ego for a moment and listen to me." Agnes may have been the size of a sixth-grader, but her voice had the quality of a middle-school principal.

In all the time he'd spent in Harmony Valley, Flynn had never considered Agnes a spitfire until now. He gave her a brief nod.

Agnes cleared her throat. "Did you know people you love stake out pieces inside your heart?"

"Like vampires." Flynn grinned.

"Focus, please. I'm not going to repeat myself." Agnes spun her wedding ring. "Some days I look at my peach tree and cry because I remember the day Manny planted it for me. Some days I spot a big motorcycle on the road and laugh because I remember how Manny tried his friend's motorcycle and could barely shift gears. Some days these are private moments. Some days I share my grief or my love with my friends and family. I'm overprotective of my personal space. Most widows are."

"Have you been spending enough time with Rose and Mildred? Because this conversation sounds more like something you'd share with them." Flynn had an idea what direction this was going in, but he wasn't going to make it easy on Agnes, him being a man and all.

"Listen up." Her thin gray brows crowded

above her nose. "When a woman's husband dies, she never stops loving him. That piece of her heart is his territory and off-limits forever. When a new man comes along, she has to find a new piece of real estate in her heart for them to stake out. But by now real estate is scarce. Staking it out is risky and scary."

"Are you talking about Becca?" Flynn was smiling on the inside.

"You have to ask?" She sighed. "And here I was so hopeful."

He took pity on her. "Becca doesn't want to fall in love again."

"And who can blame her? With all that risk and fear of losing a man, not just to death, but by becoming attached to him and being let go? It's terrifying. It's easier to move on."

He stood, hoping she'd take the hint.

She didn't. She sat. A stubborn, miniature woman in a big man's recliner. "When the lawsuit is over. When the ring is gone. When the reason for Becca being in Harmony Valley is no longer." Agnes leaned forward. "Your love needs to be stronger than her fear. Or she'll leave you."

CHAPTER NINETEEN

FLYNN HELD OPEN the door for Agnes.

Grandpa Ed was snoozing in his recliner, his breathing labored. Truman was watching a kid's sitcom, Abby nestled at his side.

Becca sat folding laundry on the couch. She whisked it out of the way. "A visit? So late? Is everything all right?"

"Agnes wants to talk about the ring," Flynn said, gesturing for Agnes to take a seat on the couch on one side of Becca while he sat on the other.

His grandfather roused. "What ring? Becca's wedding ring? Don't be jealous of a dead man."

"Not Becca's ring." Flynn sat on the arm of the couch next to Becca. "The ring Agnes is wearing. Becca's last client was an old flame of Agnes's. He wanted her to have it."

"So much for oaths of secrecy," Agnes muttered.

"I never promised." But now Flynn felt guilty.

Grandpa Ed nodded. "I wondered what brought Becca to town."

"Unfortunately, it doesn't look like good old Harold put anything about the disposition of the ring in his will." Flynn gave Becca and Agnes disapproving looks.

"And you think Harold's heirs will discover the ring missing?" Grandpa Ed was on his game.

Flynn had to give the old man credit. He was still sharp when it came to fitting pieces together.

"That puts Becca's legal hearing at risk," Grandpa Ed said.

"How did you know about my hearing?" Becca exchanged a glance with Flynn, who shrugged. "I didn't tell him."

"Do you honestly think I'd hire someone without conducting a background check?" Grandpa Ed used the recliner's controls to sit up higher.

"Yes," Becca, Agnes and Flynn said.

"Nonsense. I may be old and sick, but I'm not a fool. I called someone the day we met her."

Flynn grinned. Of course he had. It probably made the old spymaster extremely happy to gather intel on a drifting caregiver.

But that didn't solve anything. "Can we get back to the issue? I think Agnes should return the ring." Flynn gave Agnes a stern look.

"But it's not your decision," Becca chastised. "It was Harold's wish and the ring makes Agnes happy." She squeezed Agnes's hand.

"I have to agree with Becca," his grandfather said.

"If you want to keep the ring, you keep the ring, Agnes." Then Becca's voice lowered. "I'll be fine. Flynn and Edwin are going to write me letters of reference."

"You're taking a huge risk, Becca." Flynn clung tenuously to his temper. "I'm trying to protect you."

"Flynn," she said gently, turning to him. "I haven't asked you to protect me."

That's when he noticed she wore his grandmother's necklace. His reaction must have been read by everyone in the room, except Truman, because the three adults all started talking at once.

"It's very sweet of you to be watching out

for Becca," Agnes said, misreading his expression.

"Let me explain," Becca began.

She was drowned out by Grandpa Ed. "I gave it to her." He sucked in air like a new vacuum.

Flynn was sure his jaw dropped onto his chest. "Why would you do that?"

"Let's not go into why." Becca made eyes at his grandfather. "He tried to give it to me this morning and—"

"Tried? You're wearing it!"

Becca clung to the pendant. "I told him it was more appropriate to give it to Kathy."

"You're right!"

"Stop," Grandpa Ed wheezed. "I want you and Becca to have it."

For a moment, the only sound in the room was the laugh track from Truman's sitcom.

"He saw us on the porch last night," Becca explained in an urgent whisper. "I told him I couldn't accept it."

"Not until she got your permission." Grandpa Ed pierced him with a blurry stare, as if he was having problems focusing.

Flynn was familiar with the pendant's story. His grandfather wanted him to declare his intentions toward Becca. "I can't do it." If she wasn't going to do the right thing, they had no future.

Without another word to him, Becca placed the necklace in his hand and left with Agnes.

TRUMAN RAN UP and clung to Becca the next morning. "Uncle Flynn says you're going to be arrested, just like my Grandpa Joey."

"Over my dead body," Edwin roared from inside.

"Everyone needs to take a breath." Becca led Truman inside, stroking Truman's ginger hair. "Agnes is not returning the ring. Harold wanted her to have it. I'm not going to jail."

Flynn stood in the middle of the living room, shaking his head. "This is wrong and you know it."

She hadn't agonized over the ring and losing Flynn all night long just to be confronted by him again this morning. Becca considered walking out the door, but there were Edwin and Truman to consider. But she didn't move beyond the foyer. She hooked an arm around Truman.

Agnes arrived in her green Buick and hurried up the stairs. "I can't give it up, Flynn. It feels like I'm losing Harold all over again."

"Becca's right," Edwin said. "If that man meant you to have his ring, you should have his ring."

"He didn't write his wishes in a will." Flynn was wound so high, none of their arguments could reach him. "And I should point out you gave Becca a necklace and you didn't write your wishes down about that, either. It's her word against the family. Who's the judge going to believe?"

Agnes looked crestfallen. Becca took her hand, the one with Harold's ring on it.

"Are you saying you think Becca coerced your grandmother's necklace from me?" Edwin was working himself into a gasping frenzy. "I was hoping she'd give you half the necklace, just like your grandmother did with me."

"How long have you been arguing?" Becca's cheeks heated. "Please. This isn't good for Edwin."

"Becca, there's right and there's wrong. You're operating somewhere in between. You have to see this could end your career as a caregiver. These people, these heirs, are going to band together to get you. You won't be employable. And you could go to prison."

Truman started to cry. Edwin's face grew red.

"Flynn, please stop saying the *P* word. At this point, it's a civil suit." Becca tried to keep her voice calm, hugging Truman to her. "Life isn't cut-and-dried. Your grandfather paid your father to disappear from your life. Was he right or wrong? And when your father took the money, was he right or wrong?"

"He was… They were…" Some of the bluster deflated from him.

"It's a gray issue," Becca continued. "Like this. I have to stand up for what I believe in. I hope this won't go to trial. But if it does, I'll be okay." She took a deep breath, gave him a half smile. "And I hope you'll stand with me."

Flynn's expression was unfathomable. "I've got things to do." He headed toward the door.

"And that's why I'm destined to walk alone," Becca murmured.

None of them moved as they listened to Flynn drive off. Truman didn't complain that he hadn't been asked along.

Becca blew out a breath. "My Gram used to say that chocolate chip cookies could rescue a bad day." She disengaged herself from Truman.

"No one's let me have a chocolate chip cookie in ages," Edwin said.

"I'll help." Agnes followed her to the kitchen.

"Does this mean Becca isn't going to jail?" Truman asked.

No one answered him.

THE FIRST BATCH of cookies weren't out of the oven when Becca heard a car pull up in front of the house.

Agnes moved to the door. She hadn't mentioned the ring since Flynn left. "Who do we know that drives a minivan? A man." She backed away from the door to let Becca see.

If clichéd private investigators had a look, it was the rumpled, cheap suit and sharp eyes. Becca knew this was the man who'd come to see Flynn before.

"Rebecca MacKenzie." He stopped very close to the screen door. The satisfied way he said her name sent a shiver down her spine. "I was hoping to find you here."

"Who's there?" Edwin grumbled awake.

"I'm Wes Webber. I've been hired to look

into your caregiver's background." His smile gave Becca a sick feeling in her stomach, like he wanted to eat her up and pick her out of his teeth.

"Is that Webber with one *B* or two?" Edwin asked, reaching for the pad of paper on the end table near his chair.

"Two *B*s, sir. I'll save you some phone calls. I was in NCIS for most of my navy career. My nose is clean."

"Forgive me if I don't take you at your word."

"May I come in?" He raised his hand toward the knob.

Becca repressed a gasp.

"No," Edwin said.

Becca had never felt so threatened and protected at the same time, even though the screen door wasn't latched. She was glad Truman was in his room with Abby.

"Why are you here?" Agnes peeked from behind Becca.

"I got a call this morning from Harold Epstein's daughter, Diane. She says there are several pieces of her father's jewelry missing."

Becca winced. "She's lying."

Agnes clapped her hand over her mouth.

"We'll see. I promised Flynn I'd come by and tell him before the police were called in."

"They can search my motorhome," Becca said, confidence finally returning. "They won't find anything."

"You could have hocked them already. Where can I find Flynn?"

Becca was tempted to tell him Flynn wasn't available, but Flynn wouldn't forgive her, not if he'd asked the man to tell him. If ever she wanted proof as to Flynn's feelings, she'd gotten them aplenty in the past twelve hours. "He's at the construction site."

"I know where that is." He left.

Becca collapsed onto the couch.

"How dare that woman do that to you. She's going to try and frame you just like they do on those television shows." Agnes paced the living room. "Wait until I tell Mildred and Rose. They're going to die of jealousy."

"Agnes," Becca said.

"Right. Sorry." Agnes drew herself up. "I'm ready to return Harold's ring now."

"I think it's for the best," Edwin said.

For once, Becca didn't defend Harold's wishes.

FLYNN WAS IN the farmhouse talking to the drywall contractors when someone called his name outside.

Wes Webber was waiting for him on the porch.

Flynn looked past him, but no police cars were in the driveway. In his jeans pocket, his cell phone made noises announcing a text message.

"Got news about your sister," Webber said.

Flynn nearly sank to his knees in relief. He'd been expecting bad news about Becca. "She's safe?"

Joey came around the corner, sizing up Webber, still not liking him, if the low set of his brows was any indication.

"Pops," Webber acknowledged Joey, before turning back to Flynn. "Is it okay to give you this information out here? Seems like there's a lot of ears."

"Tell us." Flynn only fleetingly realized he thought of him and his father as a unit.

"She's in rehab in Petaluma."

"That can't be." Flynn felt caged.

Joey seemed to be chewing on the inside of his lip.

"Your sister is addicted to alcohol," Webber

said. "She checked in for a seven-day stay to try and jump-start her recovery and realized she needed at least the thirty-day program, the cost of which is going to hit your credit card next week."

"But Kathy has a job. She's a good mom. I never saw any signs."

Webber shrugged. "People get really good at hiding their addictions. Consider yourself lucky that she realized she had a problem before someone like your nephew got hurt."

The comments Truman made about having to put Kathy to bed and make sure she got to work in the morning took on more meaning. No wonder the kid used to walk around as if he bore the weight of the world on his shoulders. He had been.

"Her mother battles addiction," Joey weighed in. "Some of those traits are genetic. Good for Kathy."

"You were worried about your sister not calling. There are no cell phones, computers or tablets allowed during her treatment. The Serenity Club only allows phone calls on Sundays, and then only with supervision and only if the patient feels up to it. I wasn't allowed to see your sister, but you can call and arrange for a visit next Sunday."

"How did you find her?"

"Trade secret." Webber grinned. "But you may want to check her credit card charges next time."

"Thank you." Flynn stood awkwardly, waiting for Webber to leave.

"One more thing," Webber said. "This is your advance warning about your caregiver. The daughter of her last client says there are several pieces of jewelry missing. I'm getting the police involved today."

Flynn's head was shaking. He exchanged a glance with his father. "I don't believe it." He barely kept himself from revealing there'd been just the one ring.

"You're talking about the woman who takes care of Edwin? The one who drives that wreck of a motorhome?" At Webber's nod, Joey laughed. He gave Flynn a reassuring look. "She's not the type to steal."

Webber started making sounds of protest, but Joey would have none of it.

"People who steal jewelry wear brand-name goods like a badge. Mark my words. That girl doesn't have it in her to steal all that jewelry."

Joey spoke directly to Flynn. "You look into this closer and you'll find those baubles were recently hocked or sold to a jewelry store to melt down the gold. And the name associated with it won't be Edwin's caregiver."

"Since when is an ex-con a good judge of character?" Webber said.

Dane bellowed for Joey.

"You become good at reading people inside. Or you don't make it outside." Joey nodded at Flynn. "You let me know if I need to make inquiries."

Flynn felt as if someone had his back—someone besides Will and Slade.

Webber scoffed. "You shouldn't believe him. She's guilty."

"I trust my father's judgment." Flynn wasn't near as unsettled by admitting that out loud as he might have been a few weeks ago.

Webber shook his head. "When I told her we'd discovered things were stolen, you should have seen her face. She knew justice was closing in."

"You told her? You went to my house?"

"I was looking for you." He shrugged. "What's it matter?"

"My grandfather has a weak heart. If he

goes to the hospital because of you and your arrogant need to rub your greatness in people's faces, I'll be taking you to court for breach of contract. I told you specifically to stay away from the house."

The angry, wild feeling tying Flynn in knots must have shown on his face, because Webber nodded and slowly walked away.

Flynn leaned against the railing, gripping the dust-coated wood.

Remembering he'd received a text message, Flynn checked his cell phone. It was from Becca: Running an errand. Edwin insisted on coming.

Of course he did. His grandfather probably wanted to protect Becca. Flynn hit the button to call her.

The phone rang too many times. Flynn was assuming it would roll to voice mail when Agnes answered. "Flynn, Becca can't talk right now. She's driving."

"Where are you going?" Flynn asked through gritted teeth.

"You should be happy." Agnes didn't sound happy. She sounded defeated. "We're taking back Harold's ring. His daughter is trying to pin a whole bunch of thefts on Becca. We're going to set her straight."

"I don't want my grandfather going with you."

"We're almost to Cloverdale. There's no turning back now."

"I'll meet you there."

"He says he'll meet us there," Agnes relayed. "I didn't think he knew where we were going."

His grandfather's voice, labored and in command. "We can handle this. Flynn's got plenty of responsibilities back in town."

Flynn may have had plenty on his plate, but the ones he most wanted to be responsible for were leaving him behind.

CHAPTER TWENTY

"Agnes, you don't have to come inside," Becca said for what seemed like the fiftieth time as she parked Edwin's Cadillac in front of Diane's house in Santa Rosa. She looked at her ragtag supporters—Edwin, Truman, Abby and Agnes. "Give me the ring and Harold's letter."

"No." Agnes had been adamant the entire time. "I'm the reason you're in this mess."

"I'm coming in, too," Edwin said.

"Better do it quick before I lose my nerve, then." Becca went to the trunk for Edwin's walker. Flynn would most likely kill her when they returned to Harmony Valley. He'd been unable to convince Agnes to divulge their destination.

"Are we here to keep Becca out of prison?" Truman tumbled out onto the sidewalk with Abby.

Not wanting to answer, Becca set up the walker and wheeled it to Edwin.

"Yes." Edwin accepted Becca's help to stand. "And we'll get ice cream on the way home if we succeed. That's how you end all good campaigns—with ice cream."

Becca stared at the front door and then at her posse. "Last chance to back out."

"Harold loved me. Flynn's right. I don't need a ring to remind me of that." Agnes squared her shoulders and led the way.

They walked up to the front door and knocked.

While they waited for Diane to answer, Becca couldn't help but think that she'd upset far too many people by honoring Harold's wishes. Her grandmother would have said just because it was the right thing to do didn't mean it was the right way to do it.

The door swung open.

"Becca," Diane sounded surprised to see her. Her shoulder-length gray hair floated crookedly about her face in a way that screamed for a good conditioner. She wore jean shorts that displayed her varicose veins and a bright black sweatshirt with a Mercedes logo stitched over her breast.

In a wind tunnel of escaped air-conditioning,

Becca introduced her backup. "Can we come inside and talk?"

Before Diane could answer, a familiar minivan pulled up behind the Cadillac, tires squealing. Wes Webber got out. "I thought you might confront my client."

Becca squeezed Agnes's hand.

"Don't be fooled by the bluff," Edwin panted, filling the awkward silence. "I'd like to sit down out of the heat, Diane. May we come in?"

Diane let them inside. They sat down in the living room. When Harold lived alone in the house, the couch sagged and the coffee table had rings on it. There was a new cream-colored leather sofa and two beautiful pine end tables. Agnes sat hip-to-hip with Becca. Truman sat at their feet with Abby. Edwin looked around, flipped the walker seat down and sat near Diane.

Becca blew out a breath, praying for understanding. "Diane, I haven't stolen any jewelry. I hope you know I'd never do that to you or Harold."

Diane looked almost seasick. The private investigator stared at his client intensely. Becca had assumed they'd both immediately refute her statement, but neither one said a thing.

"Agnes," Edwin wheezed.

"I'm the woman you're looking for." Agnes's voice wasn't steady as she opened her fist to reveal the ruby ring. "Harold gave this ring to me sixty years ago when he asked me to marry him. And he sent it back to me after he died."

The look on Wes's face was sour.

"Diane, I owe you an apology." Becca said the words stiffly. "I promised Harold I wouldn't tell anyone, not even you, where the ring had gone, but I should have told you regardless."

"What about the other items?" Diane asked, but she was staring at Abby. "My father's antique gold watch, the gold bracelet, all his other rings."

Becca experienced a moment of gut-wrenching panic. How could she prove she hadn't stolen those items?

"Why don't you tell us what you did with them?" Edwin's lopsided smile did little to calm anyone in the room.

"Wes…" Diane turned to him. "If Becca

took one ring, she had to have taken the rest of his valuables."

"Nonsense," Edwin said.

Wes sized up the room.

"Becca's telling the truth," Agnes got riled. "And I've got proof." Agnes dug in her purse for a yellowed black-and-white photograph and the letter Harold had written her on white lined paper. "Here's the letter he wrote me on his deathbed. And this photo was taken the night Harold proposed to me at the Cliff House restaurant in San Francisco."

Becca hadn't seen the photo until that morning. In it, a very young Agnes sat with a very young Harold, arms around each other, ruby ring glinting.

"Oh, my God. That's my dad," Diane murmured. And then she scanned her father's letter.

"Please confirm that's your father's handwriting," Edwin said.

Diane frowned, but nodded her head. She handed the photo to Wes. "It's easy to doctor a photo, isn't it?"

"Are you calling me a liar?" Agnes stood. "If your father were alive, he'd be ashamed."

"That picture was taken sixty years ago.

Why didn't you marry him? Why didn't he seek you out when my mother died?" Diane was on a roll. "Or was there something going on between you all these years?"

Agnes looked like she was going to cry.

"Please, can't we keep this civil?" Becca pleaded.

"You stole the ring," Diane said. "And everything else."

"No, I—"

"You stole the ring," Diane raised her voice. "And you would never have told me the truth if you weren't being investigated and sued."

Since that was the gist of it, Becca remained silent.

"Clearly, the value of a promise means nothing to you, not like it meant to your father. He was an honorable man and I loved him. If my husband hadn't come back from that POW camp, I would have married Harold and I'd like to think that if I was your mother that you'd have learned a thing or two about understanding and forgiveness."

Agnes heaved another breath so she could continue. "Becca took care of your father when you couldn't—or wouldn't—do it. Before you go thinking badly about her, think about how important she was to your father at the end that he'd trust her with this secret. Our secret. My secret." Her voice cracked. Agnes drew her pixie height to its fullest. "You take that ring and sell it. And I hope to God that someone buys the ring and feels half the love Harold and I felt for each other. Because if you keep it, you'll look at it and see a betrayal, by your father and by Becca, and maybe even by me. I couldn't stand that, and I don't think Harold could, either."

In two pixie strides, Agnes snatched back the photo and letter.

"Call the police, Wes." Diane's voice was high and brittle, a taut wire waiting to snap and hurt someone.

"I don't think you want to do that. Does she, Mr. Private Investigator?" Edwin pinned the man with his gaze.

Wes shook his head. "Nice try, Diane. But if you continue accusing Ms. MacKenzie of theft, I'll track down every place you sold that jewelry."

"Is she a bad lady?" Truman pointed to Diane, having reached the legal time limit for seven-year-olds to keep quiet.

"That is yet to be determined." Edwin

pushed himself to standing, pulling his walker around. "I'm ready for ice cream."

Truman popped up and ran toward the door.

Becca didn't know whether to apologize to Diane or leave in a huff.

"Don't say a word." Agnes decided for her, tugging her toward the door. "I can see an apology forming on your lips. She's not worth it."

But Becca was sorry. And she had an idea what to do about it.

"DON'T EVER RUN off like that again." Worry and fear and anger had tied Flynn to the porch where he baked in the sun until Becca parked the Caddy in front of the house.

She'd texted him that things had gone well, and that they were stopping in Cloverdale for ice cream.

He should have felt relief that Becca had done the right thing. Instead, he was beside himself with worry for Grandpa Ed, and unforgivingly angry at Becca and Agnes for taking him along.

"Best day I've had in years," Edwin slurred. "Bested a con artist *and* a private investigator in one morning." Grandpa Ed accepted Flynn's help out of the car.

Becca brought his walker around. Flynn yanked it away from her.

"Hey, there's no need to be upset," Edwin said.

"There is." Flynn couldn't believe that no one seemed repentant. He glared at Becca. "You shouldn't be gallivanting about."

"I'll stop gallivanting when I'm dead," Edwin grumbled, taking the walker handles and proceeding up the walk. "Leave her be."

"Uncle Flynn," Truman ran around the car, Abby at his heels. "There was this woman. And Agnes told her off. And we saved Becca from going to jail." He hugged Flynn's legs, then turned to Becca. "I'm hungry."

Becca managed a sad smile. "You just had ice cream."

The evidence of which was in two large brown stains on his red-and-white striped shirt.

"I could use some popcorn." Truman grinned.

"Only if you pick up your room first." Becca barely had the terms out when Truman and Abby ran toward the house.

She put a hand on Flynn's arm. "I'm sorry. The investigator scared us. All of us, including Truman."

Flynn hadn't considered how they'd felt. "You should have thought it through."

"You're upset because we didn't take you along." Edwin was moving more slowly up the walk than the day Flynn had brought him home from the hospital. "You have more important things to do than babysit us."

Flynn thrust his hands through his short hair. "I wouldn't have let you go, Grandpa Ed. Or Truman."

"In this day and age, we might have gone off a little half-cocked, but it turned out all right in the end." Edwin paused at the bottom step. "Never thought three steps would seem like a mountain."

"Harold must be spinning in his grave over what his daughter tried to do." Agnes shook her head. "I'm picking up Mildred and going over to Rose's and then I'm going to tell them about everything that happened today."

"Including about the ring?" Becca teased, entirely too light-hearted in Flynn's opinion.

"Including about the ring. No more secrets." Agnes hugged Becca and then left in her Buick.

Flynn watched the Buick kick up dust down the driveway, unable to kick his anger aside. "I found out where Kathy is. She checked herself into rehab. Alcohol addition."

Edwin looked at Flynn over his shoulder, a quick look that said volumes about the worry he'd shouldered over the years. "Just like her mother. I know I shouldn't blame myself for it, but I feel as if I should have seen that coming."

"Me, too." Flynn rubbed at his short hair.

Becca lingered a few feet behind them. "I need to call my lawyer after I make Truman some popcorn."

"Go on." Flynn waved her off. "I'll help Grandpa Ed up the stairs."

"I'd like that," his grandfather said gruffly. "Do you think you might sit with me and talk awhile instead of running to repair something?"

His grandfather's request washed away the anger, calmed, soothed, but didn't manage to wash away the worry.

"I HAVE NO NEWS," Hank, Becca's lawyer, said when he interrupted the dynamic tunes of elevator music that played while she was on hold. "I need to make this quick."

"I want to settle," Becca said firmly.

"That wasn't the strategy we agreed to," Hank said, all bluster and volume.

"The private investigator Gary hired riled up the daughter of a recently deceased client. She tried to accuse me of stealing jewelry." Becca experienced a twinge of guilt over the ruby ring, but she knew that Hank could sense weakness, even over a cell connection, so she plowed forward. "I want to pay back the money."

"All ten thousand?"

Doubts slithered through her thoughts like baby snakes. "Yes."

Hank swore.

"What will the next client Gary unearths accuse me of? I can't go through life looking over my shoulder. I still believe the money was a gift from Virginia, but some gifts have to be rejected." Like Irma's heart pendant.

"Did something happen to you? You don't usually sound like this."

Score a point for rediscovering her backbone. She decided to ignore his observation.

"All right. If you're determined to accept

his emotional blackmail, how do you plan to pay Gary back?"

"A little at a time. No interest."

"Dream on."

"Hey, those are my terms."

"You'll need him to sign a document where you claim no wrongdoing and he claims to exit your life forever."

"I like it when you speak lawyer English."

"You pay me for advice, not to baffle you with terms you'll never understand." He sighed, and she could see him at his desk, tapping his pencil on the scribble-covered blotter. "Are you sure? It'll make us look bad if you make this offer and then don't want to follow through."

"I'm sure. This has become a vortex that dragged down too many people in my life. I won't let anyone be hurt again."

"WHEN ARE WE going on that trip overseas?" Edwin asked Flynn when he was settled in his recliner with a small bowl of crackers and a glass of ice water. "I want to show you where I spent my tours of duty."

Flynn couldn't believe his grandfather wanted to talk about the trip. They'd been avoiding talking about it since he came home from the hospital. "When do you want to go?"

"August. Before Truman goes back to school." Despite his slurred speech, Edwin sounded chipper. "He should come along."

Truman sat in the middle of the living room floor, munching on popcorn. "Me?"

"Yes, you." Edwin smiled. "And your mother. She should be out of the hospital and better by then." They'd broken the news of Kathy being sick to Truman. He took it like the little trouper he was—with stoic resolution. "It'll be nice to go somewhere as a family again. Do you remember that trip we took to the Grand Canyon when you and Kathy were young? I think that's one of my fondest memories."

"Will we fly in an airplane? I've never been on an airplane." Truman radiated energy.

"Yes, but August?" Flynn didn't like it. "That's the height of vacation season for Europe. Every country we visit will be crowded." Not to mention the places they planned to visit weren't kid-friendly.

"The most interesting people travel in August." He waved off Flynn's concerns. "We'll start with South Korea. Lousy place to fight a war. Hotter than an attic in summer, colder than an ice floea in winter. Rice paddies or steep mountains. There is no in-between."

"Did we win that war, Grandpa?" Truman said.

"No one ever wins a war. It takes its toll on soldiers and civilians alike." Grandpa Ed stared at the wall with the photos and accommodations of his past. "I'd like to see Algeria. Don't have any desire to see Vietnam. Perhaps Berlin. Have we talked about going to Berlin before?"

"We can go wherever you want to." Flynn was happy to have the trip within sight.

"Berlin is such a fascinating city." Edwin's eyelids got heavy. "Irma said it was beautiful."

Flynn searched the pictures on the wall. All the pictures of foreign places were of his grandfather alone or with his staff. "When did Grandma go to Berlin?"

Grandpa Ed mumbled something that sounded like, "Last year." Edwin's eyes drifted closed. Just when Flynn thought Grandpa Ed was asleep, his grandfather startled. "When did we go to Washington, D.C.? Was that last year?"

"More like fifteen years ago. I was in middle school."

"It seems like yesterday." Grandpa Ed sighed. "You haven't changed so much. Always making sure everyone likes you. You don't need to make a friend of everyone you meet."

"What's Grandpa talking about?" Truman tossed Abby a handful of popcorn.

Flynn shrugged. He wasn't sure.

Grandpa Ed turned into Grumpy Ed. "I'm trying to tell Flynn that he can say no once in a while. So what if Zenobia's faucet drips? Who cares if Felix has a creaky floorboard? Flynn's life is passing him by while he takes a hammer to every nail in town."

"I thought you wanted me to help people here!" Flynn heard Becca come in through the kitchen door.

"I do, but not every day of the week, not every spare minute of the day." He dropped his voice. "There's a woman in the kitchen."

"Who?" Truman whispered back.

"He means Becca. Don't start with the matchmaking," Flynn warned.

"You people nowadays. You think everything should come on a timeline. Job. Check. Home. Check. Marriage. Check." Grandpa Ed huffed. "Life is too short for timelines."

Misdirection was called for. "Can we go back to planning our trip?"

His grandfather shook his finger at him. "Some things should be spontaneous."

Flynn shook his finger right back. "Not trips to foreign countries."

"Irma liked Paris. I was too young for the Second World War, so it's nothing more than a city with interesting food to me."

"When did Grandma go to Paris?" Flynn had never heard mention of her trip before.

"That year." Grandpa Ed was vaguely firm.

"What year?" Flynn was fairly certain his grandmother had never traveled outside the United States.

"Flynn." Becca gestured for him to come to the kitchen. Her eyes were watery, as if she'd been blinking back tears.

"I need a glass of water." Flynn followed her into the kitchen, thinking that perhaps the excursion with Becca had helped stimulate his grandfather's brain.

"Don't argue with him." Becca wiped at one eye with the back of her hand. "It's his eleventh hour."

"Meaning?"

"They didn't tell you about this at the hospital?" When he shook his head, she searched for the words to explain. "It's when people rally. They feel energized before they pass away. It's like their system, or God, knows that everyone needs a moment of clarity before…"

Flynn's head started shaking. "No. I don't believe you." Or more accurately, he didn't want to believe her.

She put her hands on his shoulders. "I want you to be prepared. Listen to what he's saying. Make peace with his leaving. You can't fix this."

Something dark robbed Flynn of his breath. "I don't believe you," he gasped as weakly as Grandpa Ed.

Becca's gaze was filled with compassion. She hugged him, quickly, then went back to her dishes. "It's okay. I could be wrong."

But that was unlikely. Becca dealt with death on a regular basis.

CHAPTER TWENTY-ONE

AFTER BECCA TOLD Flynn about the eleventh hour, he didn't talk to her the rest of the afternoon. She'd served them dinner and left, her heart heavy.

It wasn't lighter when she returned the next morning.

Flynn didn't say a word to her as she cooked blueberry pancakes for Truman and Edwin. He headed toward the door.

She moved the pan off the burner and followed him. "Wait. I wanted to tell you that I'm going to pay Gary back the ten thousand dollars. I talked to my lawyer about it yesterday and he's going to draw up the documents."

He hadn't been expecting her to say that. His eyebrows went up. "That's a big decision."

"It is, but it felt right." Becca fingered her wedding ring. "After Terry died, he'd left so much unfinished business, so much he'd wanted to do but never got the chance to, that

I decided people should get their last wishes. And if I could help them, it would be like fulfilling one of Terry's last wishes."

"Makes sense." His tone was detached. They were back to being strangers.

Becca was heartbroken. "But being in Harmony Valley, being with you, has made me realize that every wish, every choice, has a consequence. I meant well, I really did."

"I know you did, Becca. It's good, what you're doing." His eyes wouldn't meet her gaze.

"Thank you. I didn't want you to worry about me. No one should worry about me."

He seemed to chew on his cheek, as if trying to keep words from spilling out. And then he did look at her. He looked at her with a gaze so full of disappointment that she struggled not to shrink back. "That's your grief over Terry talking and the brave front you put on and the crazy notion that you'll never love again talking."

She backed up a step, feeling lost and unsure and belittled. "I just wanted you to know."

He sighed, a sound so heavy that her shoulders nearly bowed with its weight. "I feel honored that you don't want me to worry." He walked off to start his busy day.

"Wait," she said. She had a sinking feeling that Edwin's time was near. "Maybe you should stay close to home today."

He turned to look at her. "If I do that, I'm admitting…what you said yesterday." And then he left.

Becca hadn't known what she wanted to happen by telling him everything. The need to dispel all her secrets to him outweighed the mistakes she'd made—dragging his grandfather to Diane's, telling him the end was near. She couldn't blame him for not wanting to talk to her.

She found herself back in the kitchen. The pancake she'd taken off the burner was hard and cold.

Kind of like her heart.

JOEY HANDED FLYNN a cup of gas station coffee when he arrived at the job site. "Past couple of mornings I've been thinking you need more caffeine."

Flynn accepted the cup and drank deeply without fear of it being too hot. This particular gas station was twenty minutes away.

"This morning it looks like I should have

gotten the jumbo size for you." Joey peered at Flynn over the top of his sunglasses. "Everything all right? Kathy? Edwin? That caregiver girl of yours?"

Flynn had tossed and twisted himself in his sheets all night, worrying about his grandfather. He'd freeze at every sound, wondering if it was a death knell. Every hour he'd crept down the hallway to his grandfather's room to make sure he was still breathing.

Becca had to be wrong.

Except he'd gone online and looked up the eleventh hour and seen the symptoms his grandfather was exhibiting.

He didn't want Becca to be right.

"Flynn?"

"I think…this is the end." Flynn choked on the words and immediately gulped down more coffee.

"I'm sorry." His father seemed to know what he meant.

"You don't mean that."

"I do. I may have resented him for taking you away, but I can't resent the way he raised you." Joey patted Flynn awkwardly on the back. "I cried when my mother died. She'd given up on me long before my biggest mistakes. She didn't want me there at the end. I had to wait in the hall for hours. Just listening to her laboring for breath, remembering how she used to bake cupcakes with home-made frosting, wondering when she'd give up and let go. Knowing I couldn't do a thing to comfort her." Joey stared toward the river. "Crappy conversation for first thing in the morning."

"Thanks. For sharing. And for trying. To be here. To be back in my life." Flynn drew a deep breath, praying he wouldn't start sobbing like he had when the police took his dad away. "Dad."

And then they were hugging, slapping each other on the back in the manlike ritual that decreed hugging okay.

"I don't know what any of this means," his father said. "But I will expect an invitation to special nights, like the Super Bowl. My better half, she'll want to come over on days, like Father's Day." Joey looked like he'd swallowed a live eel. "I'm rushing things, I'm sorry."

"We'll talk." Flynn knew Joey could never replace his grandfather, but he felt less alone with him in his corner.

BECCA COULDN'T INTEREST Edwin in food, not even blueberry pancakes.

She'd helped him dress and got down the hall to his recliner. He asked for coffee, but hadn't taken a sip. He didn't speak much. Communication had deteriorated to slow nods or shakes of the head.

"Someone's here." Truman went to the window.

The man was tall, with easy strides and an easy smile. "I'm looking for Edwin Blonkowski. He wrote me a letter."

This could be just what Edwin needed to interest him in the world again.

Becca opened the door. "Edwin, one of your letters…worked."

Edwin turned his head.

To his credit, the letter recipient didn't flinch or hesitate. He came forward and offered Edwin his hand. "I'm Nate Landry. Used to be sheriff up in Cottonwood."

"Got fired for arresting the mayor's son." Edwin's voice was a rusty wheel, but Becca was glad to hear it.

"My services were no longer required." His grin was slow as molasses.

Edwin waved a puffy, slightly blue hand. "Your services are required here."

"I couldn't find any job posting online."

"We just got the internet here a few days ago," Becca explained. "But I wasn't aware Harmony Valley was hiring a sheriff."

"There are funds…to hire a sheriff when… the population rises…above eighty." Edwin wheezed, having obviously expended his energy on his greeting.

Nate took in the military commendations on the wall with the barest of nods. "How close to eighty are you?"

"Somewhere between…seventy-five…and eighty."

"I drove down Main Street before I came. I think it's going to be tough to reach eighty." Nate glanced toward the door.

"Not necessarily," Becca jumped in. "They're building a winery at the south end of town. They're hiring at least three people."

Edwin's hand waved angrily. "You can wait. Live on your salary."

"I'm on administrative leave." Nate's eyes were wary.

"Paid leave." Edwin pointed at him with his finger. "I know people."

Nate stared at Edwin a good long time. "Who do I apply to?"

"Mayor Larry," Edwin wheezed. "Does yoga east of the bridge this time of day."

Nate nodded. "Thanks for the tip." He moved toward the door with that same deliberate pace that said he wasn't in a hurry and you shouldn't be, either.

"I have to admit, that was pretty awesome. Your letter worked." Becca stood at the door contemplating Harmony Valley.

Maybe she'd stay. It was a nice town. Slow paced. Whatever was between her and Flynn, she'd sweep under the rug, tuck it away like Agnes had with Harold. A memory to take out on a rainy day when she was old.

That was depressing.

"Grandpa Ed's drooling." Truman giggled, pausing while watching cartoons on the carpet at Edwin's feet to point at his great-grandfather.

Without thinking twice, Becca rushed to Edwin's side. She put a finger on his wrist. His pulse was weak, but steady. His eyes glazed, his face slack, his arms twitched. "Edwin?"

The old man mumbled something unintelligible, except for the last word. *"Irma."*

"Edwin? Edwin?" Panic tried to scale her voice into panic. Becca had to remain calm. For Truman.

Abby danced onto her hind legs so she could rest her front paws on the arm of Edwin's recliner. She stretched to sniff his face, stiffened, and then dropped to her haunches and barked.

"No." Becca had seen Abby do that twice before. Once in the twenty-four hours before she'd lost Virginia. Once in the few hours before she lost Harold. "No, no. Edwin, I need to hear your voice."

Abby went over to a corner and curled into a tight ball.

Truman walked to Becca on his knees. "What's wrong with Grandpa Ed?"

"Tell Truman there's nothing's wrong with you," Becca urged. "Edwin? Edwin?" So much for remaining calm. Her voice pitched higher than an opera singer's.

Truman plastered his body against hers. "What's wrong?"

She couldn't answer. She'd seen too much of death to lie to the little boy or herself. "I need you to get my phone and call Flynn." He'd drive them to the hospital in the time it took an ambulance to get out here. And then she'd have Truman call Agnes because they were going to need someone to watch Truman while they went to the hospital.

"HE WAS SO vibrant last night. So alive." Flynn sat at Grandpa Ed's bedside.

His grandfather's lungs rattled with each labored breath. His arms twitched, as if he was having a bad dream. Occasionally, he'd murmur something unintelligible.

His father, Slade and Will stood at the foot of the bed. Becca had her back against the wall near the hospital room door.

"What can we do?" Slade asked.

Flynn had no idea. He looked at Becca.

It struck him then, harder than a jab to his midsection. Becca was distancing herself, preparing herself for death, preparing to move on.

He didn't want her to go.

He should have told her this morning how proud he was of her returning the ring and offering to pay the money back. He should have told her every day how grateful he was that she'd made his grandfather smile and laugh, while Flynn honored his grandfather's wishes to take care of the town. He should have told her he was scared and keeping himself busy with the winery while minor repairs in town kept him from facing his fears.

She would have understood. She would have held his hand or hugged him fiercely. Then she'd have dropped her gaze and cited some ridiculous house rule.

But he couldn't tell her anything now. Words, expressions, smiles. They were all comatose in the numbness that was the hospital room.

Grandpa Ed was dying.

Becca stepped forward, as he knew she would. "Gentlemen, I suggest we take turns sitting with Flynn and Edwin. I'll take the first shift. Oh, and it would be great if someone could call Kathy."

Flynn told them which rehab facility she was in.

The men started to file out, but Becca stopped them. "Please tell Edwin that you're leaving and you'll see him later."

Slade and Will exchanged doubtful glances.

"He's still here," she said softly. "When was the last time he let you ignore him?

They did as she suggested.

Joey lingered, looking at Flynn. "Could I…?" He gestured to Grandpa Ed.

Flynn swallowed thickly and nodded.

His father moved slowly, bringing him closer to the man who'd taken his son from him. "Edwin, we've had our differences. But you made the right choice, the hard choices that I wouldn't have made. I need to thank you for that." He glanced at Becca. "I'll see you later tonight."

The only sound after Joey left was Edwin's labored breathing and murmurs.

He's dying.

"What can I do?" Flynn asked Becca, feeling more helpless than he had in years.

She pulled a chair over, sat and took his cold hands in her warm ones. "You need to be here for your grandfather with your presence and your words. Don't sit silently. Tell him when people come and go. Talk about the fond memories you've had together. Tell him you love him." She gently squeezed his hands, as if to let him know her next words were very important. "Tell him you understand he has to leave. Tell him he can go whenever he's ready."

Flynn shook his head. "I can't." He couldn't let him go.

"He's just as afraid as you are."

How could that be? Flynn was terrified. He clung to Becca.

She held his fingers tight. "He's been driving that old body for years. Slowing down. Needing more time to warm up in the morning. This is his chance to trade that body in for something less restrictive and more freeing."

"You just called my grandfather a car."

"His soul is the driver. His body is the car." Her voice. Gently soothing. Providing a metaphor that made losing Grandpa Ed easier. "I'll show you how."

Becca stood, pulling Flynn to his feet.

"Edwin, this is Becca. I'm here with Flynn." There was a catch to her voice that wouldn't have fooled Grandpa Ed on a good day. "We brought you to the hospital after Sheriff Nate came to visit."

"Sheriff Nate?"

"Sheriff Nate received one of your letters." She tossed at him, before turning her attention back to Grandpa Ed. "I'm sorry I ever doubted you in your letter-writing campaign. You're a genius."

Flynn couldn't believe someone had actually answered his grandfather's letters.

Grandpa Ed's murmuring eased.

"I know your body feels heavy," she continued. "You can be like a flower, floating down the Harmony River without a care in the world."

"Flynn," Grandpa Ed murmured.

"He's here." Becca took Flynn's hand and put it over his grandfather's. "Go on."

It took Flynn a few labored breaths to produce any words. What came out of his mouth was soft and low. "Do you remember the day Mom dropped me off to stay with you? You told me I'd never have to feel scared again. You held my hand and led me out to the porch. We looked at the river and you said life in Harmony Valley wasn't like life in the city. You told me how happy you were that I'd come to live with you." His breath felt like it had been cut in tiny chunks that stuck in his throat. "I never told you that was the best day of my life."

Becca put her arm around his waist and laid her head on his shoulder. "Keep going."

So he did. He blinked back tears and told his grandfather about all the big moments in his life that were made possible by living in Harmony Valley. He told him about how he applied lessons learned from his grandfather to his everyday life. He told him how much he loved him.

Flynn talked on and on. And when his voice faltered another picked up the tale.

He laughed with his friends over stories of their struggles to build a business. He laughed with his father at stories of the good times he'd forgotten. He laughed with Becca over stories of Truman and Abby.

But mostly, he laughed to keep from breaking inside.

CHAPTER TWENTY-TWO

S HE'D THOUGHT H ARMONY Valley was different. She'd thought Flynn was different.

There were no differences. There was grief and sorrow and heartbreak.

Edwin was dead. He'd drifted away during the night with Becca and Flynn by his bedside.

She hadn't had time to prepare, to sit with Edwin and listen to his stories, ease his fears, along with her own. She'd been too busy putting him into a routine, establishing healthy eating habits, cleaning out his cobwebs. There were no last requests, other than the necklace he'd wanted to give her. The one Flynn refused to give her.

Slade dropped Becca off at Agnes's house. Agnes was sleeping over at Edwin's with Truman and Abby.

Becca reached into her purse for the keys to the motorhome, although why she locked it was beyond her. No one locked their doors in Harmony Valley.

She rummaged around in her purse and her fingers tangled with a delicate chain. She knew what it was before she lifted it free. Irma's pendant.

Who had put it there was another question. Edwin or Truman, if she had to guess.

Not Flynn.

Her heart decided to add to the weight of sorrow in her chest. She'd resisted the attraction between them, resisted Flynn's advances, even resisted what her heart wanted.

Because Flynn was too good for her. She'd crossed too many lines with too many clients. Flynn had a zero-tolerance policy for liars and thieves.

She'd get whatever sleep she could, return the necklace and leave.

She only wished her motorhome could go faster than the rapidly accelerating grief.

GRANDPA ED WAS GONE.

Flynn sat at the kitchen table staring at a full bottle of whiskey and an empty shot glass. He'd been staring at the pair for hours, barely registering how life went on outside his window.

The occasional bird swooping past. A squirrel seeking out a stray nut. Shadows lengthening, collecting themselves, and then beginning to lengthen in the opposite direction.

Abby and Truman occasionally came to check on him—one leaning against his shoulders, one leaning against his leg. They drifted in for food and out again. Asking with their big, sad eyes when Becca was coming to help them with their grief. Grief was something Flynn had no clue how to fix.

Becca's motorhome trundled up the drive toward the house. She made a U-turn and parked.

Truman and Abby ran to the front door.

Becca came in, dark circles under her eyes, her hair as limp as her energy level. She wore a pair of black jeans and a plain black T-shirt—her idea of mourning clothes.

She dropped her purse on the floor by the door and hugged Truman. She hugged Abby. She stared at Flynn and the whiskey.

Suddenly, Flynn felt the warmth of the sun through the window, felt like he could breathe and move and live. It was Becca who made him feel that way, as if the cacophony of emotions swirling through him weren't heavy and unmanageable.

"How are you doing?" she asked when she and her entourage moved into the kitchen.

He grunted something that meant nothing.

He wanted to sweep her into his arms and never let go. He wanted to listen to her soft, calm voice telling him what to do, as it had last night. He wanted things he couldn't name.

She opened her mouth to speak. Closed it. Reached into her jeans pocket and let something metallic dribble into the empty shot glass. "I didn't want you to think I stole it. Truman or…someone…must have put it in my purse."

Flynn dipped his finger into the shot glass. His grandmother's necklace. The heart pendant was still warm. He rubbed the gently curving lines with his thumb, imagining his grandmother separating the heart pendant in two, giving his grandfather her heart, not knowing if he'd fall in love with someone else or lose his life overseas.

He couldn't remember much about her, other than her soft voice and faded ginger coloring. But she'd had guts. It took courage to put your heart on the line like that, to say, *I'll wait for you, no matter what.*

Someday, perhaps, he'd be brave enough to say it to someone. Perhaps to Becca.

She moved about the kitchen behind him. He imagined she was going to make them lunch. How could she think about others when the pain of loss felt as if it had cleaved his heart in two?

He turned to look at her.

She wasn't making lunch. She was collecting her things. "I left the grocery list for you on the counter. Truman likes fruit. Don't go spoiling him with junk food."

"Are you leaving?" Truman asked before Flynn could, coming to stand in the middle of the kitchen.

Flynn gripped his grandmother's pendant so tight it dug into his palm.

"I am. My job here is done, but…" She knelt down on the floor in front of the little boy. "I want you to have Abby. She likes being with you more than she likes being with old, sick people." Becca sniffed, firming up her voice and, it appeared, her resolve. "But only if you promise to take good care of her. No sneaking people food to her, like popcorn."

"Becca, don't go." Truman fell into her arms. "Don't go."

"I have to."

Flynn felt numb and distant, as if he was far away from the scene before him.

Truman cried against Becca's shoulder, his face scrunched and red. She stroked his hair. Abby tried to nose her way into the embrace. Flynn wanted to be there, as well.

But what right did he have? Becca had erected barriers around her heart. She knew he was hurting and she was leaving him anyway.

"First, they took Grandpa Ed to the hospital and he died," Truman sobbed. "Mama's in the hospital. She's probably going to die."

"Your mother will be fine." Flynn's voice croaked like the frogs down by the river.

"You lie!" Truman turned on him. "People lie all the time, you said so yourself." Truman ran down the hall, Abby close on his heels. A door slammed.

Flynn eased his grip on the heart pendant. "You don't need to leave Abby with him. She's your dog." He didn't like the idea of Becca being alone with no one to comfort her at the end of a long, hard day.

"Truman needs Abby more than I do." She hadn't gotten up from the kitchen floor. "While Kathy's in the hospital he'll need you and this town to help him heal."

Down the hall a door opened. The shower went on. A door slammed.

Becca stood, backing into the corner of the kitchen. "I wanted to say a proper goodbye, but if I wait for him it might be worse."

Words invaded his mind. Words like, *don't go, please stay, I need you.*

Words that remained unspoken, like, *you give me hope, you give me strength.*

He stared at his grandmother's pendant. "I'll write that letter of reference for you. Where should I send it?"

"No need." Her voice, so flat and emotionless. "I told Gary I'd pay him back. He accepted this morning and dropped the lawsuit."

Flynn hadn't been expecting that. It meant when Becca left, she'd have no reason to look back. "Stay."

Her eyes held that same trapped look as the day they'd first met. "Why?"

He couldn't give her an answer. Not because he didn't have one. He had many. But because he couldn't decide on the right one. "Where can I send your check?"

"You can't write it now?" Pain flashed across her features, pain that went straight to his heart.

She never wanted to hear from him again after this. What had he expected after he'd been so cruel the past few days? He'd justified every one of her actions in his mind, but verbally, he'd been brutal to her. Because he wanted to protect her. He'd gone about it all wrong.

Fat lot of good that did him now. She was leaving him, going out into the world unprotected.

And the irony was, she'd be fine. It was Flynn who'd be scarred and vulnerable.

He went down the hall for his checkbook, knocking on the bathroom door as he passed. "Becca's leaving. If you want to say goodbye, you need to get out."

Abby barked behind the door.

He returned to the living room with the check folded around the pendant. "Don't go."

Becca stood with one hand on the back of Grandpa Ed's fancy recliner. Flynn's Giants cap, the one Grandpa Ed had worn for days, sat on one arm of the chair.

"I need you to stay."

She shook her head. "You need someone you can trust. Someone who's sweet and love-able." She stroked the pillowed recliner. "I'll say goodbye to Truman through the door. He can text or call me anytime." She walked rigidly down the hall.

This was it. Flynn's last chance. His hands fisted in frustration. She'd say goodbye to Truman and then leave. All he was doing was circling the issue. Circling the issue. Circling love.

He loved her.

But he'd blown his opportunities to tell her. And if he said anything now she'd only see it as a sham, a way to keep her there and help him with Truman or ease his grief. She wouldn't believe that he'd been too stupid to realize what his feelings toward her actually were until it was too late.

"Truman?" She knocked on the door.

Only Abby answered.

Something cut into his hand. He opened his fist. He'd crumpled her check almost into a ball with his grandmother's heart pendant in the middle, poking through the paper.

BECCA MANAGED TO hold in the tears when she left, just like she'd managed not to hug Flynn. Truman hadn't come out of the shower to see her go. He hadn't said a word. She'd felt Flynn's disappointed gaze on her as she climbed into the motorhome.

He'd asked her to stay, but she knew it was only because he needed someone to care for Truman. If he had any emotions behind his request, he hadn't expressed them. Oftentimes the people who were with you when a loved one died were a security blanket. She certainly didn't want to fulfill that role with Flynn.

And so she drove slowly out of town. The two-lane, eucalyptus-lined highway softened beneath her unshed tears. The sun flashed between the massive trunks and leaves like a too-bright strobe light.

Becca didn't know where she'd go other than north. She wanted to get as far away from Flynn and Harmony Valley as she could.

She was so distracted, she didn't see the pothole until it was too late.

The motorhome pitched and shuddered. Dishes rattled in the cupboards.

Someone said, "Ow."

Someone other than Becca.

Becca pulled over onto the narrow shoulder of the road and turned the motor off. She walked back to the dinette set and peeked underneath the table.

A small, tear-streaked face peered back at her. He was rubbing the top of his head.

"Truman, what are you doing here?"

"I want to go with you. I'm going to be motherless soon anyway, and I like you. You tuck me in at night and make me snacks. Can't I choose you, like Grandpa Joey chose me to be his grandson?"

Becca wanted to say yes. She loved Truman as if he was her own. But it wasn't right. Kathy had an addiction she was trying to beat. When she'd come to the hospital last night she'd told Flynn she was fighting her demons for Truman.

Becca sighed. "Come out from under there."

Truman crept out, careful not to hit his head again. His apology was evident in his face. "Are you mad because I left Abby behind? I didn't want to do it, but I didn't want Uncle Flynn to be alone." He sniffed.

Becca hugged him. "He'd much rather have you. You're his wingman, remember?"

He drew a shuddering breath. "If we go back, will you stay?"

"No, sweetheart. No." Staying meant dealing with everyone and their grief. It was easier to pretend it didn't hurt.

Becca picked up her purse, reaching inside for her cell phone. A balled-up piece of paper was on top of it. Flynn's check. She shoved it out of the way, but froze when she realized a metal chain was hanging like a tail out of the crumpled paper. Gently, as if it would disappear if she opened it with any speed, Becca smoothed out the check.

The pendant gleamed up at her.

She couldn't believe it.

Becca did a quick perusal of the motorhome floor. No pennies.

And then she realized she held only one half of the pendant. The second heart was missing.

He'd given her his heart.

She couldn't believe it.

He was willing to wait for her.

Her heart swelled with love. She wanted to have Flynn in her arms this very moment.

And then the amount on the check registered: *ten thousand dollars.*

She was going to kill him.

CHAPTER TWENTY-THREE

FLYNN REMAINED AT the door until he could no longer see or hear Becca driving off.

He turned slowly, back against the wall, fighting the gut-clenching feeling that he'd been abandoned once more.

Where Grandpa Ed should have been there was only his baseball cap.

Flynn walked over and picked it up, running his fingers over the gently arched brim. He put it on and it was as if his grandfather was holding his hand again, as he had last night in the hours before he'd died.

Abby wouldn't stop barking in the shower.

Flynn was surprised Truman hadn't told her to be quiet. He hoped his nephew was all right.

Still wearing the hat, Flynn headed down the hall. He knocked on the bathroom door again. Truman was too young to require a lot of privacy. "Truman? You okay in there, buddy?"

Abby's barking became more urgent. She began scratching the door for her freedom.

Something was wrong. Flynn opened the door, momentarily blinded by a cloud of steam.

Abby ran past him, racing around the house, barking at a pitch he'd never heard from her before.

"Truman?" Flynn waved away the steam and realized that the shower was empty. As was his nephew's bedroom across the hall. "Truman!"

But the little boy didn't answer.

He didn't go anywhere without Abby. And he'd been so upset that Becca was leaving...

Flynn grabbed his truck keys and ran out the door, Abby racing at his heels.

"COME ON, FLYNN, pick up." Becca disconnected and slid her phone back in her purse.

"Do you think Uncle Flynn's dead, too?"

"No. He could be down by the river or in the shower..." Becca paused. "Did you lock Abby in the bathroom?"

"I didn't lock her in," Truman said cryptically.

Regardless, Becca was going to have to turn around. And face Flynn again. She wasn't sure which emotion held more sway—anger at him for writing her such a huge check, or love for him because he'd given her the pendant. If he'd given her the pendant. "Truman, you didn't put the necklace in my purse?"

"Huh?" Truman looked genuinely confused.

"Never mind. I think there's an intersection ahead where I can turn around. Come ride shotgun and buckle up." She waited for Truman to comply before starting the motorhome and lumbering down the road.

The more she thought about it, the more she was convinced that Flynn was more fearful of committing to a relationship than she was. He'd grown up thinking his parents had abandoned him, when in fact they'd been coerced by money. He'd thought his sister had abandoned Truman. He had no role model for a steady relationship, one based on love and trust. And Becca certainly hadn't proven she was trustworthy.

He must have given her the pendant on a whim. Otherwise, he would have said something.

A black truck appeared in her rearview mirror, horn honking. Abby's head poked out the passenger window.

She pulled over. "Your uncle's not dead." She'd hoped she had more time to think this through. About checks and pendants and hearts.

Becca had a decision to make.

She didn't think she was ready.

FLYNN AND ABBY ran to the side door of the motorhome. He yanked it open and they both leaped inside, Flynn narrowly missed stepping on the little dog.

He spied Truman. "Thank God. I was so worried. Don't ever do that to me again." He dropped to one knee and opened his arms.

Without a moment's hesitation, Truman embraced him and sat on his knee. "I'm sorry, Uncle Flynn."

"I just found him a few minutes ago." Becca's voice was distant and guarded. "I tried to call, but you didn't answer. I was looking for a place to turn around."

"I left my phone at home." Flynn's arms and heart felt full, but there was still a piece missing. A very vital piece.

"You need to write me another check." Becca tore his draft into tiny pieces and let them flutter to the carpet. "I can't accept the amount you wrote."

The check had been a gamble. But if she'd found the check, she'd also found the pendant, which she hadn't put on. His heart sank quicker than toes in the mud. "I'm sorry."

He wanted to say more, but he couldn't seem to find the right words.

She nodded. "It's just…I'll need another check. For the right amount this time. Just the hours I worked." She wouldn't look at him.

Flynn couldn't stop looking at her. Here was the second chance he needed. Thank heavens for little runaways. "No."

"No?" Her gaze narrowed to his. "No?"

"I wasn't apologizing for writing the check." *Don't mess this up.* "I'm sorry that I couldn't tell you how much I love you before now. I was scared, probably more scared than you, since you've lost more people than I have."

Truman was suddenly very still, very un-Truman-like.

"I know I'm not good enough for you and our timing is horrible. I'm missing a big chunk in my heart where Grandpa Ed used to be and I'm trying to figure out how to have a relationship with my dad. Those two things are hard enough without trying to figure out how to love someone you want to be your life partner, your one true love…your wife."

Truman gave Becca a thumbs-up.

Becca wasn't an easy sell. She rubbed her hands on her pants legs. "You don't trust me."

"I do trust you. I just never told you. I trusted you with my grandfather, arguably my life's most precious possession until I met you. I trusted you to care for him after knowing you less than a day." Flynn hugged Truman tighter. "I trusted you with my nephew, who came to us a fragile shell of himself. And I trusted you with my heart."

She swallowed.

"Becs," he said gently. "You have the biggest heart of anyone I've ever met. You care about people in the sweetest, most genuine way. A way that wins them over, because everyone can see how loveable you are."

She swallowed again.

"I'm scared, Becs. I'm scared that chasing after Truman isn't the second chance I thought it'd be. I'm scared that I won't find the right words to convince you how I feel." He drew in a shaky breath. "I'm scared that you're still so in love with your first husband that you can't find room in your heart for me."

"I'm scared, too," she admitted softly.

"Don't be scared," Truman whispered.

She gave his nephew a watery smile. "I can't bear to risk my heart for something that isn't real. Grief does crazy things to people. It makes them greedy or closed off or clingy. What you think you're feeling is most likely a product of your grief."

She didn't believe him. A cold fist of fear clenched in his stomach. "This is real, Becs. If we commit to each other and give it time, you'll see. Love is worth the risk." He offered his hand to her.

She didn't move. She didn't move. She

didn't move and Flynn nearly stopped breathing.

"I see a penny," Becca whispered. "How could that be?"

Truman found it first. Almost hidden beneath Flynn's foot. "Find a penny, pick it up—"

"It's...it's...true." And then she was in his arms, too.

He didn't know how a penny could convince her when he couldn't. He didn't waste time thinking about it. He rained kisses on her face, as enthusiastic as Abby, who also tried to join in on the love fest. "Marry me. Right now. Today."

"What?" Becca laughed, looked into his eyes, and then stopped. "You're serious."

"I love you, Becca. And the only way to prove it is to drive to Reno and get married."

"What about me?" Truman wiggled to the floor, looping his arm around Abby.

"You'll be my best man," Flynn said, never taking his eyes off Becca's dark, expressive eyes. "And Abby will be the maid of honor, if Becca loves me enough to commit."

Those eyes held his answer. She didn't look

trapped or secretive or guilty. She looked radiant and happy and in love.

Her answer came as a question. "Your truck or my motorhome?"

* * * * *

Don't miss the next
HARMONY VALLEY *romance from*
Melinda Curtis
coming in May 2014!

REQUEST YOUR FREE BOOKS!
2 FREE WHOLESOME ROMANCE NOVELS
IN LARGER PRINT
PLUS 2
FREE
MYSTERY GIFTS

HEARTWARMING™

Wholesome, tender romances

YES! Please send me 2 FREE Harlequin® Heartwarming Larger-Print novels and my 2 FREE mystery gifts (gifts worth about $10). After receiving them, if I don't wish to receive any more books, I can return the shipping statement marked "cancel." If I don't cancel, I will receive 4 brand-new larger-print novels every month and be billed just $4.99 per book in the U.S. or $5.74 per book in Canada. That's a savings of at least 23% off the cover price. It's quite a bargain! Shipping and handling is just 50¢ per book in the U.S. and 75¢ per book in Canada.* I understand that accepting the 2 free books and gifts places me under no obligation to buy anything. I can always return a shipment and cancel at any time. Even if I never buy another book, the two free books and gifts are mine to keep forever.

161/361 IDN F47N

Name   (PLEASE PRINT)

Address   Apt. #

City   State/Prov.   Zip/Postal Code

Signature (if under 18, a parent or guardian must sign)

Mail to the Harlequin® Reader Service:
IN U.S.A.: P.O. Box 1867, Buffalo, NY 14240-1867
IN CANADA: P.O. Box 609, Fort Erie, Ontario L2A 5X3

* Terms and prices subject to change without notice. Prices do not include applicable taxes. Sales tax applicable in N.Y. Canadian residents will be charged applicable taxes. Offer not valid in Quebec. This offer is limited to one order per household. Not valid for current subscribers to Harlequin Heartwarming larger-print books. All orders subject to credit approval. Credit or debit balances in a customer's account(s) may be offset by any other outstanding balance owed by or to the customer. Please allow 4 to 6 weeks for delivery. Offer available while quantities last.

HWDIR13R

LARGER-PRINT BOOKS!

**GET 2 FREE
LARGER-PRINT NOVELS
PLUS 2 FREE
MYSTERY GIFTS**

Love Inspired

Larger-print novels are now available...

REQUEST YOUR FREE BOOKS!

2 FREE CHRISTIAN NOVELS
PLUS 2
FREE
MYSTERY GIFTS

HEARTSONG
PRESENTS

YES! Please send me 2 Free Heartsong Presents novels and my 2 FREE mystery gifts (gifts are worth about $10). After receiving them, if I don't wish to receive any more books I can return the shipping statement marked "cancel." If I don't cancel, I will receive 4 brand-new novels every month and be billed just $4.24 per book in the U.S. and $5.24 per book in Canada. That's a savings of at least 20% off the cover price. It's quite a bargain! Shipping and handling is just 50¢ per book in the U.S. and 75¢ per book in Canada.* I understand that accepting the 2 free books and gifts places me under no obligation to buy anything. I can always return a shipment and cancel at any time. Even if I never buy another book, the two free books and gifts are mine to keep forever.

159/359 HDN FVYK

Name _____ (PLEASE PRINT) _____

Address _____ Apt. # _____

City _____ State _____ Zip _____

Signature (if under 18, a parent or guardian must sign)

Mail to the Harlequin® Reader Service:
IN U.S.A.: P.O. Box 1867, Buffalo, NY 14240-1867

* Terms and prices subject to change without notice. Prices do not include applicable taxes. Sales tax applicable in N.Y. This offer is limited to one order per household. Not valid for current subscribers to Heartsong Presents books. All orders subject to credit approval. Credit or debit balances in a customer's account(s) may be offset by any other outstanding balance owed by or to the customer. Please allow 4 to 6 weeks for delivery. Offer available while quantities last. Offer valid only in the U.S.

HSPDIR13R

ReaderService.com

Manage your account online!

- Review your order history
- Manage your payments
- Update your address

*We've designed
the Harlequin® Reader Service
website just for you.*

Enjoy all the features!

- Reader excerpts from any series
- Respond to mailings and special monthly offers
- Discover new series available to you
- Browse the Bonus Bucks catalog
- Share your feedback

Visit us at:
ReaderService.com